black
and blue

black
and blue

nashid fareed-ma'at

MCP Books
2301 Lucien Way #415
Maitland, FL 32751
407.339.4217
www.millcitypress.net

Printed in the United States of America

ISBN-13: 978-1-54562-596-5

TABLE OF CONTENTS

CHAPTER ONE:
Just a bag of chips

Who ever really sees us for who we are? Are we not viewed as collages of interpolated perceptions colored by held ideas painted upon the canvas of what others experience? Persons, places, objects, situations, apparent motivations and actions: all moving parts of a shifting conundrum we claim to understand and impose our determinations upon. Determinations that not only determine what we see but also the "I" who sees what we see. Conundrums upon conundrums that only evolve into conundrums of conundrums? But who is even willing to admit that the conundrum is a conundrum?

Yet this becomes the stuff of our lives. The lense by which I see "my" life and all I experience. If this is so, can I honestly claim to see me for who I truly am? And my life for what it truly is? Let alone to see you for who you truly are and your life for what it truly is...

Such was the landscape it happened upon. A Black man, or such is how most label him. Including himself. Anyway, he entered the convenience store wearing a modest suit. An unfamiliar face in a supposedly familiar circumstance. Do not stores exist for customers to enter and purchase items? For the most part, this is what usually occurs in such places.

The Brown woman behind the counter gave a stern look in her apprehension. It wasn't clear whether she was Indian, Middle Eastern, or some other ethnicity. But the fact he was Black in her eyes was significant although unspoken. So too was the fact that they were the only persons in the store.

He scanned the aisles to see where the bags of chips were. She watched. Toward the back of the store, some brands in one aisle; other brands in another aisle. He walked down the first aisle, grabbed a bag, continued to scan the selection. She watched. He then walked to the other aisle, continuing to browse the assortment of chips. She watched. He grabbed another bag and went to grab a cold soda from the cooler. She watched. He started to the counter but, on the way, changed his mind and went back to the first aisle to return the first bag.

"Hey, what are you doing!" she asked with a fierce tone.

He was slightly bewildered by the question. "I'm putting these back."

"I'm sick of you people coming in here and stealing all the time."

"Who is *you people?*""

"You know what: I'll just call the cops!"

"I am a cop."

He flashed his badge to prove it. But the storms had already collided. And who could definitively attribute which ravaged patches of destruction belonged to which storm? A presumption of guilt upon innocence. The anguish of being repeatedly wronged seeking protection from further wrongs. One Brown, one Black. And the veils of separation these distinctions behold. One woman, the other man. One business person, the other customer. One right, while wrong. Yet the other was also wronged, so did that presume a sense of being right too? The other pitted against the other, rooted in causes that long preceded their fateful encounter within this collage of persons, places, objects, situations, apparent motivations and actions.

Although only a moment had passed before she apologized, that moment had the weight of lifetimes. For he and others like him had experienced wrongs like this consistently throughout their lives. Can a few words really erase the weight of years toiled? Especially when the apology was only in words, not deeper amends.

"I'm sorry, but people have been robbing from me all week. I just want them to stop!"

The "people" and "them" was understood as the same *"you people."*

He didn't doubt her claims about being robbed, but felt offended by her suspicion. Especially since, unknown to her, he spent years putting his life on the line in the fight against crime. The premise of "innocent until proven guilty" was a framework for his policing. Even when assumptions of others' wrongdoing arose in his mind without evidence, he sought to restrain his actions to this framework of presumptive innocence, for the sake of the ideal of justice. Yet over and over again, he saw society neglect this ideal. People didn't hesitate to act in total disregard of it. He even found himself, at times, the target of this overreaching suspicion simply because of his *Blackness.*

Then came the question of dignity. In being offended, he no longer wanted to purchase the chips and soda. But was this a concession of sorts? A reaction to her prejudice that now dictated his actions and motivations?

Or should he be the bigger human? That despite her projections, he came into the store to purchase some chips and soda and should walk out doing so. Certainly, he could choose to never return to this store; such being a choice of affirmative reflection, not reaction to her apparent bias.

Neither choice offered an untainted resolution. Through no fault of his own, he was made the canvas of her projections, and could not walk away unsullied. The insult would likely linger for days before becoming a diminished memory in the lifelong catalog of bias he experienced. Even if the specifics were eventually forgotten, the collective weight of such incidents had a lasting presence.

So he just stood there. And she watched. Until the awkwardness completely dissolved the wish for a snack. With his eyes aimed low, he returned the bag of chips to the shelf and the soda to the cooler. He then exited the store without ever looking at her again.

Just another day for a Black man in America...

CHAPTER TWO:
Alleys and tombs

There were two things that became unfailingly refuges of solace for him: that photo of Uncle James and feeding his tropical fish. That old, partially deteriorated photo hung framed on a wall in his living room. A middle-aged face encasing a snide smile with glowing eyes. A lasting image of his seemingly endless wisdom. Even before the wrinkles left a lasting engravement upon his face, Uncle James' countenance beheld sagacity. Content with modest poverty, his wealth was a dignity no person or thing could rob from him. He often said if you remember who you are, no one can destroy you with their beliefs of who they think you should be. He found his "who you are," and clung to it with a stubbornness that refused to lose remembrance of it. He was always Uncle James. Always. But his favorite nephew was still in search of what it meant to be Tory, even as he dawned into the stage of being middle-aged.

The large fish tank with tropical fish was an attempt to distinguish who he was. He was oblivious to the subconscious connection between this hobby and Uncle James' penchant for fishing. A quiet spot under a tree on a lake few people frequented. The stillness of the water as he held his trusty fishing rod in hand. His back slouched against the worn polyester backing of his fishing chair. Expanses of time passing, ranging from minutes to hours, waiting for the line to be tugged. An invitation to drift inward and reflect, beyond the passing thoughts to the touchstone of the heart. And just be. How many things in this world invite us to just be?

That spot on the lake was a refuge for Uncle James, where he could be free from all the stuff of the world and their accompanying demands. Tory had the grace of going there with Uncle James only a few times, to experience his uncle's deep and peaceful content. It was something Tory longed for, although he couldn't put voice to this desire.

Yet there he was. Reduced to the simplicity of a grown man sprinkling particles of fish food on the surface of the tank. The colorful beings gliding gracefully through the water, pecking the floating flakes to ingest. There was a beauty to being free, even if temporarily, from the complexities that dominated his life. Even the talk show commentary on the radio became an inconspicuous background. There was just him. And the water. And the fish. Pecking food.

"I know it's not sexy but it's the right thing to do. Keeping up the infrastructure is a thankless job. But without sufficient and efficient means to move people and products, the cost of business goes up in ways that aren't easy to calculate -- unless you're a knowledgeable economist..." The voice from the radio paused before saying, "We'll get back to your calls after these messages."

The commercial break became an invitation for Tory's own commentary. "If only life could be as simple as swimming to the surface for food. Or are you fish masquerading a complex system of business and government...?"

His cell phone rang. The refuge of simplicity was intruded upon. The call would most likely be something from the world with its own demands. As much as he wished to ignore the intrusion, his job demanded him to be accessible at all hours of day and night.

He walked to the end table where the ringtone called. The cell phone sitting beside the gun in the holster. For years, his wife would chastise him for leaving his gun in the open. Why form a bad habit he might struggle to break once they had kids? But the kids never came. First, there were the health difficulties which made pregnancy more of a challenge. These were followed by unfolding careers that moved their lives in other directions. For Loretta, it was the opportunity to lead an innovative Black Studies department at the local college. The president gave her an explicit directive to be creative and involved with the local Black community, one which had been underserved for decades. And for him, excelling as a police officer led to promotions and special assignments culminating into becoming one of the top detectives of the Internal Affairs Division.

So it never became necessary for him to stop leaving his gun in the open. And his weapon became a regular component of his life, as normal as wearing clothes to go outside. He never left home without it. And he never forgot the power it beheld: with just the bend of a finger, he could instantly end another's life. A power invested with the pledge to only use it to serve and protect society.

Holding the cell phone to his face, he said, "Detective Givens."

The familiar voice of Anne was on the other side. He probably spoke to her more frequently than his own wife. She was a guidepost for his days. Her enduring competence made her someone he could rely on.

"Hey, Tory. We have an incident down at Water Hole. And the Chief is specifically requesting *you.*"

The emphasis on "you" implied there was more to this call than merely a request for his presence. But she knew he would rather find out what that was when he arrived at the scene.

♦ ♦ ♦

Cars. Asphalt. Intersections. Pathways that were mostly straight, but some had slight curvatures. Hanging lights with red, yellow, and green spheres. Yellow and white lines, some decayed to partial visibility. Stops and starts, with points of reduced motion. Street signs with letters. Some with numbers. Houses and buildings. Sidewalks. Pedestrians. Fixtures of a life called "urban."

For some unknown reason, he began to notice the passing landscape as he drove. His neighborhood was lined with nice homes. Lawns with trees and bushes and open space. Some with flower gardens. Others with children's toys left spread across the grass, sometimes unattended. Some homes had garages. Others contained driveways containing multiple cars. Some had basketball hoops. And some even had pools. It felt like a place of homes, a place for families. Imagery that supported a vision of the American Dream. He also noticed the skin colors of the persons there: the "neighbors" were mostly White.

But as he proceeded "into the city," another narrative arose. The landscape was afflicted by a drastic transformation. The nice family homes were replaced by tightly packed buildings with little open space. Including apartment buildings where people were stacked upon and directly next to each other with an intentional congestion. The square tiles of the sidewalks seemed to have a more prominent presence, with more bodies compressed upon them among the lingering litter. Cars formed lines along the sidewalk curbs, the luxuries of driveways being less of a commodity. The fewer trees seemed squeezed among the concrete and asphalt. Even the sunlight had less room to shine where it pierced through the heights of the buildings into the shadowed canals of streets.

And then there was Water Hole. There the dearth of openness and apparent beauty was scarred by a deeper paucity. Some buildings were decayed remnants of their former selves, abandoned and in disrepair. Left to atrophy into standing corpses among the concentration of higher poverty -- Tory never used the term "higher crime." He had seen too much in his years of policing to know that high crime was prevalent throughout all spheres of society. Violence, drug use, domestic abuse, robbery and theft, sexual assault: these were constant occurrences in all the communities he policed, from the poor to the wealthy elite. But only certain crimes fell prominently within the chosen priorities of community policing and targeted crime-fighting initiatives.

For some reason Tory noticed the stark contrasts on this drive. A drive he made almost daily since he moved to the "urban suburb" of Parker Heights. In the wake of another past police controversy, the city council passed a residency require- ment for officers to live within the city limits. Of course, there was a grandfather clause for those already living in the neighboring suburbs. This law made Parker Heights one of the preferred choices for many officers. Located on the outer limits of the city, it had a suburban feel. The higher cost of living there, along with limited public transportation, served to deter "less desirables" from the neighborhood.

"Less desirables" was the term a real estate agent used when showing Tory and Loretta their first apartment in the neigh- borhood. And when Tory made detective, they decided to exchange the monthly rent of their two-bedroom apartment for the thirty-year mortgage of their single-family home. It had now been fifteen years since they "moved on up" out of the 'hood to become one of the "Parkers."

As some in the old neighborhood would say, he had "escaped." To have a home with a lawn and a driveway, and actually some space between you and your neighbors. No, the neighbors didn't always smile like they do in the home insur- ance commercials. Or always keep the lawn cut, green, and pristine beyond the waning days of spring. But it was home. And perhaps a success: an oasis of middle class living in a life otherwise imprinted by poverty. He never did forget what it was like to grow up in the 'hood. And despite his present living situation, he never felt like a stranger in neighborhoods like Water Hole.

As he turned onto Turner Street, he saw a group of men congregating on a corner. Some sat on milk crates and chairs by the store entrance. Others stood. Most were older but a few were young. They all either had cigarettes in hand or that conspicuous bottle or can in a brown bag. The bag served as a deterrence to being arrested for "public consumption of alcohol," although it was obvious to most that the men were drinking. Some were visibly drunk. The sight brought to mind a line from a poem a good friend of his wrote: "*Were corners made for Black men to stand on / And alleys to become the pathways to their tombs.*"

"I should write to Jelani," he thought.

His arrival offered no further time to reminisce as he reached Spencer Avenue. Police barricades already blocked entry onto the street, with officers standing on post. A group of Black spectators were assembled by the barber and beauty shop on the corner, some visually upset. Tory switched on the police lights of his unmarked car as he turned to drive onto Spencer Avenue. An officer moved the barricade to allow him in.

A gas station was on the far side of the street. He parked there, beside a TV station van and a radio station media car. Their presence immediately gave him a sense that this was more than a "normal incident."

Two police cars slightly angled by a nearby alley gave him a sense that was where the incident occurred. He surveyed the area. A fenced off deserted lot sat beside the gas station. Beside that there was a large abandoned building. The lines of old steel framed windows, most which were broken, suggested it may have once been a factory.

On the other side of the street, the barbershop on the corner extended to meet a fried chicken take-out restaurant.

Beside that was a vacant shop with a "For Rent" sign in it. Next to that was a liquor store and then the alley with the two police cars by it. On the other side of the alley was an office building. It had no windows on the alley wall, but lines of windows on the street side.

There was a bus stop by the office building. Sidewalks lined both sides of the two-way, two lane street. The scene was ordinary for this part of town. But extraordinary things often happen in ordinary places.

As Tory exited the car, a short White man carrying a pad approached.

"T.G! This won't be a walk in the park. In fact, this one might go national."

It was typical of Speedy to have an interesting way of introducing one to the crime scene. When you've seen all that he's seen, you find means of bracing yourself to the constant exposure to human cruelty and trauma. For him, it was witty commentary. This was how he dealt with witnessing the continuing barrage of humanity's inhumanity to humans. Besides, he already invested twenty-eight years in this profession and was hoping to retire soon with a semblance of scarred sanity.

"Tell me what you got."

"White cop kills an unarmed Black guy," Speedy responded. "Three years ago this is just a local controversy. But given the media's present lure of the day, Water Hole just went big time." He leaned close to Tory to say lowly, "I don't mean to seem insensitive, being that I'm White, but cases like this have been happening our whole career without the media sensationalism."

The lean reflected Speedy's discomfort. He and Tory had worked together for years, including some very intense cases that fused a bond between them. But they never talked about race. Yet now they were facing a case that would place that issue in the forefront in an unavoidable way.

Yeah, they had passing conversations that walked around the issue. But a serious, heart-to-heart, completely honest discussion about race and its ramifications was something they never embarked upon. And with good reason. Such discussions could irrevocably destroy professional relationships. And their jobs were stressful enough without the added burden of working with someone you would rather not be with. Especially since there was an unspoken yet discernible discontent Speedy had about Tory garnering a higher status. Technically, they held the same rank. But in how things played out within the department, Tory was regarded as a more respected detective.

Tory was not naive about his situation. The force of about 200 police officers was a little over ten percent people of color, most of whom were Black. The civilian workforce who supported the officers had about the same ratio. There was only one other Black detective among the ranks, and one Latino detective. And Tory was the only Black in the Internal Affairs Division. Yet the city was forty-five percent Black.

Although it was subtle and subdued, Tory did feel a tension about being such a "minority" in the overwhelming White police force. While the proclaimed dogma held the color "blue" to trump all racial and ethnic differences, culturally that "blue" was more White than Black, Latino, or Asian. For the sake of amicable relations, he found it best to never stir the pot when it came to race. So his response to Speedy said one thing but meant another.

"You don't have to be P.C. with me, Speedy." Change the subject. The reason he was summoned here must be at the alley. "Is that where it happened?" asked Tory.

Speedy led the way to the alley as he said, "In plain view."

"Tell me about the officer."

"Oliver Easthill. Seven years on the force. Formerly in the Army. Doesn't seem to have a bad rep from the fellas I spoke with but he's been trying to get out of the Hole for awhile."

"The Hole" was the more common way police described the neighborhood. The poverty there was deep and pervasive. Just as it limited the prospects of residents to access the more affluent resources of society, the poverty limited the majority of criminal activity in the area to gun violence, illegal drugs, prostitution, theft, and a growing gang problem. So as much as the moniker was a play on the neighborhood's name, it also had a derogatory connotation to cops. Most who preferred to not work among the dangerous crime there.

"How about the victim?"

"Martin Little. Thirty-two years old. Did time for drug possession but had a clean record for the past few years. Call came in that he was acting weird. Erratic. Looked like he might do something."

"Like what?" asked Tory.

"Who knows."

"How about the officers? Any statements?"

"They're all mums citing the forty-eight hour rule. That means we get the lawyer's remix of their accounts."

"Any eye witnesses?"

"Detectives are questioning a few right now. But they all were at a distance when the shots were fired."

As they reached the alley entrance, the scene spoke a language of its own. Between the two police cars, he got a glimpse of the spot. A dried pool of blood with that dull, shiny film. Its crimson color contrasting against the faded black asphalt. Like something incomplete had been made complete. The unnatural rendered natural.

The now absent body had fallen not far from the office building wall, just inside the alley. Tory wondered, for some weird reason, did the victim have enough room to die? Perhaps a peculiar thought. But something in him wished that if one's untimely death could not be avoided, it should at least be as comfortable as possible.

"Easthill and his partner arrive first in that car," Speedy said referring to the first police car. "The responding unit arrives two minutes later and pulls up right behind them. Two officers."

"Was he in the alley?" Tory asked in reference to the victim.

"Initial reports say he was just by the entrance." A moment of silence. "It seems they approached Little. One officer had a taser out. Easthill had his gun. Two shots fired. Little hits the ground. Ambulance arrives fifteen minutes later. He must have still been alive cause they rushed him away. At the hospital, he's pronounced D.O.A."

So he didn't die in the alley. But it was the last place he saw before his body expired. Or maybe the back of the ambulance was. The peculiar thoughts continued.

"Were any of the officers injured?"

"Nothing reported."

"How about video?"

"One officer was wearing her own body cam. But again..."

Tory joined Speedy in saying, "Forty-eight hours." The infamous rule that allowed officers in the department a period of forty-eight hours before having to answer any questions about serious on-duty incidents that might expose them or other officers to criminal charges.

Speedy continued his reply to Tory's question about video. "The dash cams on the cruisers point away from the scene. The liquor store has a camera but it just covers the front of the store. And the gas station wants a subpoena for their surveillance footage, which we're working on. But looking at their monitors, this is not in view of any of their cameras."

"How about somebody's cell phone?"

"Nothing yet."

Speedy paused. He noticed another officer had approached and was waiting to address them. He said to the officer, "Yeah?"

"The chief wants to speak to Detective Givens in the command center." For the police chief to be on-site while the preliminary investigating was still happening indicated this was a very serious case.

Tory took a moment to look once more at the alley. *Were corners made for Black men to stand on / And alleys to become the pathways to their tombs.* If we must die, is this the place where such should happen? Upon a bed of concrete and asphalt. Within sight and smelling distance of dirty metal bins filled with garbage. Fallen on an uneven sidewalk edging an aged street. By a wall tagged with indiscriminate graffiti. Across from the skeleton of a building left in open air to further decay. In an alley next to a liquor store. Is this where we should die among all the places upon this battered earth?

The peculiar thoughts served a beneficent purpose for Tory. It prevented him from becoming comfortable and complacent with the loss of another's life. Although the years of policing made him somewhat numb to deaths caused by other humans, these had not yet become completely normal to him. Part of him was still disturbed by the unnatural loss of human life. And the odd internal questions helped keep his mind sharp in inquiring the details as to why things unfolded as they did in such cases.

He gave one last look at the blood stain on the alley floor. He then turned to follow the officer who led him to the command center trailer parked a short distance away.

◆ ◆ ◆

The officer escorted Tory into the mobile command center. People were at work on computers and phones. The officer pointed through the activity to a private office in the back. "The chief's in there. He said to go right in."

Tory moved to the office door. He knocked on it to announce to his presence and then entered. He saw Chief Smitts sitting behind a desk, addressing an officer. "...they already have that up? Geez!" In his agitation, his eyes turned to see Tory. "Let me talk to Givens alone. Come back in when we're done." As the officer exited, the chief said to Tory, "Have a seat, Givens."

Reference by last name had a way of maintaining a sense of formality and his superior rank. Although he had a civilian demeanor, Chief Smitts utilized a military approach which was reflected in his management style. He preferred to work directly with higher ranked personnel and have them deliver his directives to subordinates. Despite his high reputation, Tory wasn't ranked among the elite. So being personally summoned before the chief was another indication of the seriousness of the matter at hand. And perhaps an opportunity to earn the chief's favor. Such was necessary to receive the discretionary promotions to positions of real influence and power within the department.

"This is already turning into a nightmare. Did you get briefed?"

"Speedy gave me the basic details."

"Then I don't have to explain the media firestorm about to descend upon us." Chief Smitts leaned forward with a gaze direct. "What I need from you is a quick and clean Internal Affairs investigation. I need you to get this one right. No matter what. I'll handle the political and media circus. But I'll be frank: I got my concerns." He leaned back and continued. "The fact that a White cop kills an unarmed Black man means this will get spun a million and one different ways. They already got a Black Lives Matter at Water Hole Twitter account. So I need to put this in the hands of someone I can trust. Someone who won't be swayed by the shifting winds. You understand?"

The question was subliminally layered. Feeling it best to not engage the unspokens, Tory's reply was simple and measured. "Yes, chief."

Yet the chief offered further clarity. "If this is manslaughter, tell me that. If this is a justified shooting, tell me that. If we just can't figure it out, tell me that. But no spin. No agendas. No politics. I say that knowing the mayor's thinking about next year's election. And that all the major networks will have their people here treating this as the next case in a national epidemic of police shootings. And that activists will be on the streets probably tonight pushing their platform. But I need the facts. Just what happened irrespective of all the stuff around it."

Some clarity. Yet there was still the presence of giant unspokens which, if not mentioned, Tory felt best to not inquire about. So again, a simple and measured reply. "Yes, sir."

"Detective Dillenger will assist you on this, but this is your case. And daily briefings to me, in person, on this one. Nothing over the phone, via text, email or through third parties."

The finality in his gaze indicated the chief was done. But as Tory stood, the chief remembered one last point of information. "Also, you should know the F.B.I. will probably be on this too starting tomorrow. But our investigation is the lead and independent until we're told otherwise."

Tory nodded and exited. Yet he could not shake from his mind the big unspokens woven as silent threads between the vocalized words. Beyond all the police work dressing, framing this as an Internal Affairs matter, major questions stood out in Tory's mind. Did Easthill kill Martin because he was Black? And if so, did the chief really want Tory to go after a fellow cop? Or smooth it over as an unfortunate police shooting? Despite what the facts may show, if the chief was intent on protecting Easthill, the prospects of any punishment were significantly muted if not non-existent.

Although these concerns were part of the five hundred pound elephant in the room, Tory didn't expect anyone in the police department to state them openly. Just like no one mentioned such glaring issues with previous similar controversies. Incidents where the officers were almost always White and the citizens usually Black. And almost always, the Black citizens -- usually men -- ended up in a more harmed state than the officers. Sometimes severely hurt. Or dead.

Any honest examination of these incidents could not deny the undeniable presence of race. Including the White privilege of protection for the officers. Yet police investigations almost always treated race as no more than an incidental factor. And sometimes race wasn't mentioned as a factor at all.

But this time it felt like race could not be ignored. Not with the recent nationwide protests against repeated police killings of Blacks. Even if not mentioned in any official police capacity, the presence of race in this killing would remain prominent. And consequently, this undeniable presence would shine its light upon the factor of race in other past incidents. And perhaps upon the larger relationship the police have with the Black community. And specifically in Water Hole since it became a predominantly Black neighborhood.

This feeling was affirmed as Tory exited the command center. "Hands up, don't shoot! Hands up, don't shoot! Hands up, don't shoot...!" The chorus of voices rang strong from the near distance. A group of mostly Black men standing by the barricades, holding their hands in the air as they chanted at the police. The chant had become an anthem crying for justice. A demand to acknowledge what society long knew but wouldn't admit. That even when Blacks were doing no wrong, they could be shot by police who would face no penalty. An injustice only further ignored, and sometimes encouraged, if the victims didn't fit the mold of innocence or were resisting. A clear contrast to what normally happened to Whites. They could be obviously guilty and aggressively resisting, yet the police engaged them in ways that sought to preserve, if not respect, their lives. The tolerance of this long standing inequality had reached a tip pointing of open protest in the social arena.

"It's getting testy around here," Speedy said as he stepped beside Tory.

Although not with malicious intent, the statement read to Tory as being oblivious to the real and pressing concerns the chanters sought to convey. Yet this seemed to be the norm for most in the department. An insensitivity they were completely blind to. Nor did they seem receptive to being made aware of it.

"So what's the next step?" Speedy asked against the background of protest.

"Let's call Anne and have her pull up the personnel files of all the officers involved. Then let's go find the body."

◆ ◆ ◆

There it laid upon the examining table. Covered by a white sheet. The lights at a dim. The air sterile. The cadaver was motionless. Lifeless. Stiffening. Expelling the last remnants of life's imprint.

There's an irony to death. How a body once invigorated with vivaciousness is reduced to being an object. And even that is transitory, for the object will not last. Its decay to dust begins quickly. Fading to nothing.

The bluntness of this dynamic is evident when not viewed through the veils of memories or mental reactions to death. The body is just a body when the life that occupied it departs. And he had encountered enough bodies throughout the years, observing them without the lense of personal projections, to accept this fact.

He had seen bodies stiffened into neutral facades. At other times, he was stunned by how they were transformed into canvases of brutal destruction. Sometimes just savaged remains. In retrospect, from a witnessing perspective, the reasons why we inflict mortal harm often don't seem to justify the outcome of death. Conflict, unrestrained anger, poor judgment, or sometimes carelessness. Are these really reasons why other people should die? Or be killed? Yet such contemplation rarely happens when death is immersed in the parameters of assigning blame, guilt, and determinations of who is responsible. Including criminal responsibility.

The coroner entered with the normalcy of entering an office. The lights turned on. Tory and Speedy followed.

"I was just about to start the autopsy when you called. This one looks pretty straight forward."

The coroner pulled the sheet back to expose Martin's head and torso. His face blank and sober. Flanked by locks. His chest bare with two protruding holes.

"Two gunshot wounds in the upper left chest. One with an exit wound through the back. The other is probably lodged in a bone. The exit path is fairly horizontal, so he was probably standing upright when he was shot. Then there's blunt force bruising to the back of the head, most likely from the impact of hitting the ground. Traces of what seems to be gunpowder are on his clothes, so he was probably shot at close range. We'll let the ballistic tests confirm that and match it to the officer's gun."

"How about drugs or alcohol?" Tory asked.

"He has marijuana in his system. We already took samples to run tests to see if he was intoxicated at the time of the shooting."

"Could you smell it on his clothes?" Speedy inquired.

"No."

Tory looked at the corpse's arms as he asked, "Any signs of struggle?"

"His hands and wrists are clean. So are his shins and ankles." The coroner moved the sheet to reveal the corpse's forearms and wrists so Tory could see for himself.

There was a silence as Tory carefully scanned the body. He wanted the image to stay with him. Although it could no longer speak, there might be something it was still communicating that could be helpful to the investigation.

Eventually, Tory asked, "Any other factors you'll examine?"

"Since the 9-1-1 call said he was acting erratic, we'll check to see if he was on any mental health medication. Antidepressants, behavioral stuff, things of that nature. But other than that the cause of death seems pretty straightforward."

"Well, if any surprises pop up, please let me know."

Tory gave one last look at the body. One last chance for it to yield a lasting impression. But it just laid there. Just being dead. Its coolness dissolving to a coldness that would not be warm again.

Within that moment's expanse, it became clear the corpse would offer nothing else. So Tory turned toward the door. Perhaps death is a doorway to something else. A fitting metaphor since examining corpses often made Tory philosophical.

◆ ◆ ◆

As they drove through the streets, he wondered if it was "normal" to go from the stillness of morgues to the activity and congestion of city traffic. Yet such was their course as they headed back to police headquarters. The stirrings of the streets still echoed in their footsteps as they moved through the hallways to the small conference room where Anne awaited them. At a table covered with folders and papers, she sat with her eyes glued upon the television. The mayor was conducting a live press conference at the gas station on Spencer Avenue.

"We promise a thorough and transparent investigation. We've already contacted the State Police and F.B.I. to assist us and provide another set of eyes..." These were the words that greeted Tory and Speedy upon entering the room. Their eyes were immediately drawn to the screen. Tory noticed Chief Smitts standing behind the mayor, along with District Attorney Sandra Bailey, and others.

"Abiding by standard procedure, all the officers involved have been assigned to desk duties during the preliminary stages of the investigation. We're withholding their names for now but will make that information available as soon as it's appropriate. We're also withholding the name of the victim until we contact his family. But I will say he was an African-American man in his thirties who has died as a result of his injuries."

"Was he armed?" a reporter yelled from the crowd.

"He appeared to be unarmed but let's allow the police investigation to run its course. But let me end with this." The mayor stood a little taller with his eyes firmly focused. "We are a proud city that believes in law and order as well as treating all our citizens fairly. We also have a fine police force with officers who put their lives on the line daily. With that said, I would caution against any rush to judgment.

"Clearly this is a hot-button issue, one that will likely attract protest. The right to peaceful assembly and expression is constitutionally protected: a right we will honor and respect. But we won't hesitate to use the full extent of the law against anyone who crosses that line into criminal behavior." He paused to punctuate his point. He then concluded, "My administration will continue to provide updates as more information becomes available."

The mayor turned from the podium. Reporters immediately began to shout out questions. But he disappeared behind the members of his entourage who followed him in departure.

"Some day, huh?" Anne's irony was obvious as she turned off the television with the remote.

"Couldn't be better." Leave it to Speedy to counter with a touch of sarcasm.

"I have the personnel files here."

Tory and Speedy sat at the table. Tory knew he could always rely on Anne's preparation and attention to detail. It was extremely helpful, allowing his mind to ponder the more pressing dynamics of the investigation. Things were not always clear. Sometimes there were holes or contradictions in the gathered facts. And even these could be painted by the agendas of people pursuing their own interests.

"Let's start with Oliver Easthill, the officer who fired."

Anne pulled a headshot photo from a folder. A White man in his thirties. Round face with slightly sullen eyes. Cropped haircut. Clean shaven. You could say he looked like a cop. He looked approachable but also like someone you didn't want to mess with.

"Seven years on the force. Five years prior in the Army. He's married with two children. He has two prior civilian review complaints. One founded, he admitted to his supervisor he went too far. The other one, no judgment was rendered because the complainant didn't show up for repeated interviews."

"How long ago were those and what was the race of the complainants?" Tory asked.

Anne scoured through some papers. "The founded case was... two years ago, I think." The sought papers found. "Yeah, two years. And the complainant was a thirty-seven year old Black male. The other case was five years ago with a twenty-four year old Hispanic male. Other than that, his disciplinary record is clean. But he's filed numerous requests to be transferred from the Water Hole district."

The Civilian Review Board was created in response to another police crisis twelve years ago. Bernard Davis, the police chief at the time, instituted an aggressive program targeting street drug activity in the city's "high crime" neighborhoods. Over the course of a month, three separate incidents occurred in which Black men alleged excessive police force. They all suffered serious injuries; none were life-threatening but all required hospitalization. Avery Jackson, a nineteen year old college student, became the poster boy of police brutality in the city. He was an A student with a clean record. His disfigured face with bloated lips, swollen eyes, a broken jaw, and fractured cheek bone was featured as a full front-page cover on the city's main newspaper.

None of the Black men in these incidents had drugs on them although the officers involved suspected they did. And the all charges against them -- such as "disorderly conduct," "jay walking," "refusal to obey an officer," "resisting arrest" -- were later dropped. The district attorney at the time declined to press criminal charges against any of the officers. Although voicing serious concerns about their conduct, he stated there was insufficient evidence to secure convictions. Neither were any of the officers disciplined by the police department. But there was enough evidence to compel the city to settle civil suits with all the men, totaling about $350,000 for damages.

The political reaction to this crisis was the formation of a civilian-led body to handle claims of police misconduct. The mayor, the city council, and the district attorney were each granted a number of seats to make appointments to the Civilian Review Board. Initially, the board was only allowed to review police investigations of incidents. But after public uproar criticizing these limitations, the city council passed an amendment granting the board investigative powers, including the power to subpoena officers. This enabled the board to hire professional investigators to work on its behalf. But the board's findings were only advisory, not binding in any way. In its twelve year existence, a police chief never instituted any discipline suggested by the board that went beyond the police department's own determinations for punishment.

The only real impact of the board was that findings against officers had to be included in their personnel record. This meant any findings had to be considered when evaluating officers for promotion. Although nothing legally prevented an officer with board findings of misconduct from being promoted, it was treated as a liability. If an officer was later found in a controversy, the fact the department promoted him or her with negative findings could have unwanted political ramifications. Especially in the media.

Anne moved to another folder and pulled out a photo. Another White man with a long face and subtle grin. His jaw was pronounced, ascended by a long narrow nose. And his ears stood out among the layered hair that framed the top of his head.

"His partner of four years is Corey Peters. Eleven years on the force. Single with a clean disciplinary record. He actually has a few commendations for exceptional service. And was recommended by his supervisor for a promotion in rank which he did not receive."

Tory looked at the photo but didn't have any questions. Easthill was the only one who fired shots at Martin. Therefore, he would be the focus. Besides, Tory had done enough investigations to know all other officers involved would look to say as little as possible. To not incriminate themselves or their fellow officers. The blue wall of silence.

"Now to the responding unit."

Anne grabbed another folder and pulled out another headshot. Another White man. Stout face with a thick mustache bridged under his nose. Stern eyes with round cheeks. A knobby chin.

"Joseph Stevenson. On the force seven years. Married with no children. Clean record. He actually has specialized training in dealing with mental health crises. He employed the taser at the scene. And lastly..."

Anne pulled a photo from another folder. A Black woman. Large brown eyes and round lips. Her hair long and pulled back. There was an air of youthfulness about her face.

"Silvia McDonald. Five years on the force. She lives with her fiancee. One prior civilian review complaint which was unfounded. She was the one wearing her own body camera which she's agreed to turn over after consulting with a lawyer."

She was one of the few officers who volunteered to wear body cameras after the city council declined to make them mandatory for all officers. The council cited costs as the main reason for their decision, but pressure from the police union -- which was staunchly against the proposed policy -- was also a strong factor. As a concession, the council provided funding to assist officers who wished to purchase their own body cams. McDonald was one of the eight officers who did so.

Tory took a moment to survey the photos of the four officers. Nothing in them revealed any significant information, but it helped to start putting human faces to the facts. That this wasn't just some incident of impersonal moving parts. No, it was an interaction involving living individuals that resulted in a man's death. It had to become real to Tory.

"And none of them are willing to talk now?"

"All of them have invoked the forty-eight hour rule." Anne bent her head slightly to the side as she responded to Tory. Her gesture was clearly understood. Why would any officer not go to the fullest extent to protect one's self? And having two days to consult with others and ponder questions they knew would be asked was a luxury they had.

Finally, Tory broke the silence. "Thanks, Anne." He stood and looked at Speedy. "Maybe we should go in person to request an interview with Easthill's wife."

"I'm up for a ride."

♦ ♦ ♦

York Manor was another residential enclave for police. On the northen edge of the city, it was virtually a suburb. And segregated. For Tory's entire life, York Manor was known as a White part of the city. A lasting remnant of past housing practices that explicitly forbade people of color from buying or renting in the neighborhood. As the intergenerational legacy of people inheriting and selling houses continued, it somehow maintained its Whiteness without the blatant bigotry. Just "normal" habits of commerce and neighborhood preference that persisted upon the prior history of explicit exclusion.

Tory and Speedy rode in relative quiet. As he guided the steering wheel, Tory's thoughts wandered about the infamous 48-Hour Rule. It granted officers a forty-eight hour grace period before they had to answer any questions from the police department regarding matters of possible serious misconduct committed while on-duty. This usually meant incidents involving use of force that resulted in serious injury or death to a civilian. The rule applied not only to those who might be subject to penalties and prosecution, but also witnessing officers. It basically gave officers at least two days to prepare for an investigation. It also delayed any corrective action since it was extremely rare that the department would do anything to address such an incident without first questioning the officers involved.

The 48-Hour Rule was adopted as a concession to the police while the city was formulating legislation for the Civilian Review Board. At the time, the police contract was being negotiated. The police union argued that since the city was increasing protections for citizens via the board, the police should also receive additional protections. Thus, the 48-Hour Rule was included in the new contract.

The union deemed the rule a necessity. It argued that officers' schedules can be stressful and demanding. And when an incident occurred that could result in criminal prosecution or severe punishment, it made sense for officers to have forty-eight hours to secure legal representation and professional advice before being questioned. The union noted that police departments all over the country had similar arrangements, including some in major cities. In fact, some jurisdictions had even longer waiting periods before officers could be questioned. Some as long as ten days.

The mayor at the time downplayed the scope of the rule. He explained that with incidents involving serious charges, such as police brutality or manslaughter, it was common for prosecutors nationwide to instruct police departments to delay questioning of all officers involved. The reason being any answers officers gave in police questioning often could not be used against them in court. And prosecutors rarely conducted their own questioning within forty-eight hours of such incidents.

But public advocates were critical of the rule. They were quick to point out what they considered an obvious hypocrisy: cops were granted a forty-eight hour grace period but not citizens. Police commonly interrogated suspects within forty-eight hours of arrest, sometimes immediately after a crime. And it was not uncommon for suspects to face the challenge of securing legal representation while jailed. Why should police officers receive different preferential treatment?

Tory was torn. On one hand, he saw how the rule could serve as a reasonable allowance to officers. In theory, they were more likely than civilians to be involved in such incidents, so a higher level of protection wasn't completely irrational. He remembered stressful incidents he experienced while on the beat, some which could have easily become cases in which he was investigated for serious misconduct. Having forty-eight hours to collect one's self and prepare for questioning could be helpful. But in practice, the grace period was more often used to examine vulnerabilities in one's case and devise legal strategies to address them. Although no one would admit it publicly, officers often collaborated on a "version" of events that protected them. Even if that meant omitting or "forgetting" incriminating factors. No cop wanted to go to jail or lose one's job. And cooperating to maintain the blue wall of silence was a powerful means of protecting against such.

Tory remembered the counsel of Dusty, his first detective partner in the Internal Affairs Division. Dusty had since become his main mentor when it came to police matters. He taught that the best time to question a person involved in a crime was as soon as possible after it occurred once the person calmed down. For example, you wouldn't want to question a person right after he or she was attacked. Adrenaline and emotions would likely cloud the clarity of one's account. And if you waited too long, most people start repeatedly retelling what happened in their minds, formulating "their account" of what took place as opposed to simply stating what transpired. More time also afforded those fabricating an account greater leisure to craft and tweak their stories. But once a person has calmed down after the incident, Dusty considered that the ideal time for questioning. Such calming usually happened before forty-eight hours, so Dusty came to hate the 48-Hour Rule.

But he was clever. He reasoned that if he couldn't question the main subjects of an Internal Affairs investigation, he wanted to at least see them. He felt body language revealed more about innocence and guilt than the words people spoke. So he would often look for a way to cross paths with the subjects. Like going to their homes to request an interview of their spouse who, like any other civilian, was not covered under the rule. Dusty would justify such requests as inquiring about any factors in the officers' personal lives which may have contributed to a mental state more susceptible to misconduct.

This sometimes allowed him to at least lay his eyes on the subjects. Then based on what he saw and what his gut felt, he would engage the task of collecting evidence to support or refute the guilt or innocence their bodies conveyed.

But these were most likely the last days for the 48-Hour Rule in the city. Many jurisdictions that previously granted such phased it out or were looking to do so. The negotiations for the next police contract would start in two years. Even if the mayor at that time would be open to keeping the rule, the city council would likely not approve a contract containing it. A majority of council members already stated publicly they no longer supported the rule.

◆ ◆ ◆

Tory's mind returned to focus on the matter at hand as he turned onto the street Easthill lived on. He resided in a multi-bedroom house spread across one floor with a lawn and garage. The car with detectives sitting guard across from the house stood out because most residents parked their cars in driveways and garages, not on the street. It always humored Tory when cops' efforts to be discreet made it obvious they were cops. As if an unmarked car and plain clothes somehow miraculously cloaked the police as ordinary citizens doing ordinary things.

Tory gave a nod to the detectives as he parked in front of the house. They gave a returning look.

"Do you need me at the door with you?"

"No."

Speedy referred to the unmarked car as he said, "Then I'll let the suits know they can relax." He grimaced, exited the car, and approached the detectives.

Tory headed to the door of Easthill's house. He always became slightly nervous when making a first approach to a potentially confrontational person of interest. Although they were both cops and there was an unspoken allegiance they were supposed to share in the face of public scrutiny, the Internal Affairs investigation made Tory and Easthill opponents. Maybe even enemies. At least temporarily.

It also crossed Tory's mind that he was a Black detective investigating a White officer regarding the killing of an unarmed Black civilian. On a police force that was majority White. With the killing happening in a predominantly Black neighborhood. Many points of potential tension, even if they were navigated with professionalism and civility.

Tory pulled out his badge before reaching the door. He held it up and rang the doorbell. Moments later, the door slowly opened to show Oliver Easthill on the other side. His hand prominently upon the gun resting in his hip holster.

Tory stood still. Dusty taught him that, whenever possible, let the subjects initiate the first engagement. Don't give them anything to react to. Give them a clean canvas to display whatever they will. And observe. Remember, body language.

"Can I help you?"

Tension. An obvious unease. He clearly didn't give any indication of a willingness to cooperate.

"I'm Detective Givens with Internal Affairs."

The response was quick and terse. "I'm not answering any questions..."

"I know," interrupted Tory. "I can't ask you anything for at least forty-eight hours. I'm actually here to request an interview with your wife. At a time and place convenient to her."

The tension increased, as if he felt Tory was intruding where he did not belong. "Why?"

"To see if there's anything going on in your home or personal life that might be a factor in what happened."

"There's nothing." The words were bold and blunt as he leaned forward slightly. A restrained yet clear assertion of presence.

Tory remained cool and observant. "It's better if she tells me that herself."

"Well, she's not available right now." The assertiveness shifted to a new tactic, now maintaining his position through avoidance. Tory noticed.

"Then I'll leave my card."

Tory pulled out a card and held it out. As Easthill snatched it, Tory immediately turned to return to the car. Within a few steps, Tory heard the door being shut abruptly. Another imposition of presence.

But Tory got what he needed from this encounter. He felt Easthill had something to hide and would not cooperate in revealing it. That didn't necessarily mean he was guilty, but it clearly suggested Easthill would not be a compliant and reliable source in determining what happened. And the other cops would likely remain silent. And Martin, being dead, could offer no account of his own. The challenge would be to find other evidence, including witnesses, to reconstruct what happened. And it was better to obtain such sooner than later, since evidence not found or connected with soon after an incident could quickly become irretrievable.

◆ ◆ ◆

It was Dusty who told him, that whenever possible, don't bring your work home with you. He wasn't just talking about paperwork and phone conversations, but also the residue of police work. "Find a place to leave it all behind," his mentor advised, "find a buffer zone of release before you go home."

He was right. While immersed in the work, it's easy to become blind to how stressful it is. So much police work, especially for detectives, centers around the prevalence of inhumanity we as a society don't want to fully acknowledge. That "civilized" people kill, hurt, steal from, and otherwise harm other people within the same society. And often people they know, including loved ones. It's challenging to spend the bulk of your days, and sometimes nights, immersed in such and then go home to be a whole and humane person. The inhumanity finds ways of seeping through your thoughts and actions to intrude upon your personal life. So it's imperative to find safe ways of stepping away from the work so it doesn't deteriorate you and your relationships. It took Dusty three divorces and the ruin of a fourth marriage that ended when his estranged wife died to learn this lesson.

For Dusty, his main buffer zone became a sports bar. He made the bartender solemnly swear to never serve him more than two drinks -- no matter what. This allowed him to decompress before a visual screen of opposing teams engaged in whatever contest was on. His ranting at younger athletes struggling or excelling at feats he could not perform became a way of releasing the stress accumulated by investigating the vices of others.

Tory found his buffer zone at an isolated overlook in a city park. A place alone in the midst of an overpopulated city. Jelani was the one who showed him this refuge hidden in the urban bustle: a parking lot upon an elevated hill. It gave forth a scenic view of the buildings downtown. The sky above the metropolis serving as an open canvas to paint the pondering of thoughts explored alone or in conversation. A place to con-template the furthest reachings of the mind, if one so chose.

"But that's the irony of it. We put people in situations where they can't provide for themselves in a country that has enough to provide for everyone. And if after hitting road-block after roadblock, struggling in hardship while the fat cats are living in luxury; if someone like me decides that's enough and goes and takes what others deny me, the police arrest me for robbery while turning a blind eye to the societal forces that led to me stealing."

"But we could use people like you on the force. You would make a good cop."

Jelani took a moment to grimace. He found humor in Tory making his plea donning the police uniform Jelani knew he would never wear.

"The fact that I see this game for what it is is exactly the reason I can't become a cop. I can't be part of it even if it means staying in poverty."

"But things can change."

"How much has it changed since you've been on the force? Are poor people of color being arrested and prosecuted any less while the elite, who create situations of poverty and sometimes steal themselves, go along untouched? I know that may seem like urban conspiracy theory to you but that doesn't mean it's not true."

He smiled with his wired framed glasses. The broadness of his face was vibrant with life, as he stroked his thickening beard and mustache. His shoulders, lean and wide, were a befitting mantle for his wit and long locks. Slender and tall, he possessed sharp eyes that allowed him to survey the terrain of existence. Beholding a sharp mind, he was quick to analyze and interpret what he observed. To Tory, he felt like a close cousin more than a long-time friend since childhood. A bond that insinuated they were of the same family but had different parents. And, therefore, different quirks which informed their similar yet distinct personalities.

"Were corners made for Black men to stand on
And alleys to become the pathways to their tombs,
Scarred by pavement cut in squares

That crack and break as trampled upon.
And in the city, the traffic doesn't stop.
Although the surface is rough
Bondage is fragile:
Our lives are that very sidewalk.
Yet somehow, within the brokenness of life,
We search for places to congregate in joy.
Even if upon the convergence of corners,
Indulging in self-destructive acts.
Dying to be happy,
Falling in alleys that become our mausoleums."

It was just like Jelani to spontaneously shift from one topic to another. "It's not quite done, but isn't what I have so far tight?"

To him, the apparent disparate points were connected. If Tory remained quiet, Jelani's stream of words would reveal how they were related in his mind. And with Jelani, the words were sure to come. Any silence within his presence was only temporary.

"That's what I would do if I had the means."

"Be a poet?"

"I am a poet. Or a street philosopher whose chosen mode of teaching includes poetry. But poet-philosophers, the real ones, most of us live and die in poverty. So that's not what I meant about making money. No, the corner: *"Were corners made for Black men to stand on."* I would open a corner store if I had the means."

Tory smirked. Jelani noticed this and smiled.

"You think I'm joking but I'm serious. The corner store is an unofficial institution in the 'hood. In the right hands, you could have more impact than the mayor. Maybe even the president.

"First off, I wouldn't sell malt liquor. No matter how much money I could make selling it. As a Black owned business, I would force the brothers and sisters to upgrade their choice of alcohol."

Tory burst out in laughter.

"I'm serious. Look, I'm realistic: I know I can't get them to stop drinking altogether. But if we keep drinking from the bottom of the barrel, we'll never... I can't think of the word I'm looking for."

"Rise up?"

"Nah, we need to have like an awareness that we can rise up before we actually do it. And I'm talking about being open to that awareness. That'll never happen if we stay stuck on that malt liquor. We have to at least take it up a level.

"But more than that, I would put a fruit and vegetable stand outside. Even knowing in advance people are going to be robbing me all the time. But think about that: if people are stealing healthy food from me to eat, at least now we're starting to be a little healthy."

"But they're stealing."

"I told you why. Because we've been placed in a situation that compels us to do so. I'm not saying that's a hundred percent the reason. But if we eliminated poverty today, you'd see an instant decrease in robbery, violence, all kinds of crime. When people have something of their own, they're less concerned about taking other people's stuff."

Jelani paused as if to reflect upon his own wisdom before continuing.

"But I would do the fruit stand with good quality produce. Not that crap the supermarket labels as fruits and vegetables. And I would keep the store clean as heck. Let people see we can have something and take good care of it. Even the outside, I would sweep the sidewalk everyday."

"What else?"

"The prices would be fair, not ghetto taxing the poor. And if I had a brick wall outside, I would commission it monthly to different graffiti artists in the neighborhood. It would be like our own art space. A street gallery.

"And then, which connects to the poem, I would actually hook up the corner hangout spot. I would buy the brothers chairs instead of crates. Maybe even have a table with the umbrella so they could have some shade during the day. I would leave some conscious books on the table, an encouragement to have more serious conversations. And a free condom dispensary."

"Now you lost me."

"Nah man, this safe sex -- I mean safer sex thing is something we gotta get real about. Plus, if they see I'm providing them a community service, they'll show more respect for my store. I could get free condoms from the health clinic. They get boxes of those things every week for their patients."

Jelani smiled, having concluded his dissertation. Tory smiled and then began to laugh. A laughter contagious that eventually infected Jelani.

"Just because I'm laughing doesn't mean I'm not serious about every word. Word to the mother!"

The memory made Tory smile. He peered over the heights of the darkened buildings tinged by the glow of the street lights below. Physically he was alone but the presence of Jelani was with him, an intimacy within the larger vague urban landscape. Their vivid conversations always had a way of washing away the residue of police work. The memories of these talks did so to a lesser degree. Tory could feel a partial release of the building tension he had been carrying in relation to the Martin Little shooting since the afternoon.

But then came the image of the young body now laying dead. Then the front door opening to see Easthill standing with his hand upon his gun. Then the turning of the street corner past the group of Black men drinking and smoking. Then the dried stain of blood upon the alley's concrete. Then a bag of chips and a soda in his hands as he looked to the floor in the convenience store.

The stream of uninvited mental images was interrupted by an inserted thought: if Jelani was still around, I would partner with him to open a store. Tory's increased salary along with a kid's college fund that would likely not be used for that purpose would suffice as seed money for their venture.

But Jelani was no longer around. And wouldn't be so for a long time. If he ever came back. He might never come back. I need to write to him. I also need to go home now to my wife.

CHAPTER THREE:
The idea of justice

The drive home was uneventful. He pulled into the driveway and parked in his spot beside the garage. He grabbed his keys and entered through the back door. The house was quiet and in darkness. She probably wasn't home.

He checked the refrigerator door to see if there was a note since she didn't text or call him. And there it was in her distinctive cursive script. "At the protests. Be home later if not arrested..." followed by a smiley face.

They had an agreement that she would never communicate via text, cell phone, his office phone, or email anything regarding her community activism. They both knew these could be monitored by the police at any time and without notice. He preferred to know as little as possible about her organizing work. If he didn't know, he could truthfully not answer any questions about it. It was known in the police department that Loretta was very involved in community organizing. Including past campaigns that were extremely critical of the police.

Loretta. She had become an unremovable pillar in his life. Although they had ventured onto different paths, she was an undeniable guidepost for him.

They met at a church meeting a little over 23 years ago. She was more serious about Christianity then. For him, it was more social. But he was drawn to her determined spirit and summoned the courage to introduce himself. He admitted years later that he only started going to her church's Wednesday night Bible class to get to know her since, at the time, he attended his own church irregularly. But a connection emerged between them whereby he finally asked her out on a date.

They went to see a PG-rated comedy. She always remembered the movie's title, he always forgot it. But he did remember it was rather boring with only a few funny moments. He also remembered that they went to the Moonlight Café afterwards. And what they ordered. She had a chicken breast platter, a strawberry milkshake, and a chocolate cake for dessert. He ordered a jumbo burger with fries. He would have gotten a dessert but didn't because he wanted to make sure he had enough to cover the bill just in case she didn't offer to go dutch. She didn't.

Her "stinginess" made him a little mad, especially since he already paid for the movie tickets, with popcorn and soda there. But he wasn't going to say anything about it on a first date, one he really liked except for her not paying for anything. Fortunately, he had just enough to cover the bill. And she didn't even offer to leave the tip. He was slightly embarrassed to leave only a dollar and some change so he tried to make it look like more by partly covering it with a napkin.

But he was drawn to her "old school" sensibilities. She never hesitated to say that she trusted her grandmother's values about men. She was very vocal that she would only date a good Christian man. Neither did she believe in dating just for the sake of dating. Or in long engagements. She held no qualms about stating that she was an independent woman who believed in equal, Bible-guided relationships. And that she wanted children, and had to have at least one girl.

As the months passed, she admitted she had some doubts about Christianity. Not Jesus' teachings, rather the structure of the church and the accompanying dogma and politics. And unending drama. This came as a relief to him, who admitted he wasn't the most devout Christian. For him, religion was more a family tradition than a personal conviction.

Yet he did see the benefit in striving to be a good man with few vices.

But they fell in love. Eventually all the facades and charades that people hold of how they are supposed to be with each other dropped away. And they found themselves *together* in a truly intimate and effortless way. That's why he wasn't surprised that night she let him sleep over, their naked bodies cuddling each other throughout most of their sleepless voyage to dawn. And as the sun rose, she joked, half serious, "You know this means we have to get married now, cause that's what this would mean in biblical times. And my grandmother's days of shotgun weddings."

Although his response was only a loud laugh, in his heart he agreed. Whereas past sexual encounters became personal accomplishments and pleasure-centered events, this time it truly felt like the consummation of a beautiful union. One he wanted to embrace and never lose. One he wouldn't let get away.

So the next day he went to a jewelry store to purchase a ring. A silver band beholding a small cut diamond. Not knowing her ring size, he took a guess, securing a promise to be able to exchange the ring for one of the right size if it didn't fit.

He then went to wait for her outside her Thursday morning class. She was in graduate school at the time. His smile was booming as his eyes met hers upon exiting the class. She was happy to see him, oblivious to what was about to occur. He played it cool, cause that's how cats from the streets are supposed to do it. Accompanying her to the dining hall, they joined a couple of her friends for lunch among the throng of hungry students. Eventually, the mass of sated bodies dwindled to a sparse few, including the happy couple remaining at a table in a far corner of the hall.

In the middle of her rambling about some conceptual argument she was preparing for history class, he walked around the table, dropped to one knee and pulled out the jewelry box. She was instantly overwhelmed with tears, saying yes before he could even finish the sentence, "Will you marry..." Her scream of excitement echoed through the hall. The remaining students and staff turned with concern, but this quickly melted into a witnessing delight.

He still played it cool. Street debonair. He carefully took hold of the ring. Gracefully grabbed her hand with the extended ring finger. Gave a lover's coy smile. But all the suave veneer came to an abrupt end when the ring wouldn't fit over the knuckle of her finger. She burst into uncontrollable laughter as her joyful tears continued to fall. He also laughed, to be enveloped by her hugging body draping him in amused appreciation. There was no room for shame or embarrassment in this moment of pure joy. Pure love.

As the witnesses applauded, she held the ring in her hand. They kissed and held each other in a moment that was nectar sweet. But when she pulled away, he became nervous. He didn't want the ring to get lost before they exchanged it at the jewelry store. She went to the bathroom to wash her face, refusing to release her grasp of the ring. He took the time alone to take a deep breath of delayed anxiety. And then to worry about losing the ring. When she returned empty-handed, he nervously asked where it was. She displayed it hanging on a necklace around her neck.

He asked if she should put the ring back in the box to return it to the jeweler. No, she insisted on wearing it proudly around her neck for all the world to see. So the bus ride across town became one of him constantly peering at her necklace in hope that it wouldn't fall off. Or be ripped away by a bold robber. Or somehow magically disappear.

The jeweler was happy to exchange the ring. But this she dismissed. It was only a half size too small, so she wanted the band expanded. Therefore, instead of a free exchange, Tory had to pay extra to have it stretched. Something she, in retrospect, acknowledged was a bit silly. And he never let her forget it, in a playful lover's way. That along with how he had to pay for everything on their first date.

The wedding was small but unforgettable. She broke with tradition by summoning him to her bridal chamber prior to the ceremony. After clearing out all the bridesmaids and her grandmother with the beaming face, she stated she had some things she wanted to make sure were said before they wedded.

"Cause I know I'm the one who insisted that we not date long before getting married. But if you're not ready, I'm willing to push things back."

"No, I want to do this. Really."

"Cause it's only been a year. And I only want one marriage in my life. With no divorces." He nodded in agreement. So she continued. "I would rather be real with each other than play pretend. And I don't mean just for today. I mean that for every day of our marriage. I lean on my grandmother's words when she says a true commitment to each other is more valuable than being happy. Happiness comes and goes, but when someone is there with you no matter what, that's what makes a marriage work.

"Being there doesn't always mean getting along with each other. She and my grandfather were married for forty-four years. And she said for about ten of those she couldn't stand his guts. But they were married. And not liking your husband doesn't amount to adultery, the only reason Jesus gave for why people could divorce. Are you listening to me?"

"Absolutely."

"I'm not trying to say we should hate each other but I want to know... Rather, I want to let you know that after we put these rings on, even if I end up disliking you immensely, I'm not divorcing or leaving you. That somehow, some way, we'll have to find a way to work it out or get along. That even if a period comes where things are real tough, I'm never leaving you. And I hope you'd do the same for me."

"There's no one better for me than you, Loretta."

"But people change. They're supposed to change if they're truly living. My grandmother told me not more than a month ago: "The man you marry today, don't expect him to be the same man you'll die with. He's gonna grow and change. In some ways, he'll be better. And some ways will need some fixing. But "death do us part" means you're committed to staying the course with him till death. Even if he comes to need a lot of fixing." Her smile spurned him to grimace.

"She said that's how it was with my grandfather. Before he became the absolute treasure he was as an old man, there were periods when he was the opposite. But that was part of his growing and maturing. And by my grandmother sticking it through, she got to see him become a diamond."

Loretta then stood close to Tory and looked him squarely in the eye. "So I just want to be clear that's where we are. That even if your asshole tendencies take the lead, I'm not leaving you." He was surprised to hear her use that word in a church, but her point remained poignant. "Even if that means we'll have our share of battles and periods where we just don't get along. But once you get your stuff together, rest assured, you won't have any problems with me. I'll be a good wife cause I'm already perfect."

Her smile inferred the jest of her closing words. And as their eyes rested in each other's gaze, they both smiled. In that moment, he felt so in love with her that he couldn't put into words what was bursting forth to be expressed. So he sighed. The silence affirming their shared understanding which was mutual and fulfilling.

The memory receded as he stood before the refrigerator. Staring at the imperfect circle with two dots and a crescent. Loretta's smiley faces always looked like they were leaning slightly to the right. Her skewed perfection.

"At the protests. Be home later if not arrested..." Right. He figured there would be something her group would do in response to the shooting. To ease the nervousness he felt, he headed to the television. If anything concerning happened it would surely be mentioned on the news.

The first visual that appeared on the large screen was informing. A reporter was standing by police barricades set up by the gas station. A group of protesters, mostly young Blacks, were chanting and yelling nearby. Officers, clad in riot gear, stood in the face of the anger vented in their direction.

"The scene has been tense all night," said the reporter, "but a more angry mood has taken over in the last hour. There hasn't been any violence, but certainly a lot of screaming and yelling directed at the cops. The number of protesters has dwindled but not the intensity. One wonders if things will escalate into violence..."

As the reporter continued, someone could be heard entering through the back door. With his attention partly tuned to the television, he looked in the direction of the kitchen for Loretta's entrance.

"People are mad and "sick and tired," as one resident said, of what they regard as a long history of police abuse and mistreatment..."

Loretta entered. He muted the television with the remote in his hand. She remained in the doorway, looking at him and then the television. He could feel the stress upon her.

"Not a good day?"

"I left a half hour ago. The young people are really angry and there wasn't anything we could do to calm them down."

He paused before speaking, knowing what he had to say would likely worsen the mood. But he had to tell her. They had an understanding that they did not have to divulge everything. In fact, certain things he couldn't disclose and with other things it was better that she not know. But when something felt like it would be a secret to not reveal, those things he made it a point to confess to her.

"Guess who's been put on the lead to investigate it?"

He didn't intend for it to sound boastful and hoped it didn't come across that way. But her response was quick and sharp.

"What's there to investigate? He killed an unarmed Black guy. Or did the media leave out that he had a weapon? Or that he was in the midst of attacking a cop with his bare hands?"

"You know it's not that simple."

"For the police and the media, it never is. But the people we spoke to said he was killed for being Black."

Issues like this remained a point of strain in their marriage since he decided to become a cop. It didn't impede their love for each other but it made their love uncomfortable at times. It really is easier to be at odds with an enemy or stranger. To bear such with someone you truly love can be an immense burden. Even if a temporary one, passing like the burdens that had come and gone before. With her commitment to community activism and his profession as a cop, these conflicts arose regularly. Just as contentious incidents between the Black community and police were frequent occurrences.

Yet he would defend his position. "Then I trust the facts will bear that out."

"They already have." She would not relent and was willing to have this argument if he wanted. "The real question," she asked rhetorically, "is will there be justice? Or accountability? History says no. But we'll see if things are different this time with a *Black* cop investigating."

"You mean detective," he uttered in response to what he felt was a demeaning insult.

She rolled her eyes with a fierceness. Many times they had debated whether Black officers, or concerned officers of other races, could affect change in a system built upon and sustained by White supremacy. And she would be clear in their discussions to not limit White supremacy to just bigotry or extremism. At its essence, White supremacy holds White life and culture to be superior to, regarded more valuable than, other races and cultures. A supremacy often achieved, in part, by denigrating other races and cultures, relegating them to lesser positions and worth. Within this view, any instance in which a Black life was treated as less had White supremacist tendencies, even if done without explicit prejudice and hatred. Even if done with a graceful and polite facade. Even if done unintentionally.

Not even he could deny that with so many incidents involving extreme force by police against Blacks, Black life was not treated with the same regard as White life. Even with some cops being more sensitive to how they engaged Blacks, this increased sensitivity did not diminish the harmful impact of incidents when Black life was treated without equal regard.

She was ready to counter his response. But a greater war demanded a reserve of her energy from the present battle. A battle that would eventually fade into the background of the domineering love that remained the basis of their relationship. So she waved the white flag.

"I'm going to bed. Tomorrow will be another long day followed by another night of much needed protest."

There was a little dig at him who only attended protests as a cop assigned to police them. She rolled her eyes once more and started toward the bedroom. But before exiting, she turned to offer one last word. Her surrender to love demanded it.

"Just for the record: I still love my husband. I'm just at odds with his profession right now..."

"... at odds with his profession right now," he overlapped. And to the familiar refrain he added, "Again."

She took a moment to stand there before exiting. The ringing of his cell phone offered a distraction to the lingering animosity. He answered it.

"Detective Givens."

"Givens, this is the chief."

"How you doing, Chief Smitts?"

"Listen, I need you to go meet with the D.A. first thing in the morning. Seven-thirty sharp, at her office. She wants to talk to you about the case. I'll explain why when I see you in person tomorrow."

Bewildered, Tory responded, "Okay."

"I have to go. I'll see you tomorrow."

In the midst of saying, "Good..." he heard the phone disconnect. But he continued the statement anyway, "... night, sir."

A moment of digesting the unexpected as distractions offered an apparent refuge. He unmuted the television to give audio accompaniment to the sight before his eyes: ice cream was on sale. The supermarket commercial advertising the sales of the week was more comforting than the killing of an unarmed Black man for reasons not yet known. Reasons even impacting his home life with his wife.

Although you try not to bring the work home, sometimes it follows you there.

◆ ◆ ◆

When he entered the bed, she was already laying with her back to him. Although this was her normal way of sleeping, it always felt more pronounced when they went to bed after a squabble. It only added to the collage of stuff whirling through his mind. He knew it was unlikely that he would have a night of continuous sleep to greet the dawn with.

He became accustomed to the sleepless nights. It wasn't quite insomnia but not that far removed. He would lay on the mattress, dropping in and out of semi-states of unconsciousness as a gamut of thoughts dominated his mindscape.

This night, the argument with Loretta was the first intrusion upon the solitude of his drowsiness. Not so much the words spoken earlier as much as the unsaid points of contention vocalized in past disputes.

Can a cop working in the system diminish and eventually overcome the White supremacy within in it? Part of the problem was the utter blindness of the police force: most cops wouldn't even acknowledge the possibility of White supremacy permeating policing. And the few who did often painted such an assertion as overreaching, as if it overlooked improvements made to better race relations in policing.

Loretta always said this was a common narrative. That mainstream America, which includes the majority of Whites within it, is invested in the idea that this country gets a little more just, a little bit better every single day. They cite the abandonment of more extreme expressions of bigotry and open hatred as a significant culmination proving improvement. They hold that most "innocent" Whites, and the social and cultural institutions of this country, are approaching or have already reached the point of being "post-racial." A state where people are not "judged by the color of their skin but by the content of their character."

Dr. Martin Luther King, Jr. echoed those last words in his famous *I Have a Dream* speech. Loretta often noted how within this speech he explicitly criticized "the unspeakable horrors of police brutality." There were other points of stinging commentary he offered before articulating his oft-praised dream-vision of America. Points many people never read or chose to ignore by focusing on the dream at the end of the speech. But in leading up to that historic climax, King bluntly declared that Blacks were still not free, even as he was speaking one hundred years after the Emancipation Proclamation. That Blacks lived as exiles in their own country. That when it came to the promissory note of the Constitution, Blacks were given a bounced check stamped "insufficient funds." That the unalienable rights of life, liberty and the pursuit of happiness proclaimed in the Declaration of

Independence were still denied to Blacks. A denial not limited to the more extreme forms of White supremacy prevalent in the South: King's criticism also included the so-called integrated North whose professed advancements still left Blacks without freedom, equality, and the fruits of true citizenship.

For Loretta, this speech asserted a powerful creed. Not just the eloquence of King's dream but also the call to combat the injustices inhibiting this dream from its inherent and attainable reality. She took to heart his acknowledgment of "the fierce urgency of now." And how the pursuit of what is right must utilize a soul force not sullied by wrong deeds. The speech set a standard of purity and uncompromising conviction that served as a benchmark for her life. An unyielding reminder that until racial oppression is adequately addressed it will be virtually impossible to judge one by the content of one's character. And in many cases, this oppression, along with its accompanying prejudices, would totally blind others to the character Blacks possessed.

She also held that the ideal should not be used to gloss over the continuing factors which prevent the actualization of the ideal. This point resonated deeply with Tory. That it was irresponsible to promote a race neutral approach within a society that viewed everything through the lense of race, even if unknowingly. This dynamic was present even among some who sincerely wished for more just relations between the races.

The contemporary shift in language and manners did not mean society had reached a state in which one's character dictated how one was perceived. The more explicit and obvious racial terms of the past simply underwent an evolution of expression while maintaining the same values and norms. An evolution that still reserved space for expression of the old ways. The new terminology and facade were just a more sophisticated code. One draped in a politically correct veneer and social savvy aimed to purport an illusion of better conditions for Blacks and other people of color. Yet the new code still maintained a limited lexicon for Blackness, most of which remained overwhelmingly negative and inferior. And even where the new language included some previously denied positivity for Blackness, it didn't prevent the ongoing predominance of injustice Blacks have suffered since the "good ol' days." How much had really changed with the new coded language and norms?

For Tory this was personal. He never lost sight of the fact that he was from the 'hood. And this was accompanied by the daunting truth that things there remained just as unjust today as they have always been. Some aspects of the injustice have been more exposed. Other aspects continue to be glossed over or hidden. Yet the brutal injustice of concentrated poverty and intense suffering afflicting predominantly Black urban neighborhoods persists.

But so many problems in the 'hood have always been there. Even the shooting of Martin, if it's proven to be police brutality: that's nothing new in the 'hood. As a youth, Tory was treated roughly numerous times by police upon the premise of far-reaching suspicions. Being out late, hanging with friends, being in the "wrong" neighborhood: these were deemed sufficient "reasonable cause" to be stopped and questioned by police. And sometimes searched. And sometimes manhandled -- a few times, very roughly. These police actions were only recurring injustices based on stereotypes that Blacks were dangerous and guilty with criminal tendencies. Stereotypes Tory continued to see acted upon by various colleagues throughout his years as a police officer.

If such stereotypes were held to be true, there was no need to treat Blacks with the same care innocent people are due. If they were disrespected, wronged, hurt, or even killed in the policing of their "criminal tendencies," what harm was really done? Within such reasoning, even if they didn't do anything wrong *this* time, they probably did something wrong before. Or will do so soon enough. And even if one encounters a "rare" individual Black who never did or ever will do wrong, the presumption of guilt was something he or she had to expect given the prevalence of negative qualities among *those people.*

Only the beeping of his alarm clock brought the parade of thoughts to a temporary halt. He hit the snooze button and turned to see Loretta readjust to resume her sleep. He laid there for a moment, knowing that an additional few minutes of sleep was a dream deferred. Instead, he disabled the alarm and sat up to accept the fatigue that would hang over his day.

◆ ◆ ◆

The early morning drive through the streets offered a temporary diversion from the weariness he knew would collapse upon him at some point in the day. For now, the deficiency of sleep offered him a quietude of mind. He was too tired to continue the unending barrage of thoughts that intruded upon his sleep time. The mind was more settled for now. Besides, he was awake while most of the city remained asleep. This gave him a sense of invigoration.

Anticipating the meeting with the District Attorney, his mind naturally gravitated to city politics. For him, there was a no more trustworthy expert on the subject than The Professor. Just by recalling his name, Tory could see with his mind's eye that regal face of roundness that beamed deliberate intelligence and matured wisdom.

When Tory told Loretta he was thinking about becoming a cop, she suggested he talk to The Professor. He proved to be a valuable mentor to her and was a major reason she pursued a career in academics instead of public policy work in the world of think tanks. She stated directly her preference that Tory not become a cop. For reasons political as well as selfish.

"Yeah," he remembered her saying, "I don't want to come home one night to find out my husband was killed. There's no way I would ever tell you what to do. But if you get The Professor's blessing, it will ease my heart."

It felt strange going to a complete stranger to discuss such a major life decision. But within the first minute of meeting The Professor, Tory was overcome by the power of his personality. Although he sensed he might be challenged in difficult and intimate ways, Tory felt safe being vulnerable with this wise elder. He had the flair of a storyteller in exploring the historical, political, and social dynamics of what might seem to be just mundane factors. Sitting with him, Tory understood why Loretta often connected personal matters with the larger fabric of history and society. All these qualities were vividly displayed in Tory's first meeting with him.

"You can do it," The Professor eventually uttered. "I think you have noble reasons and good intentions. But in my heart, I feel you're too intelligent for what you'll end up facing. You could make a more powerful contribution to our people doing something else." It was tempered, but a blessing nonetheless.

While escorting Tory out of the office, The Professor said his door would always be open to him. And it was. Numerous times throughout the years, Tory went to him for counsel, support, and sometimes some very needed hard-handed correction. He also became a go-to-guy for legal matters. Not so much from a lawyer's perspective, rather how the application of the law informed how to proceed in the day-to-day realities of being a police officer. He was also one of Tory's unfailing pillars of guidance for the array of issues that arose from being Black in a White-oriented police force.

Tory remembered going to The Professor to discuss the election of Sandra Bailey seven years ago. She surprisingly won the Democratic primary for District Attorney despite her history of staunchly conservative politics. She then easily cruised to victory in the general election. The Professor explained that the city's politics never veered far from its conservative right-leaning traditions, even if dressed as a left-center orientation among contemporary Democrat politicians. In the long-term view of the city's politics, both major parties had extended periods of holding hard right stances.

This history went back as early as the Emancipation Proclamation, when many prominent local politicians admonished Lincoln's Republican Party. All the prominent politicians at that time were White and remained with or joined the Democratic Party. Thus, this party became the political vehicle by which to restrict and control the city's Black population. Some politicians even touted a hardline rhetoric of sending Blacks "back to where they came from" -- often without stating specifically where that would be. Blacks, however, were needed to maintain a sufficient supply of low-wage workers for the city's manufacturing companies, as well as domestic workers for affluent Whites.

When Presidents John F. Kennedy and Lyndon B. Johnson aligned with the civil rights movement, many local politicians considered that political treason. This spurred a migration back to the Republican party for many with con-servative strains. In contrast, Blacks who had previously registered in the party of Lincoln shifted to the Democrats. Thus, the dominance of local conservatism became draped in Republican dressings.

The national decline in manufacturing finally hit local streets in the 1990s. As a result, the overall political landscape became more aligned with corporate interests and the city's conservatives found a home in both parties. Therefore, The Professor found little surprising about Bailey's conservatism surfacing in a Democratic Party discreetly abandoning its lib-eral orientation. It also didn't hurt that, if elected, she would become the city's first female District Attorney. Such would serve as a nice historical mantle for local Democrats to boast about in the decades to come.

For the police community, Bailey was certainly an ally. She was in favor of increasing the police force and aggressive crime fighting on the streets: code words for more vigorous policing in the city's "high-crime" poor communities. One of her most repeated campaign slogans was: "We need to get the criminals off the streets and in jail." Although she didn't yell it with that old-fashioned furor, her calm modern reserve reflected traditional conservative values of a hard-handed criminal approach toward Blacks.

After winning the seat, there were always whispers of her ambitions to become the city's first female mayor. Therefore, it wasn't surprising that she and the mayor, a fellow Democrat, had a contentious relationship behind the scenes. The prospects of her aspirations became more viable with the decreased popularity of the city's two-term mayor and her increased favorability. The mayor's administration suffered a number of setbacks over the past two years. There was also a rising impression that the mayor wasn't getting anything of significance done.

After parking in the guest lot, Tory passed through security quickly. The halls were quiet as he made his way to the District Attorney's Office. He was five minutes early. So after identifying himself to the receptionist, he sat in a chair and perused various messages on his cell phone. Minutes later, he was told to enter through the large arching wood doors. Walking into the huge wood-paneled office, he saw Sandra Bailey sitting behind her desk with her hands folded on her waist. He felt he was under her careful watch the moment he opened the door. As he approached her, she stood and extended her hand.

"Good morning, Detective Givens."

"Good morning, Mrs. District Attorney."

As they shook hands, their eyes locked. She had a strong penetrating sight. Her pale face framed by cropped hair, the dyed blonde receding to darker roots. There were remnants of youthfulness among her aging features. Her presence was commanding, an aura reflecting she had been through many battles and was eager to meet the more to come. It was clear she intended to dictate the tone of the meeting: she would make all the first moves and lead where the conversation went.

After releasing his hand, she said, "Thanks for coming so early. Please have a seat." She sat down. Tory sat down in a chair on the other side of the desk.

"I'll get right to it. I told Chief Smitts I want my office to take the lead in the investigation. Legally, I have the right to do so. But since he made the request, I agreed to meet with you first before making a final decision."

She paused briefly, as if to allow her control of the situation to resonate. Tory remained cool, trying not to give even a glimmer of a reaction.

"I'm sure you know this case is already garnering national attention. The potential criminal and political dynamics cannot be ignored. With all due respect, I wouldn't hesitate to take over the case if your boss was leading the investigation."

"Chief Smitts or Assistant Chief Gulley?"

"Both." Her reply was blunt and sharp. "Police Chief and Head of Internal Affairs are political positions. Appointed, but still political. Despite what their intentions may be, they're both politicians working for an elected politician who's running for re-election next year."

"The mayor?"

"Exactly. You give politicians a national stage, they'll play their cards for what best suits their ambitions -- not necessarily for justice. The fact that an unarmed Black man was killed in broad daylight becomes a pawn in their game of politics. How do I know you're not part of that?"

He was slightly taken aback. Here was a politician, very adept at the game of politics, criticizing the same game she cunningly played. During her campaigns and time as District Attorney, she had never shown more than a bland concern for

Blacks. Like others, she did a minimum amount of political courting so as to not totally offend the forty-five percent of the city's electorate who was Black. She never stepped forward for any "Black" issues and was hardly seen in Black communities outside campaign season.

Her concern for the killing of an unarmed Black man seemed to ring of hypocrisy. But, of course, he couldn't say that to her. He knew he had to offer the same type of responses he gave in police circles. So he kept his reply reticent and professional.

"My record speaks for itself."

"It is impressive, along with your reputation. But things are different now. We're dealing with stakes that can drastically change the course of people's careers. Including yours." She was very crafty in her attempts to turn up the temperature. But he had years of on-the-job training in the art of remaining cool.

"I'm aware of that but my focus is on determining what happened yesterday. And only that."

"Perhaps you have the luxury of doing that. But prosecutions happen in the aftermath of what occurred and all that follows, encompassing a larger scope." She took a moment to rock back in her chair as she looked Tory squarely in the eye. Then she floated it out, "Would you have any disagreements to my office taking over the investigation?"

The question was equivalent to being checked in chess. But he already had a response to avoid a possible checkmate. "That question is better suited to my superiors."

"You don't have even an inkling of an opinion?"

Check again. But he would evade defeat for at least another move. "I just want the truth to be known and justice served."

She smiled, as if victory was near. "Ahh, yes. This is supposed to be about justice." Another statement with layers open for interpretation.

"Well," she continued, "the meat of any police investigation can't take place until the forty-eight hour period has expired and the officers involved have to at least sit in an interrogation room. Besides, my people will need at least that much time to prepare if I do take over. I'll make my decision by this afternoon. I'm sure Chief Smitts will inform you of it."

With her purpose served, she stood to send Tory on his way. "I do hope if my office takes the lead you'll be willing to assist us."

Tory stood as he said, "I'm more than willing."

Again, the professional reply to give even if it wasn't one hundred percent genuine. She extended her hand to put an end to this chapter of the game.

"Thank you for your time, Detective Givens."

He shook her hand and offered the corresponding courtesy. "Thank you for meeting with me, District Attorney Bailey." Then he turned and exited.

◆ ◆ ◆

"Ahh, yes. This is supposed to be about justice." The remark reverberated through his mind as he headed toward police headquarters. But what is justice? A term cited often, although the details of individuals' implied meanings vary vastly. And even these are often theoretical, having little practical value to the everyday lives of people. Yet still many hold justice as a cherished principle, something that should govern our lives individually and collectively.

The wandering thoughts settled on the memory of the most impactful conversation he ever had about justice. Approaching the midnight hour in his old neighborhood, it happened just outside a corner store. He remembered buying a beer through the store's bulletproof window. He put a five dollar bill in the rotating chamber of the window, turning it to the cashier inside. He stated what he wanted. The cashier placed the bill to the side before going to grab a beer from the cooler. He then placed the beer with the appropriate change in the chamber and turned it back to Tory.

After a significant increase of nighttime gunfire in the area, the owner decided to lock the store doors after ten p.m. On the weekends, when the store remained open twenty-four hours, all purchases occurred through the bulletproof window till six a.m. This became the preemptive option to protect the overnight profits in the face of the nocturnal danger. A danger Tory and others had become accustomed to navigating with very little protection.

He remembered opening his beer as Jelani said, "Break it down for them, homeski. They be sleeping on the genius of the elders."

"I don't know if I'm a genius, I just read a lot. Plus, I'm a little tipsy right now so I don't know if I would listen to me too closely."

Barry roared with a contagious laughter that infected the small group present. His jolly face beamed with glee, framed by a mostly white beard. His shoulders were broad. A testament to the many years he spent hauling trash on a city sanitation truck. That was until one day he took a bad fall that left him nearly incapacitated. After two years on worker's comp, surgery, physical therapy, endless doctor visits, and almost endless medication, his back never fully recovered. So he was designated "disabled."

At first there was heart break. The permanent loss of his previous strength and some of his mobility really brought to light the finality of this life. But after a period of feeling sorry for himself, he took solace in some of the treasures he collected while picking up trash.

Prior to the back-breaking and exhaustive days as a trash man, he loved to read. But the daily physical and mental fatigue left him without the focus and clarity of mind to follow a good book. Instead the simple-mindedness of television and movies became the replacement. Yet if he saw an interesting book while out collecting the garbage, he would take it. In certain neighborhoods, people left undesired items that others might want beside the garbage. These were up for grabs until the trash truck came. Over the years, he would take a book here and there. He ended up amassing three boxes of books, all in good condition. They were now awaiting the man unable to work and with plenty of time to read.

Within this booty was a copy of Plato's *The Republic*. Barry wasn't much of a philosopher, but he knew this book was a classic. He felt if there was ever going to be a time when he might be able to comprehend such, it was now. So, without any expectations, he dove into the translation of the Greek masterpiece. He ended up developing a great admiration for Socrates although he didn't agree with his every point.

"The main theme of Plato's *Republic* is Socrates' definition of justice."

"You lost me already," chimed in Radar. Others burst into laughter.

"You just a simple motherfucker."

"And drunk as hell."

"No, simple would be that if Plato wrote it, it would be his definition."

"Socrates was Plato's teacher."

"Okay. That makes a little more sense."

"Will y'all just let Barry educate your dumb asses. That's why so many of us stay ignorant. We don't know how to shut up when someone has something valuable to say."

"My bad, Barry."

"Well, like I was saying, the theme of *The Republic* is Socrates' definition of justice. And it's expansive. Spread out over ten books, which are like chapters. But basically he says justice is the balance of the parts of the soul. When there's imbalance, there's injustice. And that it pretty much plays out the same for an individual or a society."

"So what are the parts of the soul that need to be balanced?"

"The rational part, the emotional part, and the lustful part."

"I'm all about that lust, dawg!" More laughter.

"Stop interrupting him!" Jelani chimed in again. The laughter died down.

"Socrates holds that we all have these three parts, but we need to have them in balance in order to live justice." There was a momentary silence, as if the validity of this point could not be denied. Something that resonated with all gathered.

"He goes on to illustrate this point in the case of a city-state, how it is governed, cause he says it's easier to see how justice works on a larger scale. But the same principles apply to the individual as well.

"He calls the ideal state an aristocracy. Well, actually before I begin that, he says the best way to bring about a just city, transform a society that's unjust into being just, is to kick out everybody over the age of ten."

"Then who would rule?"

"Those who are educated in the true sense of what education is supposed to be: that which turns one to Truth. But there's a deep point in wanting to kick out everybody over ten. Think about it. By that age, or maybe a little older for us in modern times, we formulate the framework for how we'll proceed as adults. And once that framework is formed, how many of us are really able or willing to shift to another way of thinking? Of living?"

Barry paused. No one responded, fearing they might step into a philosopher's trap. Urban nighttime quiet.

"Once we become oriented to an unjust way of life, Socrates says it's better to start all over with a new genera-tion who hasn't been corrupted. Because once the corruption begins, things only continue to decay toward tyranny. There may be some improvements along the way, but the overall tide continues downward.

"So, for Socrates, the ideal state is an aristocracy. But it's really a righteous monarchy ruled by a philosopher-king."

"Jelani would probably like that."

"Let him talk."

"In this city, people fulfill the roles they are capable of and trained for. You have those who should rule, a military who should protect the nation, and a general workforce. So only the rulers rule after they've been educated and prepared to do so, with an emphasis on them studying philosophy to become wise. If a military person or a worker ends up in a ruling position, that's a sign of decay. Socrates says part of the balance required for justice is that people stay in and fulfill the roles they are in."

"I don't know if I would go for that: people putting limits on what I could be."

"That's what I thought at first. But then I thought about the fact that I've never lived under a righteous ruler. It might not be so bad just being a worker if things were good."

The statement touched a chord with those gathered. Despite their varying ages and experiences, could any of them say they knew what it was like to live under a leader who lived justice and righteousness? And served the people through these virtues?

"When the decay of justice begins, the just monarchy descends into timocracy."

"What's that?"

"It's a society in which people treat honor, power, and success as more important than wisdom and justice. And this is reflected in the government. As people with these values obtain ruling positions, the purpose of government gets lost and injustice begins to spread. Socrates says mistakes by just leaders and disunity among the people will play a role in the fall to timocracy.

"From there, the imbalance only increases. People put their individual pursuits of wealth and power over the collective well-being of society. The divide between the few rich and the masses of poor widens, leading to the spread of more crime. And with more people chasing their own ambitions, you end up with more people doing things for which they are not fit. So the quality of work decreases. And so too the overall quality of life.

"When children in such a state see their parents lose wealth or struggle in poverty, it fuels a drive in them to seek their own desires. They begin to lose their rational sense. Their lives become dominated by emotions and desires, until you have oligarchy: where wealth becomes the most important thing in society.

"The problem with this is that wealth is concentrated among a few. And as it becomes even more concentrated, the masses become even poorer and begin to revolt. And not just armed revolution. In fact, more will revolt against the institutions, the norms, and values of society."

"Like you just don't give a fuck."

"That's the state of democracy: where freedom becomes the most important thing. Even if people are poor, they want the freedom to do whatever they want, however they want. They hold to this desire even if they don't have the means to fulfill it; and no longer have the rationality to see how this doesn't make sense. But with most people being poor, the pursuit of freedom is carried out through bodily desires. Cause even if you don't have money, you can be pleasured by your body with food, sex, drugs, and other physical enjoyments.

"Once people with this democratic attitude become the rulers, the desire for pleasures becomes overly glorified in society. The government then becomes more concerned with giving people opportunities to pursue pleasure instead of tending to the collective well-being of all."

Tory couldn't restrain the thought that spontaneously spoke itself. "For so much of our lives, we've been taught that democracy is good. The best form of government because it's free."

"Socrates thinks otherwise. I don't agree with everything he says, but it does make me think about what is it our democracy really is. Like if it's truly capable of manifesting justice." It seemed as if the entire city, even the unending background of urban bustle, became silent to let these queries resonate.

"And when the pursuit of desire becomes so extreme within a democracy, tyranny arises. In tyranny, any limits upon any freedom of any form are deemed unjust. But instead of this approach truly making people free, it creates its opposite: slavery. People become enslaved to their desires, blind to the rational and emotional parts of their being. Even when people are getting what they want, their blindness can't see how being led by their desires is creating imbalance and suffering.

"The rulers in a tyranny will present themselves as champions of the masses against the elite. Yet these same rulers will be intent on removing all threats to their power, including the wise who think more in terms of what is best for society. The tyrants will also invest a lot of money in the military, to defend their interests. They won't hesitate to kill or imprison anyone who resists them. Even members of their own family. Obviously, one can see there is no justice in such a state."

His final point made, Barry took a drink. The mood on the corner was introspective. Contemplative. Despite the regularity of drinking, smoking, and joviality on street corners, this type of inquisitive search for meaning and understanding occurred more often than many realize.

Although most present already knew the answer to the forthcoming question, the tradition of street corners required that it be vocalized.

"So where is this country in all of that?"

"I would say it's a democracy with serious tyrannical tendencies, not far removed from complete tyranny."

Another silence.

"But to bring it back to what started this whole thing," Barry continued, "the question of justice. I can't say I completely agree with Socrates that we should start all over with just people under ten. Maybe I'm more hopeful than him in thinking that people stuck in an orientation of injustice, of imbalance, can change to reach the balance required to be just. Especially if we can be honest enough to admit that our unrestrained pursuit of desires and so-called freedom has only made us more and more unhappy. And less free. If we can admit that, the imbalance of our souls will be obvious. And so too how illogical it is to continue on in this way. Then we can begin the business of reestablishing balance within ourselves and our society. And that can lead to justice."

Tory's focus returned from the nighttime memory to the day-lit streets he was driving through. The point about balance within being a key to justice in society weighed heavy on his mind. Yet this principle was absent in so many efforts to attain, regain, or sustain justice. And this is within a society that regards Socrates as one of the major figures in Western civilization. It seemed as if the words of this renowned thinker were only deemed significant in philosophical theory, being largely ignored in the day-to-day realities of governing this country.

◆ ◆ ◆

He sat in a conference room with Speedy and Anne. Speedy had a mug of decaffeinated tea. Anne, a cup of coffee and a remote control. An array of papers and photos were laid across the table. The apparent clutter organized in the mind of Anne who was leading this screening of surveillance footage in connection with the Martin Little shooting.

"None of the gas station footage shows the shooting but two cameras show witness reactions. In particular, this one shows Officer Peters directing a man to go inside the restaurant right after the shooting."

Their attention turned to the television. Upon the screen was a paused video capturing the street and sidewalks. It encompassed the closed shop for rent and the fried chicken restaurant, but the alley where the shooting occurred was just beyond view.

Distinct upon the screen was an eccentrically dressed middle-aged man. He donned a colorful cowboy hat and large sunglasses. Facing the alley with his arms stretched in a questioning manner, he seemed engaged from a distance. A few other people, standing in front of the fried chicken restaurant, also watched the action happening offscreen. At the bottom of the grainy video was a time stamp. It read: "April 19, 2016 - 3:37PM."

Anne unpaused the footage, the middle-aged man stepped forward. He stood in front of the closed shop yelling in the direction of the alley. The footage had no sound. And his distance from the camera made it impossible to read his lips, so there was no way of knowing exactly what he was saying. But he seemed very concerned. All the sudden, he ducked as the other spectators ran into the restaurant. It was reasonable to assume this is when the gun shots were fired. Moments later, a few people poked their heads out the restaurant doorway. The middle-aged man stood, making unrelenting questioning motions. It seemed as if he was questioning someone's actions. As if asking: "Why did you do that?" That it wasn't necessary. Or right.

It wasn't long before an officer entered the shot with his gun drawn and pointed to the ground. Tory quickly scanned the photos on the desk to see that the man resembled Officer

Corey Peters. He pointed at the restaurant and yelled for the middle-aged man to go inside. Continuing to question, the middle-aged man retreated to the doorway. Officer Peters walked back toward the alley and out of the shot.

Referring to the middle-aged man, Anne said, "He basically continues to stand there for the next few minutes."

"Do we know his name?" inquired Tory.

"Reynold Collins, but he's known in the neighborhood as just "Ralphie." He's a fixture in that area."

Ralphie. Tory took a mental note of the name and his grainy visual on the screen.

"None of our guys questioned him?" interjected Speedy.

"The local detectives are trying to track him down. He has a history of petty crimes: selling loose cigarettes, buying alcohol for minors, things like that. The detectives said they're not surprised he didn't hang around to be questioned. They checked the last address they had for him, but he moved from there about a month ago."

"If they track him down, we want to talk to him ourselves." Speedy nodded in agreement to Tory's request.

"I'll let the detectives know. And then there's the dash cam footage. The footage from Easthill and Peters' car faces away from the alley but it captures Ralphie and shows Officer Peters crossing to him."

Anne hit the "next chapter" button on the remote. The dash cam footage of a police car facing out the windshield emerged upon the screen. The car, parked at an angle, captured the sidewalk from in front of the liquor store and beyond. The time stamp stated "April 19, 2016, 15:34 hours."

Ralphie stood in front of the closed shop questioning what was happening offscreen in the alley. Others watched from in front of the fried chicken restaurant. Again, Ralphie's words could not be deciphered because of his distance from the camera and there being no sound. Tory was quick to notice this.

"There's no sound?"

"The microphones on both dash cam systems are broken."

Ralphie suddenly ducked as the spectators by the fast food restaurant rushed inside. Eventually, Ralphie stood, his questioning motions appearing more demonstrative in this footage. It seemed more obvious that his remarks were directed at the cops. The focus of his eyes followed Officer Peters as he approached and entered the camera's view, holding his drawn gun toward the ground. From behind, Officer Peters is shown pointing and yelling for Ralphie to go to the restaurant. Ralphie backed up, continuing his pleas from the restaurant doorway.

As the footage continued to roll, Anne added, "The responding unit parked right behind this car, so its dash cam basically shows the back of this car."

"Why are the mics on both patrol cars broken?" Tory could guess the likely reason, but he wanted to know if someone offered an explanation.

"You know why," Speedy replied. "Or has it been that long since you've worked the streets? I used to break mine all the time when I was on the beat. I bet you half the fleet has "broken" microphones."

It was a moot point now. The evidence was the evidence. Even if the cause for its incompleteness lay, in part, with deliberate acts by officers to protect themselves from potential culpability. Having audio of the exchange between the officers and Martin would have proven valuable. Its absence afforded more leeway to the officers in their accounts of what happened.

"Is this the best we have for video footage?" Again, Tory asked another question he already knew the answer to. If there was better footage, Anne would have started with that. But still, he had to ask.

"This is it, unless something else pops up."

"Don't forget, we're still waiting on the body cam footage from MacDonald," Speedy added. But that was grasping for straws. There was no way of knowing what that would offer until they could see it.

After a moment of contemplation, Tory turned to Anne to ask, "Beyond the selects you showed us, is there anything showing Martin Little? Even the gas station footage prior to the shooting?"

"No. The video guys said they screened it from an hour before. They think he must have approached the alley from the other direction. But I have all the uncut footage if you want to check again."

Another dead end. "Thanks, Anne."

They had nothing that showed Martin. Nothing that might suggest the state he was in prior to the incident. This meant they would have to lean heavily on interviews with his family and friends to garner any clues regarding the mental state he may have been in when the shooting occurred. And that would begin now.

Tory turned to Speedy to say, "Let's go see Martin's sister."

CHAPTER FOUR:
The criminal America always assumed I was

He was never nervous in these parts. He didn't grow up in Water Hole, but in another "poor, high crime" section of the city. The similarities were undeniable. The monotony of uniform buildings crammed together within the encasing of sidewalks. Damp and decayed colors tinting coarse and hard surfaces, interspersed with small patches of dirt and grass. The trees seemed in a state of perpetual neglect: alive but denied enough sunlight and water to fully blossom. Perhaps that reflected the aura of the people: abundant with gifts and potential, but not sufficiently nurtured. Mostly surviving instead of thriving. Yet still they were vibrant with life, finding ways to touch glimpses of fullness within glasses that were only half full. Or a quarter full. Or nearly empty.

He pulled into a spot among the scattering of cars parked along the sidewalks. He exited into the street. Speedy nearly tripped, catching his foot in a crack on the curb just outside the passenger door.

"Not enough decaffeinated tea, I guess." They both smirked at the attempt at humor. It was little moments like this that sought to bring a touch of humanity to the grind of constantly treading on life's unpleasant side.

Tory led the way across the lawn of weathered concrete in front of the apartment building. People moved to and fro. Even the stationary ones seemed in motion amidst the stirring of movement around them. Yet something seemed to remain eerily the same, as if the totality of the activity was running in place. That was one of the paradoxes of the 'hood. Despite the constant hustle of survival and struggle, so many remained stuck in a morass of unyielding conditions. Conditions which, for most, were beyond their control.

The building's lobby was dim and dingy. The elevator cramp, with rusting spots on the ceiling. The ding of the bell sounded faint as the doors opened to the fourth floor. The hallway felt sterile aside from a few door mats outside the apartment doors. Turning the corner, they neared the destination. Tory knocked the knocker on the metal door. Approaching movement could be heard on the other side, followed by a female voice.

"Who are you?"

Tory pulled out his badge as he replied. "Detectives Givens and Dillenger from the police department. We're looking for Mandy Little." He held his badge higher toward the door's eye hole. The door was opened slightly to the length allowed by the chain lock engaged from within. A pair of wet, red eyes peered through. The door was then shut, the chain lock removed, and then opened again to allow their entry.

There she stood. They assumed it was Mandy. There was some resemblance in the face to Martin. She was short and chubby with a round, loving face. But it was clearly scarred by the suddenness of tragedy. A mascara of melancholy shrouded her eyes. Yet they remained strong. They were the magnet of her face. And discerning, having seen much within her years. Perhaps too much, especially now with the unexpected death of her brother.

"Come in. And please excuse the mess."

She led the way through the short hallway to the living room. It was cluttered with an assortment of adult and kid items. A large television was on displaying what appeared to be a syndicated sitcom.

Upon entering the living room, they were greeted by his eyes. His body faced the large screen, holding a remote, while his head was turned toward the entrance to sate his curiosity. Chubby with a cheerful face, his young body was draped in an adult-sized LeBron James jersey. A wine-colored Cleveland road jersey with the gold "23." There was an innocence about him, yet the twinkle in his eye suggested he had his moments of youthful mischief. He too had a facial resemblance to Martin.

She motioned the detectives toward the sofa as she addressed the boy. "Why don't you go watch that in the room."

"Okay," he said. Then he turned to the two strangers to ask, "Are they from the media?"

"Just go in the room, Chunky!" He started toward the bedroom with the remote in hand. "But leave the remote." If there were any doubts about their relationship, the stern motherly tone in her voice affirmed that he was her son. He handed her the remote and exited into another room. "And close the door." He had been through this routine before. The door was already in motion, closing upon her last word.

She muted the television and then turned toward the detectives. "Please sit down."

Tory and Speedy sat upon the sofa. She sat on the love seat set at a right angle to them. Speedy pulled out a small pad and pen, remnants of the old style detective habits he refused to relinquish in a more digital age.

This was a meeting undesired. Who welcomes sitting with detectives to discuss your brother who was killed by a cop yesterday? Despite this being the situation, her home training kept her in the arena of proper etiquette.

"Pardon my cautiousness at the door. I was told they're releasing Martin's name this morning, which means a lot of media will probably be trying to reach me for some type of statement."

"We understand."

A high-profile killing is not granted the same privacy and courtesies as other deaths. And with the shooting already registering as a national case, Tory knew she would be inundated with media intrusions that could not be avoided. Probably overwhelming, along with the weight of mourning. Yet still he had to interview her. She might have timely information vital to the investigation.

"Thanks for taking the time to meet with us. We know other detectives asked you some questions so pardon us if we ask some of the same things. We're just trying to piece together what happened, including anything that might have been a factor leading up to the incident. Even if something seems like it might not be that important, please don't hesitate to share it. Sometimes those things can be very helpful."

"Okay."

"Please state your full name and relation to Martin Little."

"Madeline Little, I'm Martin's..."

The swell of emotions quickly surged until the damn of tears broke forth again. Tory grabbed a box of tissues from the nearby coffee table and handed it to her. He had been through enough of these types of questions to know when to pause, so as to not break the delicate equilibrium of functionality she was navigating.

Tory and Speedy sat in a respectful silence until Mandy regained enough of her composure. "I'm sorry. I just miss my brother so much... I've been crying all night since..." Her voice drifted off again.

"It's okay. We can take a moment to let you gather yourself."

Although it was gripping to witness her pain, he knew it was best to maintain an emotional distance. He needed his mind to stay focused and clear, to analyze the information she may offer. He would try to be gentle but that wouldn't stop the pain. He was there to discuss matters that tugged at tender wounds too fresh to have formed scabs. The blood of anguish was still wet and trickling forth.

The torrent of disturbed breaths and ripe emotions began to settle. There would be no calm in the midst of this storm, only enough restraint of the disturbance to continue. In an ideal set of circumstances, he would wait a few days for the storm to diminish. But with so many moving parts of the investigation, he had to proceed. And she knew this.

A deep exhalation and then, "Okay. I'm ready."

Speedy stepped in to ask, "Are you his younger or older sister?"

"Younger."

"And he lived here with you?"

She turned to Tory to respond to his question. "Yes. After he finished his drug treatment I made him come live here with us because I didn't want him..."

Her voice drifted off again. Another period of turbulence in the storm. The sad irony of why she paused became apparent when she uttered the conclusion of her sentence. "...I didn't want him to end up back in jail or dead." And yet death found a way to snatch him anyway.

"Who else lives here?"

"Just my son, Chunky."

"Does Martin have his own room?"

"This was basically his room. It's just an one bedroom apartment. Me and my son share the bedroom. He kept a dresser in there, but this pull-out sofa was his bed."

"Did he stay anywhere else?"

"He would sometimes spend the night with his girl-friend, Wanda."

Speedy interjected, "Do you know her last name?"

He and Tory's questioning rapport was such that the sec-ondary questioner would only interrupt to get needed details that might be forgotten in the flow of conversation.

"No," Mandy responded, "but I've known her for awhile from the neighborhood. She recently became pregnant, which is why Martin was trying so hard to get a job. So they could get their own place."

Pregnant girlfriend. Trying to get a job. Tory took mental note of these significant points.

"Do you know where she lives?"

"She shares an apartment with her roommate on Powell Road. I have her number on my phone."

Speedy made a note on his pad as he said, "Maybe you can give it to us before we leave?" Tory nodded in agreement and then resumed in taking the lead of the questioning.

"Do you know why Martin was down at Spencer Avenue yesterday?"

"Probably job hunting. He's been trying real hard but getting a lot of rejection because of..." Mandy quieted again.

Tory could see she was uncomfortable, so he offered what he presumed to be a likely reason. "His criminal record?"

"He wasn't a dealer! Never was!" She fiercely defended her brother from what she felt was an extreme misperception of him. "He had a drug problem and was just doing something to try to get drugs when they busted him. But he's been clean ever since."

"Do you know what he was using?" Tory knew the answer from Martin's file but wanted to see what she would share.

With face frowned, she admitted, "Cocaine."

Her answer was incomplete. Whether she would confess the rest would affect the credibility through which he assessed her answers. So he gave a prompting.

"How about marijuana? And was he using that recently?"

"Probably. But he could control that. It was the cocaine that ruined his life."

Her honesty assured his confidence in her trustworthiness. But now to another sensitive yet important issue. "How about his mental health? Records show he had problems in the past."

"That was in the past. Lately, he was just really, really stressed out." Tory looked her squarely in the eye. Again, she seemed honest. "I tried to encourage him, tell him to keep his faith and be patient. But he was losing hope that anyone would hire him with his criminal record."

Tory could relate. He had personally witnessed this dynamic play out with a number of relatives and friends. Including tragically for Jelani. But another sensitive issue had to be broached, more so to see if any reaction indicated she was hiding something.

"You kind of answered this but I still have to ask. Do you know if he was involved in any kind of criminal activity lately?"

"Absolutely not," she replied adamantly. "He wanted to be there for Wanda and their kid."

He had no reason to doubt her reply. He had one last question, since he was still grasping for leads. "Do you know if he had conflicts with any police officers or detectives?"

"Not that I know of. He was serious about staying out of trouble and starting a family with Wanda." A family that would now be formed without him.

The main thing that stood out from Mandy's answers was the fact that Martin may have been under a lot of stress. That alone shouldn't be a reason why he was shot. But it rose the possibility of his stress being a factor that led to an escalating situation with the officers.

As was their rapport, Tory turned to Speedy and asked, "Anything else from you?"

"No, just Wanda's phone number." That meant Speedy felt Tory covered all the necessary bases.

Tory pulled out a business card and handed it to Mandy. "If anything else comes up, you can call this number to reach me. Thanks for your time."

"Let me get my phone to get Wanda's number."

As Mandy walked into the bedroom, Tory scanned the room. His eyes settled upon a photo on the wall. In it, Martin wore the same LeBron James jersey Chunky had on. Martin smiled broadly and gave an animated pose with Chunky under his arm. A stark contrast of happiness to the residual image in Tory's mind of the expressionless corpse upon the examination table.

The thought was interrupted as Speedy nudged him and said lowly, "Look."

Tory's eyes moved to the muted television. A mug shot of Martin was being displayed under a "Breaking News" title. His name in bold letters along with bullet points. "32 years old." "Served time in prison for cocaine possession." "Completed treatment for drug addiction."

His gaze of disappointment in the mug shot was another contrast to the picture of happiness on the wall. But the televised image took on a more sinister tone beside the chosen descriptions.

Mandy returned to the sight of Martin's mug shot on the television screen. She was instantly traumatized. Numbed beyond the point of tears or an emotional response. She merely stood there. Frozen in grief.

◆ ◆ ◆

The drives between destinations often offered time for contemplation. As Speedy roamed through this phone, Tory's mind wandered through memories. His childhood puppy, Casper. His grandmother's corn muffins. The red sweater he loved to wear until one day he lost it on a school trip. And then Jelani. He too had a hard time finding a job, which eventually led to him leaving the city.

After years of building tension with his parents, namely his father, one of his aunts allowed Jelani to move into the basement of her house. No time limit was set but it was supposed to be a bridge to him getting his own place. Things really flared up at his parents' home when he decided to take a year break from college. And, as his father predicted, the break became permanent.

Jelani felt he was a man, but his father insisted on him abiding by his parent's rules -- even a curfew. He constantly disobeyed his father's edicts, which resulted in unending fights. Including one that came to clenched fists being raised but, fortunately, not thrown.

After moving into his aunt's basement, he was faced with the challenge of making money for himself. She agreed to feed him and gave him a starter loan, but beyond that he was on his own. While applying for full-time jobs, he embarked on a range of side jobs to get by. He worked as an on-call food preparer for a catering company. But that never amounted to more than five days a month. Sometimes he could get a few days of work at various construction sites. And around Christmas time, he worked as a part-time holiday loader for a shipping company.

Despite his perseverance, Jelani couldn't find a permanent and steady job. He was constantly borrowing money from friends, rarely able to pay them back. And the credit card he got in college was maxed out. He was caught in a financial situation that seemed to offer no way out.

He even tried selling weed briefly. He argued it was no more poisonous than alcohol and would probably be legalized nationwide within the next ten years. But when he reflected on how it was part of a larger cycle of self-destruction, with rival crews fighting over territory and it serving as a gateway to harder drugs, he quit the drug game. Luckily, he was able to leave it without any drama.

He considered going back to school but his heart wasn't really in it. The only reason it registered as an option was because he couldn't get a job. Besides, life experience was the best teacher for an "urban philosopher poet." But, as he would often joke, the pay is bad and the benefits don't kick in until you die.

Jelani continued to put in application after application for more steady and consistent work. He rarely got an interview, none of which amounted to anything. Again, he would put his ironic spin on it: how many places do you know when you walk in the door someone greets you with a name like Jelani? He professed repeatedly to Tory that he thought his name alone was the cause for many people tossing his resume in the refuse pile without any consideration. That's why he never doubted his talent and intelligence. Although he couldn't prove it, in his mind, he wasn't being given a chance despite his competence.

Tory tried to convince him to become a cop numerous times. But they both knew Jelani didn't have the demeanor to be an officer. If anything, he would end up getting fired for standing up for the community instead of maintaining the ranks of policing decisions he felt was unfair. Or unjust.

Jelani continued to live by the conviction of his values which asserted every human has the right to live without compromise. Even if this left him on a path with little hope of escaping unending poverty and residing in his aunt's basement. That was until she kicked him out. Such wasn't uncommon for situations like his, when the grace of time given "to get on your feet" became many years.

So when one of his favorite cousins in Louisiana invited him to move down there, Jelani accepted the invitation. Perhaps a new start in a different place would offer an opportunity to find better financial footing. But after five months of being down there, Jelani disappeared. When Tory, concerned, called the number he had for Jelani, it was disconnected. It would be another two years before Tory received any word from Jelani. And in a form that was mind-blowing.

The handwriting on the envelope seemed somewhat familiar but the return address was a correctional facility. Tory opened it to unfold two looseleaf papers scribbled in his friend's penmanship. It began, "Dear Tory, I have become the criminal America always assumed I was..." Tory would forever remember these words.

The memories came to an end as Tory pulled into his parking spot at police headquarters. He had to focus. They would be meeting the lead F.B.I. agent working on the Martin Little case, who was already meeting with their boss. Tory and Speedy were told to join them as soon as they were done questioning Mandy. So they made their way through the halls to Gulley's office.

◆ ◆ ◆

The etching was bold upon the frosted window of the door: Assistant Chief, Brian O. Gulley, Internal Affairs. The letters swung out of view as the door was opened to reveal Gulley sitting behind his desk. His eyes were upon the guest who sat in a nearby chair as Anne displayed some documents.

Tory led the way inside as he said, "You wanted to see us, sir."

Gulley motioned for them to enter. "Come on in, guys." The guest stood to shake hands with Tory as Gulley continued. "This is Agent Phillip Carruthers, from the F.B.I. These are Detectives Tory Givens and Simon Dillenger."

"But everyone calls me Speedy.

"And you can call me Phil. A pleasure to meet you both."

"Same here," said Tory.

"Welcome," Speedy added.

Agent Carruthers was tall and slender with a distinguished demeanor. Yet he seemed approachable. And very confident.

"Anne was just finishing her briefing," Gulley mentioned. "Maybe the next best thing to do is to take Agent Carruthers to Spencer Avenue."

"We can do that," replied Speedy.

"Why don't you see if he would like some coffee for the road?" suggested Gulley.

"Or decaffeinated tea. I've been off caffeine for four years counting." Speedy smiled with pride.

"A coffee would be nice."

"And Anne can make those copies for you before you go."

"Will do." Anne headed off to the copy room.

Gulley stood and extended his hand to Phil. "Whatever you need from our team don't hesitate to ask."

"I won't."

"Givens, give me two minutes before you go."

"We'll be at the snack room," Speedy said to Tory, turning to lead Phil out of the office.

Gulley motioned for Tory to have a seat as he sat behind his desk. He took a moment to rock his chair back and forth slightly, a long-time habit. He then broke the silence with his deep voice.

"So, how did the meeting with the D.A. go?"

"It went fine." Tory knew Gulley's questions always led to something. So the smart approach was to offer brief responses until his follow-up questions made clear what his objectives were.

"Just fine?" Gulley took a moment to give that probing look he was famous for. Then the next question. "Did she mention she wants her office to take over the investigation?"

"Yes." Tory sensed there was more going on behind the scenes. Perhaps things he would prefer to not know. But he wasn't in a position to censor his boss.

"So you see the politics are already in play with this one."

Gulley's piercing gaze indicated he was about to unload. Tory settled more into his seat to brace himself for whatever might come. In the prevailing police culture, it was part of one's unofficial duty to bear any venting by one's superiors.

"First, the chief makes you the lead investigator without consulting me. Which I don't mind, I would have chosen you. But it's not coincidental that a Black detective is placed in charge of investigating the shooting of an unarmed Black guy." Tory tried to hide his discomfort. He was unsure what these words were leading to. "Then the D.A., who's been putting out feelers to challenge the mayor next year, is looking to overtake that. Legally, it's within her right. But the circumstances don't warrant it. Unless you consider the heap of media attention this will garner her as a viable reason."

It certainly felt like a dig at the District Attorney. But Tory wondered if this series of complaints would soon find fault with him.

"You're not a baby, Givens. So there's no need for me to hold your hand. But just a warning: there's a lot of sharks lurking in the waters right now."

Tory wasn't sure what to make of this statement with subliminal layers. So he kept his reply simple. "I understand, sir."

Gulley, sensing the tension he may have created or amplified, tried to ease it. "Even I have to pay the piper a little bit with this one. But let's not forget what's at the center of this storm. We got a dead Black guy and a cop whose career is on the line. So stay focused and keep your cards real close to the vest."

It was typical for Gulley to attempt to end all his interactions on a friendly note. He was clearly trying to imply he was on Tory's side among the present dangers. For now. But Tory was not naive. Gulley's words indicated that professional politics were emerging as a more dominant factor than determining if the shooting was justified.

"Thanks for the warning, sir."

The unofficial code deemed an expression of gratitude was due to his superior. Tory waited a moment longer to ensure Gulley had nothing else to say. He then stood to exit, feeling less at ease than before he sat in that chair.

◆ ◆ ◆

Tory often found it helpful to take a second look at a crime scene after all the police activity was gone. To see what it looked and felt like without all the yellow tape and barricades, evidence collecting, and the sense of spectatorship a police perimeter created. He wanted to see the normal rhythm of the place, if possible. And in the 'hood, except in the most extreme of cases, the locale quickly returned to its own rhythm.

Spencer Avenue was just another street a day later. Even with the memorial assembled at the alley. There was the office building with people moving in and out at varying paces. A liquor store for any alcohol-related wants. A fried chicken spot if you ate greasy food. And the barber / beauty shop on the corner, which appeared fairly new. It not only seemed to be a place to get your hair done, but also a venue where people congregated and socialized. Across the street there was the gas station with its small convenience store. Beside that, a fenced off lot and abandoned building. Deserted real estate was a regularity in Water Hole. Sometimes serving as forbidden playgrounds for kids during the day, and private spaces for concealed activities at night.

Tory parked in front of the fenced off lot, right across from the liquor store. The vehicle and pedestrian traffic was moderate to light. Tory led the way across the street. Phil and Speedy walked side by side. Phil carried a folder of various photos and papers.

Speedy oriented Phil to the sequence of events, referencing the actual locations. Tory surveyed the street. It seemed like just another place in the 'hood. Nothing distinct that would forecast it becoming the scene of a national controversy. But that too seemed to be one of the qualities of the 'hood. Within it, anywhere could become a place where anything extraordinary could happen, to then quickly return to the indistinct normalcy of urban life. The latter had not yet completely happened, but it wouldn't be long before it did, Tory thought.

His eyes fell upon the memorial. A collage of flowers, burnt out candles, and teddy bears. Someone had spray painted the letters "R.I.P." above the corner wall where the items lay. There were also the initials "F.T.P." Tory knew what they stood for in this context. Not File Transfer Protocol, but Fuck Tha Police. A sentiment he had felt strongly many times prior to becoming a cop. His sentiments never reached that extreme since putting on the uniform, although at times he felt extremely disappointed with the police as a whole.

"I've seen a number of cases like this..." Tory returned from his own internal monologue to hear Phil. "When you get down to the bare emotions of it, it's often fear and over-re-action. If the cop could do it over, he probably would use a lesser form of force. And they often walk into the situation knowing better. That de-escalation is better. But they get caught up in the moment and..." The words not said completed the sentence.

"You think that's what happened here?" asked Speedy.

"Just my initial impressions. You have an unarmed Black man, four cops on the scene and no reports of violence by the suspect." Phil pulled out a crime scene photo as he continued. "But whatever happened will now get colored through the lenses of race and politics. And the agendas of people trying not to go to jail while others want someone to be held accountable. The truth of what really happened will quickly get lost. And those in the best position to admit it usually don't because they want to protect themselves."

"I hear you," Speedy chimed in.

"But that's just my personal, unofficial opinion. There's no way I can put any of that in a report without sufficient evidence. Which in this case, is what? The words of the officers, who you still can't question?"

"Tomorrow we can."

Phil looked at Tory as if all was already lost. But his words tried to sound more gentle. "You give a good lawyer twenty-four hours, he or she will find a way to spin things in their client's favor. That or the cops take the fifth, and you're still stuck with insufficient evidence."

It was understood by the three men standing in that alley that the police union would ensure the officers found good lawyers. They worked in law enforcement and knew how these dynamics worked. How the culture of blue always sought to protect its own first. Always.

Phil then admitted the obvious, "With all due respect, unless something unforseen pops up, this is probably going to go down as just another unfortunate police shooting. Even if charges get brought up, there's probably no chance of a conviction. That's been my experience."

Phil pulled out another crime scene photo. A shot of the alley floor with the pool of Martin's blood. Using a prominent crack in the asphalt as a marker, he compared the photo to the actual spot in the alley. The crack remained, all traces of the blood were gone.

◆ ◆ ◆

He had some time before his lunch appointment with The Professor. So much was running through his mind. A dead Martin. *My wife is still upset with me.* The politics of the investigation. Memories of Jelani. *I need to write to Jelani.*

He went to a quiet café he frequented for refuge. A booth in the corner before the lunch rush offered an escapade from the pulls of the world. The waitress delivered his usual. A large coffee with two milks and a chocolate croissant. He sat alone against the wall, visible and yet unseen.

He pulled out his phone and started scanning through photos. There it was, he found it. The one he took with Jelani twenty years ago at a summer barbeque. The younger versions of them captured in the image smiled at the camera. As if smiling at whoever might be viewing the photo at whatever time in the future. A glare from the sun reflecting off of Jelani's shades. Tory holding up a plate of food and a cup. This was Tory's favorite photo of them. Without a doubt. And it would probably always be his favorite.

After a few sips of coffee and a smile of pleasant remembrance, he motioned through a series of photos until he reached what he now sought. A photo of a handwritten letter on loose leaf paper. He zoomed in to read its beginning.

"Dear Tory, I have become the criminal America always assumed I was..." These words were forever etched into his heart the first instant he read them. The dim of the kitchen as he leaned upon the counter. Tears fell along the inner side of his eyes as he gave a blank stare at the unfolded paper. There was a tension within his finger tips of wanting to tear the letter to shreds to reject what it signified. But there was also an unwillingness to destroy this remnant from a lost friend now rediscovered. His best friend. He had to pause before reading the rest.

The mathematics of the situation were evident. The return address on the envelope added to these words multiplied by the years of no communication equaled Jelani must be in jail. Or prison. Jails were for short-term incarceration. Prisons were where you went to do serious time.

Since then the letter weirdly became a memento. A remnant of a sacred friendship possibly forever lost to the circumstances of life. Oddly enough, the potential permanent loss of the friendship made it feel more special. Urging a deeper retrospective of the bond they appreciated yet somewhat took for granted: assuming their companionship from days past would always be. Despite the unfortunate turn of events and how it would have been easier to just disappear behind unknown prison walls, his dear friend Jelani reached out to him. Tory knew this was deeply difficult to do, perhaps in ways he would never fully comprehend. But it was a sign their severed companionship still had some value.

Although they interacted as equals, the tone of their relationship was such that Jelani acted as the wiser older brother. Explaining things in a comprehensible manner to the younger Tory who was still coming into his own. Being supportive of his growth, Jelani was an example of living this greater maturity. And courage. Even in the midst of trying hardships that could have been averted by compromising one's values, concession to society's norms was never an option for Jelani. Such capitulation would have been worse than death.

A bite from the croissant. A moment to notice the taste of the chocolate. The now more mature Tory began to read the letter again, scanning the small screen left to right and then downward left again as he read.

"Dear Tory, I have become the criminal America always assumed I was. It's not all my fault. I can't blame myself for the economic situations I repeatedly found myself within. But I am completely responsible for how I chose to deal with them, including doing something I knew at the time I should not do.

"Let it suffice to say that I'm still alive, although life is certainly more reduced living behind bars. And I needed a couple of years to build up the courage to confess my downfall to you. In fact, even when I finally decided to write this letter, this is probably the seventh or eighth version I've written. I wanted to come to you correct: no bullshit. I owe you at least that much since I feel I've failed you in so many ways. As much as I've tried to find the words to say what I'm saying, the larger part is beyond what words can say. But at least let this much be said: you are my brother and I will always love you. I just hope you feel the same way for me.

"But yeah, bro, I'm doing a bid on drug and gun charges. It's probably best I don't say more than that in writing since I'm pretty sure prison staff read all my correspondence. But if you want to write back, I put my address below. Or even if you want to call or visit, come any time, I'll be home. (That was meant as a joke.) But I guess most importantly I just wanted to reach out, make some kind of effort at reestablishing communications with you. But I also understand if you choose otherwise. You're probably still a cop, hopefully with a kid, whose life may have headed in a different direction. If so, I understand.

"Sincerely, Jelani Maurice Tucker. Imprisoned philosopher / street poet."

"P.S. *When the sun don't shine,*
Don't blame the sun.
Maybe your head is in the sand.
Or you've become too preoccupied with the clouds
That will pass away,
If you wait long enough."

Silence. Reading that poem always put Tory in a state of deep internal silence. It wasn't Jelani's best work, but it was among the ones that affected him most intimately.

A loud honking horn brought him back to the city he was seeking to temporarily escape. He looked at his watch. It's about time to head to the college. Well, maybe a little early. In fact, if I leave right now I can pick up some flowers for Loretta and drop them off at her office before I see The Professor.

◆ ◆ ◆

He could hear her voice drifting into the hallway as he approached her door. It must be her time for student office hours, he thought. Knocking lightly on the slightly open door, he glanced at the bronze name plate upon it: "Professor Loretta Givens, Head of Black Studies Department."

As he entered, their eyes locked on each other. The look of love, as mild spontaneous smiles emerged upon their faces simultaneously. That was one of the beauties of their love, a beauty of love, that it can conquer any sense of separation once it is remembered. Sometimes the passing of time from a point of conflict was enough for the memory of love to seize them. And here they were, only hours after their disagreement, being captured by love. Again. Neither of them resisted.

He sat down holding the bouquet of flowers he brought. She continued on the phone, motioning with her eyes that she would be done shortly. "I'll be there after my afternoon class. Then we can move the signs and banners over to Spencer Avenue. And did you ever hear back from his uncle to see if he's going to speak...?"

His eyes caught sight of the large portrait hanging behind her desk. A canvas painting of Dr. Martin Luther King, Jr. donning a pastor's robe. Loretta constantly reiterated the importance of remembering King as a pastor first. His social and political activism were fruits of his service to Christ. It seemed the artist captured him in the midst of his powerful oratory. One could imagine the commanding force of his words reflected in the dramatic composition of his face. And underneath the draped shoulders were inscribed the words: "The whirlwinds of revolt will continue to shake the foundations of our nation until the bright day of justice emerges." Words from the *I Have A Dream* speech as Loretta had informed him many times.

Loretta commissioned a local artist to do the painting. She wanted a bold yet undisturbing reminder hanging on her office wall of what her work was really about. She considered herself a disciple of King's work. Nonviolence was more than just a conceptual framework for community organizing: it was a way of life based on ancient principles that preceded King. His point of entry into this relationship with truth came through the gospel of Jesus. And like King, she studied the roots of Nonviolence's modern re-emergence through the life of Mohandas K. Gandhi. The later's communion with truth came through Indian spiritual teachings, as highlighted in scriptures such as the *Bhagavad Gita* and the *Ramayana*.

She clearly had a different spiritual orientation than Gandhi. Yet this did not prevent her from receiving one of the most impressionable lessons she learned from studying him. She sought to emulate his dire need to not just talk about and study the principles of Nonviolence, but literally fight to apply them to all aspects of his life. A fight waged without force and destruction: instead through the strength of humility, the wisdom of heart, and the courage of purity. That just as he utilized these spiritual tools to deal with an unjust government, he had the same tenacity in employing these in his relations with family, friends, neighbors, co-workers, etc. And, perhaps most importantly, in his relationship with himself.

Heeding this precious lesson, Loretta confessed many times regarding the injustices she fought in society: that traces of these same iniquities dwelled within herself. She often found them hiding within her own selfishness and negative qualities. Some which she had known for some time she needed to address, some realized through the struggle of living the principles of Nonviolence. So for her, like Gandhi and King, the fight for justice began within. With constant introspection and honest reflection to deal with her own impurities. Thus, she could become a pure vessel for justice, love, and truth. A vessel for these to manifest in the world, not someone who sought to compel these into being.

"No, I'll have Clara call him, she kinda knows him." She looked at Tory again, indicating the person on the line was going on unnecessarily. "But let me go. I'll see you later."

Loretta hung up the phone, her eyes immediately locking upon Tory's eyes again. They both smiled. She loved to receive gifts from him. He loved to see her joy. But their gaze evolved into a game as they both knew the next step in their routine of reconciliation. He was supposed to offer the flowers to her. But he intentionally didn't, instead holding them in his hand. Her response to his playful delay was to stare at him more intensely, silently encouraging him to deliver the peace offering. But he wouldn't.

"Well, actually these are a gift for Speedy to celebrate another month of detective matrimony."

She rolled her eyes and turned her head to give him a glance out the corner of her eye. He smirked and finally placed the bouquet upon the desk, with the attached note clearly in her view. She would normally say "How sweet of you" or "You didn't have to." But to chastise his mischievousness, she denied him any words that would coax his romantic ego. After moments of silence, he noticed her intentional omission. She smiled. He eventually smiled too and bowed his head, a sign of him enjoying their jestful interplay as well as his surrender. Accepting her victory, she opened the note to read it. She then read it aloud.

""Sometimes I hate my job too."" More smiles. "Don't we all."

Although playfulness was the mood of the moment, she wouldn't deny him the final reward. Besides, she thought he was a good kisser. So she walked around the desk to kiss and then hug him. A moment of love's joy.

"So how's your day going?" she asked as she pulled away.

"It's going. How about you?"

"Craziness and drama. We have a rally planned this evening and then a candlelight vigil. And, as usual, with not enough help."

As much as it was registered as a compliant, after decades of this being the norm she was resigned to this always being the case. In fact, she would probably go to the grave never having had enough help. But on to another topic. "Do you have time for a quick bite?"

"I'm actually on my way to have lunch with The Professor."

"More confidential police business. Or were the flowers really for him?" More smiles. "Well, I'll see you at home some time tonight. Unless I get arrested."

Although the joke was no longer funny, it never got old. It was another subtle reminder that her work didn't come without risks.

Then the forgiving wife kissed the good husband on the cheek and sent him on his way.

◆ ◆ ◆

August. If Tory had to pick one word to describe The Professor, that would be the word. His presence was commanding in an inviting way, and despite his effortless regalness he never made you feel small. Instead, he took every opportunity to uplift people. He lived with an explicit intent to have people realize their greatness by speaking to that in them. If someone so wise praised the greatness in you, it made you feel encouraged to realize that within yourself. And fulfill it.

His greatness was complimented by an accessible humility. Such as the simple rooftop café he assembled atop the building that housed his office. The roof surface was ragged and uneven, with repaired spots as obvious blemishes. The small table with fading paint was set near a short discolored wall. There were three non-matching chairs with all-weather cushions. One chair was slightly unsteady due to a shorter leg. Potted plants and flowers formed a collection nearby, a struggling garden due to his mediocre horticulture skills. None of the plants seemed very alive. In fact, some were already immersed in the process of their pots becoming their graves.

The scene was a stark contrast to the elegant office below granted to him as chair emeritus of the Black Studies department. But his majesty was not diminished the least by this rooftop serving as his present domain.

Only a select few were granted admittance to this sanctum, where he would offer one-on-one sit downs with trusted seekers of guidance. Formality and pretense were forbidden here. Within this intimacy, he would cut to the heart of what was being addressed with the precision of a master surgeon. Tory only requested these meetings when he was pressed with serious challenges. Once assigned to investigate the Martin Little shooting, he didn't hesitate to request a meeting with The Professor at his earliest convenience. Fortunately, today was free. That is, as long as he promised to bring lunch.

"The criminal law, as it presently stands, doesn't consider racial bias -- conscious or unconscious -- as a primary factor in such a case." The Professor leaned back with the taste of jerk chicken still upon his lips. He reached into his suit jacket for a toothpick to commence his post-meal habit of cleaning his teeth.

"This case will focus on use of force. Did the officer have an "objectively reasonable" belief of threat at the moment he used force?" Tory took note of this point. "Legally, it doesn't matter whether it was an actual threat. This is why whether Martin was armed or not won't matter in the court room. For an officer carrying out police duties, *objectively reasonable* belief of a threat in the moment of the interaction makes the shooting justifiable. Even if in retrospect it is realized the officer wrongly perceived a threat that wasn't there."

"So what is reasonable?" asked Tory.

"*Objectively reasonable* is the language the Supreme Court uses. Basically, this encompasses two sets of circumstances." The Professor leaned forward. Tory knew this meant a detailed explanation was at hand. He also leaned forward to better focus his attention.

"The first is the defense-of-life standard: an officer protecting one's own life or that of another innocent party. The second being a suspect engaged in a violent crime: force can be used to prevent the suspect from escaping. From what you've told me, I doubt the officers will try to say Martin was engaged in a violent crime. So most likely their defense will lie in the defense-of-life standard. Easthill saying he used force because he had an *objectively reasonable* belief Martin was a threat to the officers.

"With Martin being dead, there probably won't be another strong account to counter Easthill's justification. And remember, it's his *belief* in the moment he fired his gun. Even if in retrospect it's shown there was no actual threat."

The Professor stroked his beard to let the points resonate. Tory remained attentive. Legally, it was a simple principle which had far reaching ramifications. It basically limited the court's concern to the mindset of the officer, whether it was reasonable -- dismissing any other factors. Yet who determines what is reasonable in a series of varying circumstances among people with differing beliefs and levels of understanding?

To some, the shooting would seem unreasonable given the history of strained police relations with Blacks. Others would quickly side with the officer, perceiving Martin as an ex-convict with drug problems who must have done something to provoke the cop's bullet. But, if Tory was following The Professor correctly, these positions become irrelevant to what Easthill thought in the moment. As long as it wasn't beyond the scope of what a jury or judge considered reasonable, the shooting would be deemed justified.

"The law gives a lot of leeway to the cops."

The Professor nodded in agreement. "Expecting that the executive branch -- in this case, the mayor -- will exercise due diligence in hiring and training cops who will act with responsible judgment. And if the executive branch is failing, the legislative branch can use the power of the purse or write new laws, including new criminal codes, to address the situation."

The Professor took a moment to dislodge a piece of meat from between his teeth before continuing. The thought of relying on the mayor or city council to take responsible actions to address incidents like this didn't comfort Tory. They clearly had other priorities until controversies like these erupted. Then, temporary attention would be paid to the matter until it faded away into the background of day-to-day politics. Unless an incident was big enough to garner media attention, neither the mayor or city council were concerned about daily relations between police and the community. Especially in "high crime" communities.

"Historically," resumed The Professor, "the courts have not used criminal law to restrict police from making split-second decisions to protect themselves and society. So the courts are less inclined to convict a cop who made a bad judgment, but will allow civil penalties to be imposed for mistakes. Which is why Martin's family is pretty much guaranteed to be offered a settlement from the city and won't be denied the opportunity to sue Easthill for wrongful death."

Tory spoke what he felt was the summation of The Professor's legal explanation, which was in no way surprising. "Then he's most likely going to walk away scot-free."

"In criminal court," added The Professor, as if to prevent Tory from falling into pessimism. "But there's the potential of a civil suit against him: that is if he has enough money to make it worthwhile to sue. And there's also the police department's own internal disciplinary process."

The Professor's eyes sharpened, as if suggesting what may be the only course for any semblance of justice within the existing framework of laws and politics. "For example, he may have violated department policy or protocol which may justify him being fired. Like a de-escalation policy or violation of procedure once a suspect has been contained. Would I rather he went to jail if he's wrong? Absolutely! But that's not likely under the present laws. But if there's a way to get him off the force if he's wrong, do it. It won't end police misconduct but it's a step in the direction of justice."

There went that word again. Justice. Does retribution for wrongs committed have a connection to balance of the components of the soul? It wasn't a question Tory was prepared to ponder now, or even present to The Professor.

Yet the presence of the question remained even as the conversation shifted to lighter topics. How's the marriage? How are your parents? Are you two thinking about adopting since Loretta is probably too old to do the pregnancy thing now? Before leaving, The Professor escorted him down to the office to look up the citing for the Supreme Court decision that established the standard of *objectively reasonable*.

◆ ◆ ◆

Tory sat in his office, his eyes fixed upon his computer. The screen displayed a summary of the 1989 Supreme Court decision for *Graham v. Connor*. The introductory briefing didn't provide enough details to sate his curiosity, so he found an internet article which provided more information.

The case revolved around an incident that happened in Charlotte, North Carolina, on November 12, 1984. The main subject was Dethorne Graham, a thirty-nine year old maintenance worker for the North Carolina Department of

Transportation. He asked his friend William Berry to drive him to a convenience store. Graham, who was a diabetic, felt an insulin reaction coming on and wanted to buy some orange juice to treat it. He rushed into the store but there was a long line. Fearing he wouldn't be able to purchase the orange juice in time, he rushed out of the store and back into Berry's car.

Connor, a police officer sitting in a patrol car outside, became suspicious of Graham's hasty exit from the store. Connor followed the car and made an "investigative stop" a short distance away. That means he pulled them over. Berry, the driver, mentioned that Graham was a diabetic and suffering from a "sugar reaction." Connor still made them wait as he called for back-up and to have a police unit find out what happened at the store.

As Connor made the call, Graham got out of the car, ran around it twice, and then sat on the ground where he passed out. When back-up officers arrived, Graham was turned over and handcuffed behind his back. Berry asked the officers to get Graham some sugar, but his pleas were ignored. Instead, he was carried to Berry's car and placed face down on the hood. One of the officers said, "I've seen a lot of people with sugar diabetes that never acted like this. Ain't nothing wrong with the motherfucker but drunk. Lock the son of a bitch up." A clean version of these words were quoted in the Supreme Court decision.

When Graham awoke, he asked the police to check his wallet to see the diabetic decal he had inside it. They refused. Instead, one of the officers told Graham to shut up, pushing his face into the hood of the car. He was then grabbed by four officers and thrown head first into a police car. One of Graham's friends brought some orange juice to the scene, but the police refused to let him have it.

Finally, Connor received a report that Graham had done nothing wrong at the store. But the damage was already done.

During the "investigative stop" he suffered numerous injuries: a broken foot, an injured shoulder, bruises on his forehead, cuts on his wrists, and an unending ringing in his right ear. No criminal charges were brought against any of the officers, so Graham sued Connor and the other officers in federal court. His suit alleged they violated his Fourth Amendment rights by using excessive force.

It's also worth mentioning, which won't be a surprise to some, that Graham was Black.

As the case moved through federal court, district and appellate court judges ruled in favor of the officers. So Graham appealed to the Supreme Court. Ironically, the Supreme Court sided with Graham but not by deciding the case in his favor. Instead, the majority decision cited that the lower courts inappropriately used a "due process" legal test to render their decisions. The case was remanded back to the Court of Appeals to decide the case under the new *objectively reasonable* standard.

When the case was reconsidered, Graham lost again under the application of the new legal test. One can infer that the appellate court judges accepted that it was reasonable for the cops to assume that it was criminally suspicious for Graham to rush out of the convenience store and into a car. And that the judges also accepted as reasonable the cops assuming his abnormal behavior was the result of being belligerently drunk although they were told it was a diabetic reaction to having low blood sugar. Also deemed "objectively reasonable" was the harsh physical treatment he received which was partly, if not completely, responsible for the injuries he suffered. That is unless one wants to assign all the blame for his injuries on his diabetic condition and the fall he took because he was unable to get sugar in time.

Tory opened another window in his internet browser and typed in "fourth amendment." He clicked on the first link and took a moment to read the text:

"The right of the people to be secure in their persons, houses, papers, and effects, against unreasonable searches and seizures, shall not be violated, and no Warrants shall issue, but upon probable cause, supported by Oath or affirmation, and particularly describing the place to be searched, and the persons or things to be seized."

Tory remembered how vigorously his favorite teacher in the police academy drilled this constitutional right into the minds of his students. "This is a nation of laws, and our job is to uphold and enforce them." He declared the Fourth Amendment to be a vital pillar of good police work. Particularly the section decrying "unreasonable searches and seizures" since the department's subpoena policy addressed the later part.

Yet the issue arose again: who determines what is reasonable since the amendment doesn't offer a specific definition? Such determination can vary from individual to individual, but shared themes would likely emerge among groups with common lifestyles and experiences. Terms of reasonableness devised by middle class Whites would likely contain distinct differences than those of Blacks living in poor urban communities. So what to do when such differences clashed? This made Tory contemplate: if there is no universal standard of what is *objectively reasonable*, should it be applied universally?

He remembered a point Loretta made consistently over the years: the police must be members of the communities they serve. She argued the basis of community extends beyond just a common skin color or shared neighborhood of residence, it also encompasses the values people hold. The city government made minimal movements in this direction. Over the years, the city's initiatives included campaigns to recruit more "diversity" onto the police force, the Civilian

Review Board, and more community outreach activities by the police department. Yet still the prevailing dynamic in the 'hood remained the same: the cops were mostly White middle class while the residents remained "urban" and Black. And even most of the non-White cops on the force operated with the "blue" values of White officers.

The difference in values went beyond mere skin color and economic orientation. It also included the differing dynamics of how people engaged each other and situations. Irrespective of how the larger White culture perceived it, the urban Black orientation was not more violent, confrontational, aggressive, or criminal than the dominant culture. But those who didn't understand it could easily misinterpret it to be, especially with so much social messaging proliferating and reinforcing such views.

Tory knew these stereotypes to be false. He grew up in the 'hood and could more easily defuse tense situations there by acting within the context of its prevailing values. Situations that people from outside the 'hood could sometimes misconstrue and, thus, unnecessarily escalate into intense conflicts and violence.

When officers operated within "outside" orientations, it became *objectively reasonable* to assume the 'hood was more dangerous. Sometimes the officers' ways of interacting with residents unknowingly contributed to increasing tension, and the sometimes resulting conflicts. But in the mind of such officers, it was *objectively reasonable* to respond to situations in the 'hood with more of an eye for danger. And it followed, that their response to threats -- actual or perceived -- would increasingly involve the use of greater forms of force. Sometimes deadly force. Yet the law was saying any incident of potential excessive force was to be viewed through the officer's perspective. Even if that perspective was biased.

A sentence Chief Justice Rehnquist used in the decision further haunted Tory: *The "reasonableness" of a particular use of force must be judged from the perspective of a reasonable officer on the scene, rather than with the 20/20 vision of hindsight.* Should this be the legal approach even if an officer's perspective leaned toward a use of force that wouldn't be necessary if he or she dealt with citizens in ways more compatible with their orientation? It was possible to do this and still perform the duties of an officer, which included the solemn duty to serve and protect the people. Tory knew this from his own experiences of dealing with people of varying orientations. Dealing with people in ways that resonated with them made de-escalation a more viable option. Such an approach wouldn't end all use of police force, but could reduce it significantly.

And why would the law disregard a clear *hindsight* perspective in cases when an officer's *on the scene* perspective was wrong?

It seemed overreaching that only the officers' perspectives were deemed relevant in the eye of the law. By making this the legal baseline, the law was contributing to a mentality among police in which they only had to worry about their own perspectives. Officers could completely disregard the perspectives of all others involved as long as their perspectives didn't transcend the bounds of *objectively reasonable*. It was disconcerting to Tory that the law citizens were supposed to obey could totally dismiss their perspectives in matters of police use of force.

Tory looked back at the computer screen. His eyes fell upon a citing of the name "Graham" in the text of the decision. He wondered if this incident could have been avoided if Connor gave ear to Graham's and Bell's pleas that Graham was having a diabetic reaction? Part of hearing this would have included understanding the perspective which held it logical to not wait in a long line in a store. Or to not open the juice before buying it, given the drama -- immediate and lingering -- that could cause. Or even that Graham's anxiety regarding an oncoming diabetic reaction possibly clouded his thinking and shouldn't be solely construed as immoral calculation. Or that, as a Black man in America, a cloud of suspicion was hung over his head; and this cloud made the choice to rush to a friend's home a logical decision.

The presence of this cloud was evidenced by Connor's pursuit of Graham, assuming his hasty exit from the store was a basis to suspect he did "something" wrong. A "something" that was still fresh in Tory's mind, given his experience in the convenience store yesterday. More than thirty years after Graham's incident, he continued to encounter others' perspectives hanging a cloud of suspicion over his head. Even as a high-ranking detective.

Tory pondered if Graham ever saw Connor's police car outside the store. And if so, did Graham trust the police enough to approach the patrol car, explain his situation, and ask for help? Should not citizens feel comfortable to go to police officers when in need of assistance? Is that not a parcel of the sworn duty "to serve and protect?" And would such trust have been enough to prevent this unfortunate and unnecessary incident from occurring?

The journey of thoughts then came back to Martin Little as Tory's eyes fell upon an autopsy photo on his desk. In the stoic image of Martin's still corpse lay the reason Tory was reading the Graham decision. How much of the unfolding of the incident yesterday was fueled by two individuals engaging a tense situation from different perspectives? Perhaps perspectives so vastly different their misinterpretation of the other collided into a deadly outcome.

Tory wondered how Martin's behavior, described as weird and erratic, would have seemed to him as a person who grew up in the 'hood. Even if it appeared weird and erratic to him, would his 'hood-influenced perspective been more amicable to a resolution that didn't involve a gun?

And did Easthill, perhaps unconsciously, totally disregard Martin's perspective? A perspective that may have saw the cops as a threat and made him more tense? The law holds only Easthill's perspective was legally relevant, so he didn't have to give any mind to Martin's perspective. Yet did this lay, or significantly contribute to, the framework for what eventually resulted in shots being fired?

The law and society, as a whole, give more weight to Easthill's perspective. He was given a police badge and a gun. He was invested with the authority to stop, question, arrest, and use physical force on others. An authority protected from criminal liability as long as his actions didn't go too far into the unspecified realm of unreasonableness. Although some may offer lip service that says otherwise, Easthill was given the right and backing to completely dismiss Martin's perspective. Even to impose his perspective upon Martin: he did shoot an unarmed Black man while suffering no injuries himself. And probably did so because, in his perspective, he deemed Martin was a threat. A threat, whether real or imagined. A perspective, real or imagined, that left a real lasting imprint on the lives of so many...

CHAPTER FIVE:
*A Martina for a real **man***

There was a sudden knock on the door followed by a talking entrance. "That might work...."

Tory looked up from his computer screen to see Speedy, on his cell phone, step before the desk. "Let me just check something to make sure." Speedy covered his cell phone to say to Tory, "I got Wanda, Martin's girlfriend, on the phone. She says she's free until four p.m. if we want to go meet her."

"Let's go now."

Speedy uncovered the phone to say, "We can be there in twenty minutes if that's okay with you... Good. Let me just write down your address..." Speedy grabbed a pen and paper from the desk as Tory put his computer to sleep.

◆ ◆ ◆

She agreed to meet them at the entrance of her apartment building. As they moved through the courtyard of the building complex, Speedy dialed her number. Tory noticed a slim figure standing by a doorway and wearing a hoodie pull out a cell phone and answer it. Moments later, Wanda and Speedy realized who was on the other side of their lines, their eyes meeting from a distance. The figure wearing the hoodie approached.

After introductions, all agreed to Speedy's suggestion to sit on a nearby bench to talk. Wanda sat on one end of the bench, Tory near the middle. Speedy said he would stand as he pulled out his small pad and pen.

The softness of her face was hugged by the rim of her hood. Whatever baby weight she had was concealed by her large hoodie and baggy pants. But if you looked carefully, you could see a touch of that maternal glow unfolding upon the contours of her face. Her sleepy eyes were framed by thick glasses, weary eyes that seemed to have not had much sleep. She kept her hands in the hoodie's pockets, maintaining a reticent stillness. Somewhat aloof. Life comes, life goes. This seemed to be reflected in her reluctant countenance.

Her voice had a gentle quality. Tory had to ask her to speak louder at times to hear her over the jubilee of kids' voices in the playground nearby. She seemed nervous and apprehensive at first, very curt with her answers. So Tory took a patient and assuring approach until she settled into a sense of comfort.

"I think things were starting to weigh on him. Not so much the baby, he was looking forward to that. He already named him Martin Jr. if he was going to be a boy. Or Martina if she's a girl." That made her smile briefly. "But it was just, how to provide for a baby and us? I only work part-time so we definitely needed another income. And having a criminal record made it hard for him to find a job."

"Do you think it was more than just stress? Like a more serious mental health issue?" She hesitated, her eyes turning away slightly. Tory noticed this and proceeded with care. A honest reply might prove essential to the investigation. He looked her squarely in the eyes and spoke with a gentle encouragement. "You look like you want to say something."

"I don't want to embarrass him. Or say something that's going to make him seem worse. Like in the media, how they're portraying him to be this thug drug dealer and addict when he hasn't done drugs in years."

"Even weed?" asked Speedy.

"That helped him relax," she said in his defense. Behind the glaze of her eyes was a piercing agitation. Speedy's question was relevant but Tory would have waited before asking it. In her defensiveness, she seemed to be closing up. So he sought to assuage her anxiety by returning to his gentle and assuring approach.

"Look, you don't have to tell us. But anything that helps us better understand what he was going through might help us to understand what happened on Spencer Avenue."

She took a moment to gaze at Tory, concealing her deep breath in her stillness. Then a yearning exhalation. As if to convey that she had to tell this to someone. It was important. So she leaned forward, a stare to the ground as she began to confess.

"Last Tuesday he spent the night with me. I woke up in the middle of the night and he was in the corner, crying. I tried to comfort him but he wouldn't stop. Saying how he felt like he failed me. That he wasn't a man cause he couldn't get a job. That maybe things would be better if he just died..." She paused in the tragic irony of the statement. "He didn't seem stable. But in the morning, when he woke up, he was more positive. More like himself. Saying he couldn't give up. That God would make a way, he just had to keep trying. Then he printed up some more resumes and went out to "pound the pavement," as he would say."

She sat more erect, having said what needed to be said. Whatever would come of it would come. Speedy looked at Tory, having a question in mind but not wanting to intrude upon this moment of disclosure. Tory signaled with his eyes that he wanted to allow the moment to settle before continuing, so Speedy withheld the question. A spontaneous outburst of kids' laughter in the background was a stark contrast to the present gravity.

"Did he seem depressed?"

Wanda looked at Tory, tilting her head to the side as if a full answer went beyond any response she would volunteer. "He said he felt some of the same feelings like he did in the past. But he felt he had it under control."

"Did you believe him?"

"I wasn't around him when he was going through his stuff before, so I just took him for his word."

"How about anger? I believe he had anger issues in the past."

"Again, that was before we got together."

At first, that seemed to be all she would say on the matter. Yet the natural pause of Tory's patient pace of questioning paid off.

"But he said," added Wanda, "he felt some of the inklings from before. Like this building rage. Building, not full. But he could control it, he said. That's part of why he smoked, it would calm him down. And then his uncle Devin was helping him with that too."

Tory made a note of the name: Uncle Devin.

"Have you ever seen him act out in anger?"

"He would get mad sometimes like anybody else."

"Anything unreasonable?"

"No," she said defensive again. "He would get frustrated more than angry."

Tory paused. He didn't want her to retreat into defensiveness. And he felt she probably gave all she was going to give on the topic. There was a protectiveness in her devotion to Martin.

He decided to move on. "To come back to the day of the shooting. Do you know why he was down at Spencer Avenue?"

"In the office building he was shot by, there was a security agency he went to because he heard they were hiring."

Tory and Speedy looked at each other knowing the significance of this. They had been searching for a person or some piece of evidence that could indicate Martin's state around the time of the shooting. And finally, in what may have seemed like an inconsequential piece of information to Wanda, a treasure was given. That is if he ever made it to the security agency.

"Do you know if he ever got there?"

"I assumed he did." The question seemed a little stupid from her perspective. That's where he was going and that's where he was shot.

"Did he contact you after having gone there?" asked Tory.

"Or even right before?" interjected Speedy.

"No. We talked in the morning and that was the last time I heard from him..."

She didn't expect the effect the words would have on her as they rolled off her tongue. But they reverberated in her mind: *the last time I... the very last time...* She couldn't even complete the thought. Sadness. A building of tears she refused to show publicly. Especially to them. Although they seemed nice, they were cops. And a cop killed Martin. And probably for something stupid and unnecessary. She knew him, he wouldn't have done anything to get shot. Not with his son or daughter on the way. Not with her being in his life...

Although Tory couldn't decipher the specific reason for her retreat, her curt and distant replies made it obvious: she had shut down. So after a few more questions Tory brought the interview to a close.

After thanking her, he and Speedy walked to the car. They both knew without saying what their next destination was: the office building by the alley to find that security agency.

◆ ◆ ◆

What is it like for someone to have been here yesterday and then be unexpectedly gone today to never come back? The thought weighed on his mind during the drive to Spencer Avenue. His departing sight of Wanda left a lasting impression.

Her face bent low to the ground, as if an unseen weight was upon her hood and shoulders. Left to carry what may be the most lasting legacy of Martin: a baby to be born with a deceased father.

But there was no time to engage the thoughts now. He caught sight of the growing memorial as they walked past the alley to the office building. Just inside the entrance was a display listing the companies within. Baxter Security. No other company seemed obviously connected with security, so Tory and Speedy proceeded to the third floor office suite.

As they approached the suite door, a bearded man exited, visibly upset. Tory caught the door before it shut.

"Nice catch," smiled Speedy. Tory raised his eyebrow in appreciation of the joking praise. They then walked inside.

The suite was cramp and very cluttered. There was a small reception area with a desk and open doors to two adjoining offices. Behind the receptionist's desk sat a woman, her head down among the looming stacks of folders and papers on the desk. She didn't look up, so Tory decided to alert her to their presence. "Excuse me..."

With her head still down, she quickly interrupted with a phrase she must have been saying all day. "If you're here to apply for the security guard position, we're no longer taking applications."

"We're actually from the police department and have some questions regarding the shooting yesterday."

Tory had his badge out by the time she looked up, slightly surprised. "The Martin Little shooting?" Tory and Speedy nodded affirmatively. She put her work aside for the moment to give them her full attention.

She was a pale and aging lady, aggressively employing make-up in her war to retain a youthful appearance. Dressed formally, she had command of the space. With a keen eye to decipher which guests to engage and who to send on their way. Yet there was a gleam within her expression: the detectives' forthcoming inquiry aroused her curiosity.

"Oh. Well, I didn't see anything. I was in here when it happened."

Speedy held out a photo of Martin for her to see. "Here's a picture of him if you need it."

"I remember him. He came in here, although Mr. Harris wasn't exactly nice to him."

"Who's Mr. Harris?" Speedy asked as he put the photo away.

"He just walked out. He's the boss. He was standing here when that Martin guy handed in an application. Looked right at the question about criminal history and said, "We're not hiring ex-convicts.""

"What happened then?"

"Mr. Harris went back in his office and shut the door. And Martin just stood there, for like a minute. I tried to ignore him at first but he just stood there. So heartbroken. I said I would try to get Mr. Harris to give it another look. But I think he knew there was nothing I could do. Then he left."

Tory asked, "How did he seem when he left?"

"Devastated," she replied bluntly. "But what could I do? We just lost a major contract because one of our guards was caught stealing. So Mr. Harris has been adamant that he's not hiring any ex-cons."

Tory looked at Speedy, who signaled with his eyes that Tory could continue with the questioning. "When Martin left, did he seem angry or mentally unstable in any way?"

"Just devastated." That word again. "And then to hear he was shot dead after that. I think Mr. Harris feels a little guilty. I know I do."

Tory noted her admission but it wasn't important to what he needed. He needed to know how close this occurred to the time of the shooting. "What time did this happen?"

"In the afternoon. Maybe like three or three-thirty. I don't remember the exact time."

Tory and Speedy looked at each, their eyes acknowledging the significance of this. "Could we talk to Mr. Harris?"

"He just left for the day and is supposed to be out of the office till next week. I could try calling him but he's notorious about not answering his cell phone, especially when he's upset."

Tory read between the lines. Mr. Harris probably wouldn't want to talk to the police. And Tory would only question him to confirm the time of his encounter with Martin. But the receptionist seemed trustworthy, so it wasn't essential. Instead he pulled out his business card and extended it to her.

"I'll leave my business card." He turned to Speedy to ask, "Anything else from you?"

"I just need your name, mam."

"Barbara. Barbara Sterling."

◆ ◆ ◆

Upon returning to his office, Tory received a call from Chief Smitts' secretary. The chief wanted Tory to give his in-person update before the protests scheduled to happen that evening in Water Hole. He promised to be at the chief's office in fifteen minutes.

After using the bathroom, he stood before a sink. He drenched his hands in the running water to wash his face. Then a stare at his reflection in the mirror. An officer in uniform passed by behind him toward the exit. He noticed the officer's race. He was White.

As the door shut, Tory gazed through the mirror to see all the urinals were unoccupied. All the stall doors were open. He was alone, but not in solitude. There seemed to be so many presences impinging upon his life in this moment. Persons and personalities. Ideals and agendas. Ambitions and despair. Justifications and outrage. And more. All were in the bathroom with him without tangible forms. A swirl of knots jumbled in tangles that threatened to only become more of a mess if one sought to unravel them. But if they were not untangled, the person at the center of this disarray would be lost in the whirl of the wind. A quickly forgotten and unwilling martyr.

It was already becoming a struggle to see Martin as a person instead of an idea thrown about by others colored by their own perspectives. Yet Tory felt a duty to his person. Whoever he may be. Or was. A duty felt even if he was hampered in what he could do to bring him justice.

For some reason, the line of empty stalls took on the feel of a row of prison cells. He felt the containment of the closely spaced bars even if he could not see them. And restriction. His movements given a latitude of autonomy within a small defined space. A space designed and defined by others. I need to write to Jelani.

He remembered his visit to the prison in Louisiana. The visiting hours were strict. Only on Saturdays and Sundays until two p.m. And no visits were allowed on the last weekend of the month if it was the fifth one. He normally worked weekends and his supervisor at the time was not one to grant time off unless it was for a serious reason. So he considered it a special grace that his supervisor gave him that Sunday off.

An early morning flight placed his feet on that hot southern soil. He then rented a car at the airport to complete the ninety-minute drive to the rural prison. But he got lost along the way. His late arrival meant he would only have twenty minutes, at most, to visit with Jelani. He tried to see if being a cop could get him a few extra minutes. The guard overseeing the visiting area was sympathetic but it wasn't his call. He relayed the request to his supervisor. It was respectfully denied.

Tory, disappointed, sat inside one of the booths. A black handset was the means of verbal communication through the thick glass encased by a stone wall. His nervousness built as he sat before the empty chair on the other side. The five minutes of waiting felt much longer. Like an intense moment being stretched toward eternity. Until a familiar form wearing a bright orange outfit appeared. Different yet familiar. And missed.

He looked significantly older, as if he aged more than the years that had passed. His presence seemed stricken, afflicted beyond the flesh and bones that still carried his life. A stern stare acknowledged the awkwardness. Neither of them ever envisioned they would be meeting in such a setting. I mean, maybe if Jelani was incarcerated as a political prisoner. But as a convict for an actual crime? The situation seemed imposed rather than a natural outflow of what his life was intended to be.

He broke the ice with silence. His head tilting to the side with a smirk. Tory grinned. He then grabbed the handset on his side of the glass and held it to his face. Tory followed.

"Thanks for coming to see me. It means more to me than you think."

Tory nodded. Something inside him wanted to cry. Something else inside proclaimed that was the last thing he needed to do. That he needed to appear strong and positive to support Jelani. That's what he should do as a friend, despite how he felt.

"I got lost, that's why I'm late."

"It's fine."

More silence. Not knowing what to say, he slipped into a common custom. "So how are you doing?"

"Are you just trying to make conversation? Or are you *really* asking me how I'm doing?"

Tory wiped his eye to catch the escaping tear before it started to stream down his face.

"This shit is hard. I'm literally breaking in here. But that's what it's designed to do: break you. How else could you keep a living man in captivity without him resisting? Revolting?"

He leaned forward, his elbows resting on the counter surface. His eyes poignant and direct. An attempt to speak intimately through the sterile barrier. "I been in here for years and still cry almost every night. So many in here do. When the lights go out, you just hear sobbing. Some of these same cats who are so hard when the sun is up, who are straight up murderers. Broken."

Jelani stroked his forehead with his middle three fingers, as if they were searching for something to grasp. Tory was numbed to silence.

"I guess I should tell you how I ended up in here, since I know we only got a few minutes. The short version is I just got sick of struggling. Of doing the right thing and only remaining stuck in the same situation with no other options. Up there, down here, it was the same shit. So I said, "Fuck it. Whatever's available, I'll take it." And with my cousin already being in the business," he raised his eyebrows to indicate what that really meant, "it was right there. So I got involved.

"But that was my mistake. I let the wrongs of this society dictate my move from righteousness. I should have just kept doing what was right even if it was a struggle. Even if most of society, most of the world didn't give a damn about me. At least I had shelter and enough food to not starve to death.

"But I got tired of having nothing. Always having to beg. Day after day, year after year, with no prospects at hand. I mean, if a person does what's right, does what society says they should do, isn't society supposed to reciprocate? Something? And I'm not talking about being rich, just a steady and sufficient lifestyle.

"So when the cops raided us, I was in there cooking the stuff with my cousin. And having illegal guns in the house only added to the charges. There was no point in fighting it, so I pled guilty hoping that might get me some leniency. But we were Black guys selling to White folks, including college students -- one of whom sold us out. Wore a wire for the cops to avoid doing time for possession.

"The judge gave me 19 years, and my cousin got 22. They got some of the other guys in our crew too, lesser sentences for just selling. But we were deemed the "masterminds" of the operation so they made an example of us."

Silence again. Their eyes avoided each other. Tory, to absorb the tragedy of the story. Jelani, to bear the shame of having disappointed his friend. His little brother. Although Tory knew it wasn't his fault, he couldn't help but wonder what he could have done to affect a different outcome. In retrospect, things he previously deemed inconsequential seemed to take on a more profound relevance now. Like maybe he should have harassed Jelani more into taking the police test. Or maybe he could have lived more frugally and used the money he saved to rent a space for Jelani's corner store. Or used some of the money going into his retirement fund for the store. Or...

The stream of thoughts were interrupted as Jelani spoke, still with eyes looking elsewhere. "The funny thing about this is that, in theory, this is supposed to be rehabilitating. But all I can see is that I'll spend the next big chunk of my life locked up, only to be put back in the same situation years later. Still having nothing, with even less prospects. If I couldn't find a steady job before, how much more impossible will it be having drug and gun convictions? And being older? That's if I even make it out of this place. Not everyone does."

"You will," Tory mustered up.

"Hope and reality share different dimensions here."

Tory was wounded hearing these words. Just the thought of his best friend dying in prison brought torment. Yet he couldn't deny the validity of Jelani's statement: people do die in prison. He knew in that moment that their friendship was forever changed. What was would never be again. That what they had was essentially lost despite what fragments might slip through the very real barrier of prison. It then dawned on Tory that this visit was no longer a reunion as much as it was a memorial to their shared past.

"So how are you doing?" The question now being reversed.

Tory shrugged his shoulders, as if admitting the overall pleasantness of his life was insignificant to what Jelani was enduring. But he was spared from having to vocalize such as a guard stood behind Jelani. It was obvious what this meant. Visiting hours had come to an end.

They both frowned slightly, wishing they had more time as tears swelled in their eyes. They wished they could stay, have this moment be extended. But other forces determined otherwise.

"I gotta go, bro." Jelani didn't even attempt to stop the tear that fell from his eye. He extended his hand to the glass, pressing his palm firmly against it. Tory did likewise, as if some form of human warmth would pass through the cold, thick glass. Jelani then quickly hung up the handset and walked away.

They both knew that to extend the departure would only make it more painful. Tory sat there for a moment as his hand withdrew from the glass, his other arm drooping the handset from his face. He wiped away the fallen tears and placed the handset back on the wall. He gave one last stare at the empty chair on the other side before summoning the will to stand. One last stare.

Staring at his reflection in the mirror. The trance broken as he heard someone enter the bathroom. Another White officer in uniform. They nodded hello to each other and then returned to their separate activities as the officer entered a stall. Tory checked his cell phone. It was time to go see the chief. So he stepped away from the reflection of his memory to face the reality the present was drawing him to.

♦ ♦ ♦

Chief Smitts leaned back in his chair behind his desk. Tory sat erect across from him.

"So what do you have so far?"

"Not much. From what we can gather, Martin seemed to be under a lot of stress. He was having a hard time trying to find a job so he could provide for his girlfriend and their coming child. Shortly before the shooting, he applied for a security job but got turned away because of his criminal record. I'm wondering if that, with the stress he was under, led to him acting erratic. He had mental health issues in the past."

Tory's complete analysis was more expansive and probing. But he always felt it best to stick to tangible facts and evidence when discussing matters with his superiors. He knew they were usually more concerned with what could be used to build or disprove a case, and less concerned about what actually happened and why. Having spent many years as a detective, he knew the components of a case didn't always share the same space as what actually happened.

"How about his encounter with Easthill? Any details?"

"All the witness accounts so far are from a distance and offer nothing conclusive about why he shot Martin."

"Anything to suggest why he pulled out his gun?"

Tory recognized the intent behind the question. One of the factors in deciding if this was a case of excessive force was if Martin did anything to escalate the possibility of danger prior to being shot. If so, Easthill's actions would more likely be viewed as justified even in light of Martin being unarmed.

"Witnesses say Officers Easthill and Peters tried to talk to Martin but he continued to act erratic. That he even yelled at them to leave him alone. But nothing so far to indicate specifically why Easthill chose to grab his gun."

"Well, maybe he'll offer some answers tomorrow."

Chief Smitts' body language shifted as the matter most pressing to him had been addressed. He seemed less anxious now. To Tory, it seemed what was most important to the chief was if one of his officers had crossed the line into police brutality. The fact that Martin died, why he was really shot, and the politics surrounding the shooting seemed less significant. Even the tone of the chief's voice seemed to treat these "lesser matters" as an aside.

"You should know the D.A. decided to take over the criminal investigation, which has the mayor and others upset. But she's agreed to allow you to sit in when they question the officers." He then leaned forward as if to make it seem this matter was just as important as the previous one. "This is still an active Internal Affairs investigation and I'll need a report from you regardless if they press charges. So continue on as you normally would, deferring to them when necessary."

Tory knew the implications of the criminal investigation changing hands. It basically relieved the police department from the responsibility of taking any corrective actions. Any findings by Internal Affairs would fall secondary to the determinations made by the prosecutors. If they declined to press charges, it was pretty much assumed that Internal Affairs would follow suit with a similar or lesser finding, even if the investigating detectives felt otherwise. Also, in the context of the police culture, the shift limited the scope of punishment Internal Affairs was expected to recommend. It would be surprising to suggest more than mild discipline, if any, since the criminal aspects of the matter now lay with the District Attorney.

"The lead prosecutor is Lucas Garfield," continued Chief Smitts. "He's a bit of a bulldog. I don't know if he'll let you ask any questions, but I want you at the interrogations of all the officers tomorrow. We can follow-up with our own questioning if needed."

Then another aside. "Also, you should know they're releasing the names of all the officers involved within the hour."

Although Tory agreed the public had the right to know the officers' names, doing so now would only increase the protective silence among the police. The reactionary tension from releasing their names would move them to be more defensive toward the media and general public. And certainly the prosecutors. He almost preferred that the names be withheld until after the interrogations tomorrow. The officers would surely be more guarded now within an atmosphere they regarded more hostile.

◆ ◆ ◆

The fish tank had become a place of refuge. The encased water with the colorful fish floating within it became a respite from a world constantly flaring with stress. Although the grasping pulls of the world were still present, dropping the colored flakes of food upon the water gave a temporary relief. And he needed the relief. Without it, it wouldn't be long before the constant toil of his life broke him.

The fish tank and the photo of Uncle James. For him, these offered refuge. He remembered Uncle James liked fishing. He never took a liking to it. To him, it was boring. And he didn't like the feel of the squirming scaly creature jerking for life as he removed the hook from its mouth. But fishing was a virtual paradise to Uncle James who seemed to do it religiously in his later days.

Uncle James. If he was still here, Tory would have sought his counsel with this case. The immensity of it seemed to consume his every waking moment like no other case before.

There was no guarantee his uncle would have addressed it directly. He had a strict habit of not offering advice about things he felt he didn't know enough about. When presented with such, he would usually shift the focus to something else. Like when Tory went to him because he was having mild anxiety attacks about his upcoming detective exam.

"I don't know anything about being a detective. Or anxiety attacks. But I know a good wife makes a good home. Like with Marcia..."

His voice dwindled away to a happy reminiscence. Such a peaceful smile. Marcia, Tory's aunt by marriage, had died about two years prior to this conversation happening. After she passed, Uncle James made it a point to hang photos of her in every room of their house. Even the bathroom.

"For twenty years I treated my marriage like it was an entitlement. What I was entitled to get from her. It was only after she was diagnosed with cancer that I treated my marriage like a responsibility. That I had a duty from God to serve her without expecting anything in return. Sure, I did plenty of things for her before but always expecting something. Or cause I got something. But that isn't love, it's selfishness.

"And I could be so petty at times." He chuckled. "We must have had over a thousand arguments -- literally, a thousand -- about her stealing the covers in the bed at night. She didn't do it intentionally, she would do it in her sleep. And I would wake up with just a little bit of cover on me. Just furious!" He chuckled again. "She offered a reasonable suggestion. That I have my covers and she have hers. But I said no. That if you do that, I'll throw those covers in the garbage! Stubbornness! I said there ain't no reason a married couple should have two sets of covers. We wouldn't need such if you just stopped taking all the dang covers!"

He and Tory laughed. The obvious absurdity was hilarious in retrospect.

"I was dead serious. One time I got so mad, she decided to sleep without covers. Just to appease me, I guess. Maybe she thought it would make me sympathetic to her. It didn't. But after doing that for a few nights and getting a cold, she made up her mind that she would just bear me getting upset but stay warm at night."

His eyes were alight with joy reflecting on the silliness of something he once took so seriously. And for so long. "Even the morning we got the diagnosis, I woke up mad cause she had all the covers. *Ah-gain!* I didn't complain about it because I knew she wasn't feeling well, but we both knew why I was upset.

"But look at the beauty of that. I was a fool. A damn fool. And in her love for me, she allowed me to be a fool since I refused to be corrected. But still she continued to do all the beautiful things she did for me as a wife, out of her expansive love for me. I was the one who was small-minded."

Tory appreciated the honesty of his uncle's confession. He also sensed Uncle James had a deliberate intent in sharing this. A warning to heed for the younger man still evolving within his own marriage.

"I can remember how, when we were in the doctor's office; how after he said that c-word, the silence that fell upon us. How ashamed I felt. That here we were twenty years into a good marriage, and I'm still acting like a child over some damn covers."

He paused to let the words sink in. It was clear to Tory that the concerns he brought, however serious they may have been, were secondary to this more important lesson Uncle James felt he needed in his life right now. And, perhaps unconsciously, there was a greater lesson in the midst: to not lose sight of what's truly important in the distracting clutter of lesser things. Was a test for detective more significant than ensuring he wasn't sacrificing portions of his marriage over things he would later realize as unimportant? Even things that were obviously foolish but not realized as such because of his own present blindness?

"I tell you, Tory, that day I realized how much Marcia loved me. Not because of anything she did that day, but because of all the things she did for me over all the years without me fully reciprocating. I took so much for granted. So much. And knew better. My grandmother taught me from an early age: "Don't let no good deed end in you. When someone does something good for you, always return the blessing with a blessing. No matter how small it may seem." And saying "thank you" ain't enough, especially when the other person is always doing something for you." He smiled resting in the sweetness of this wisdom. "That there is a gem of a lesson. But I wasn't applying it to my wife, the woman I vowed to be with till death do us part.

"After that day, the day of the diagnosis, I committed to serve her without ever expecting anything else in return. That I was eternally in debt to her for all she had done for me. And in doing that, actually serving her, I finally learned how to love her *just because* -- which is how she loved me. Not needing a specific set of reasons or agenda to be loving. It took me twenty years of marriage, after a few years of courting, to finally learn what it meant to truly love someone.

"I tell you, nephew, those last two years, despite her failing health, how little I could do to ease her suffering; those last two years of losing my wife were the best years of my life. I know that might sound weird, but it's true. Completely devastating but the best."

There was a glow about him as he seemed to stare into the memory of that time. And Tory felt blessed to just be witness to it. Then, as an epilogue, he added, "Don't wait twenty years to start living this. Start living it now. Every day. Every moment."

It seemed as if the light of this realization was still shining in his eyes in the aged photo hanging on the wall. And maybe, in some weird and seemingly unconnected way, this was exactly what Tory needed to hear right now. To love. That nothing's more important than love. To honor those who serve and benefit your life. To reciprocate the small as well as the big things people do for you. To not take things for granted because time is always creeping toward an end. To truly appreciate people now before it's too late. That in realizing and living these simple yet profound virtues, even the loss of a caring and loving spouse can become beautiful. With a lasting beauty. That blessings can still be found in the unavoidable tragedies that will afflict our lives.

Maybe something good can still come from the present tragedy of Martin's killing. Maybe. And if that's possible, it's important to remember to keep an open eye for such. An open heart.

◆ ◆ ◆

The resonance of the thoughts faded to the sound of the television. With his attention so focused on the fish and the memory of Uncle James, the newscast became an ignored background. But now Tory's focus was drawn to the screen where a press conference was being held in front of City Hall.

A group of people stood behind the man in a suit speaking. Most of them were Black and held signs referencing the Martin Little shooting. Some even wore t-shirts with Martin's face upon them. It didn't take long for Tory to notice Loretta among the group. Not far from Mandy and Chunky.

"He was shot like a dog in the street," the man said boldly.

His dark flesh furrowed upon his forehead as others behind him vocalized their support. Text on the bottom of the screen identified him: Alton Lewis, Lawyer for the Little family. He was a dynamo of force and precision, continuing on with an unabating eloquence.

"And for what? He was unarmed. He wasn't committing a crime. In fact, he was down there to apply for a job. Someone striving against the odds to be a positive, law-abiding, contributing member of society.

"Did he have a criminal past? Yes. That was a consequence of his drug addiction, something he overcame by going for treatment. But did the cops know this when they shot him? Did they know he was a reformed person determined to do what was right? Or did they just see another Black man and assume him to be a danger? A threat? And guilty? Therefore, there was no need to regard him as a full-born citizen of this country, entitled to the same rights and protections all citizens of this country deserve. No need to regard him as innocent until proven guilty."

He paused, the group behind him chorusing their endorsement of his powerful words.

"So I'll end reiterating our demands. That a special prosecutor be assigned to oversee this case." The group agreed. "That the F.B.I. come in, not to assist but lead the investigation." The group agreed again. "The same police department that regularly mistreats and abuses our community cannot be trusted to investigate themselves. And, finally, that this cop be tried in court for the murder -- that's right: the murder -- of Martin Little!" The group erupted into exuberant applause. "If a regular citizen did what Officer Easthill did, he would already be arrested and charged with murder. Being a police officer should not be used to justify injustice!"

The group applauded loudly. His extended pause indicated he was done. He then turned to look at an older man among the group who nodded back. "Now let us hear from Devin Scott, who can speak to the personal loss he feels for the sudden death of his nephew."

People applauded as the older man stepped forward. His circular glasses dotted upon the beard ranging over the lower half of his face. He wore a large blue dashiki with gold embroidery and a matching kufi upon his head. He was deliberate with his movements, making every motion with care. He took a moment to gather himself before speaking. Then his deep voice emitted from his mouth.

"I echo everything Mr. Lewis, our family lawyer, said because this loss has been absolutely overwhelming. I've been there to support Martin, really chastise him, when I saw him throwing his life away on the streets. But I didn't realize then he had a problem: he was a drug addict.

"It took him hitting rock bottom, getting arrested and going to jail, to finally go to drug treatment and start to get his life together. That with his beautiful, loving sister, Madeline, and her son -- we call him Little Chunky; how they took him in to live in their home. That's what set him on the right path. But he got even more serious when he found out he was going to be a father. To see him going through that transformation, making the commitment to be a man in the fullest sense of the word; to have him be killed in the midst of that... it's more heartbreaking than I have the words for.

"That cop killed a *man!* Someone striving to live up to his responsibilities and..." He paused searching for the words, to eventually blurt out, "That's just wrong!" The group vocalized with concurring emotions. "And I would say the same thing if anybody killed him. But for it to be a cop, someone who's supposed to protect us, that just makes it hurt in ways that cut deeper."

His voice fled under the pain. He tried to summon it back but it wouldn't return. So after standing there speechless in deep emotion, Alton stepped forward to put his arm around the uncle shaking with grief. The image was deeply moving. Even Tory was moved to sympathy.

"Thank you, Devin. So please join us tonight for a candlelight vigil at the place where Martin was shot, followed by a rally. And come in peace."

CHAPTER SIX:
Moving images through the night

After a brief dinner alone, Tory made his way through the evening dusk back to police headquarters. He knew Loretta would be at the protests in Water Hole. And he worked better in his office. It would be quiet, with less distractions.

He noticed the slight echo his shoes gave as each step struck the tile floors of the hallway. He grabbed a cup of tea to accompany him into the office. With just the desk light on, he left most of the room in a dim. Then he began to remove various items from his bulging Little file and spread them across the surface of the desk.

Before delving into the case, he pulled out his phone to check it. A flashing icon indicated he had missed a call. Listening to the message, he frowned: Devin Scott had returned his call. Tory immediately dialed his number, knowing he might not answer if he was at the ongoing protest.

"Hello, Mr. Scott. This is Detective Givens again. I somehow missed your call. But as I said in my previous message, I'm investigating the shooting. I was hoping you would give me a few minutes of your time to answer some questions. My phone will be on and with me, so you can call me any time to set up a meeting, even if it's late. You have my number. Thank you." Hanging up the phone, he placed it on the desk.

He was stumped. The desk displayed an array of pieces of the case, but they weren't adding up to a clear sum. In situations like this, his mentor Dusty advised him to begin again, start anew.

Tory grabbed the copy of the police report Easthill wrote after the shooting. This was the last thing he did as a cop before his period of silence. As expected, it offered little beyond the obvious. But he did write "the suspect ignored police commands." And that "he lunged at me in a threatening manner, at which I discharged my gun in self-defense."

It was known among officers to give as little information as possible on such reports when dealing with something that might prove to be controversial. His supervising officer could request a revised report with more details but he was under no obligation to submit it until the forty-eight hour period expired. Underneath Easthill's report were the reports of the other officers. They were also vague beyond the obvious.

Tory then laid out photos of the crime scene. Various shots of the sidewalk and alley from different angles. The police cars stationed by the sidewalk. The pool of blood on the alley asphalt. A wide shot of the scene taped off by yellow police tape. Photos have a language of their own and sometimes reveal things hidden. But he could decipher nothing from the photos that whispered more than what was already known.

Then to the people involved. He skimmed through the headshots of the officers, placing the portrait of Easthill before him, on top of the others. He looked through various autopsy photos. A profile shot of the corpse laying upon the examining table. Various angles framing Martin's dead face. Close shots of the bullet holes in his chest, the broken discolored flesh swollen as puffy craters. Tory pulled out one displaying his naked corpse from mid-torso to his head and placed it beside Easthill's portrait. He then scanned through a few of the photos Mandy had given him of when Martin was alive. He selected a couple with Martin wearing a LeBron James jersey. Maybe he was a LeBron fan.

He stared at the three photos of Martin he chose from the rest. He was looking for any visual indication that might signify something not yet known. He picked up the photo of Martin's uncovered chest and face. He scanned it carefully, hoping it might divulge how Martin died. And why. Since he was still alive when the ambulance arrived, their priority was to rush him to the hospital for care. And rightfully so. But this meant there were no crime scene photos of him in the alley. And most likely no civilian photos either since the officers would have immediately set up a perimeter to keep people away. This left Tory without any hints of how he lay on the ground. Or the expression on his face. Where his arms and legs laid. Whether his hands were clenched. Sometimes these gave signs of things human words sought to conceal. Or signs human silence wouldn't admit.

Tory's focus on the photo was such that he almost fell into a meditation upon it. In the dimmed quietude of his office, there was only him and the image. Only him and the picture of the corpse. Therefore, he didn't notice the rapid footsteps approaching and increasing in volume. His mind engrossed by the two craters on Martin's chest. Thus, he was completely startled by the knock on the door, followed by Speedy poking his head into the office.

"They're rioting in Water Hole and want all available officers to assist."

◆ ◆ ◆

The patrol car sped through the streets with flashing lights and blaring sirens. As they entered the Water Hole section of the city, all signs of traffic suddenly disappeared.

Speedy had a firm grip on the steering wheel. The riot helmet he was wearing had the visor raised. He and Tory both wore official police jackets. Dark colored with "POLICE" in large white letters on the front and back. Tory sat with a worried look as he held his riot helmet in hand. It felt awkward to have to wear a helmet designed for military combat as a civilian cop responding to a civilian incident.

The sirens, roaring engine, the sound of the tires spinning across the asphalt served as conversation. That was until Speedy spoke. Although relevant, his words seemed to come out of nowhere.

"From what I could gather from the wire, some people rushed the liquor store with rocks and started breaking windows. Then the vacant shop next to it and the restaurant. When the cops moved in, more rocks were thrown. Then gunshots. Then chaos as people started running everywhere."

"Gunshots from who?"

"Who knows." These were just details of an impersonal event for Speedy. To Tory, they held more significance. "Did you hear from Loretta?"

"She texted me back to say she's home."

"Good." What was happening could remain just an event. Not something personally affecting his partner. Or at least that's what Speedy thought.

He decreased the car's speed as they approached Spencer Avenue. It was blocked off by a police barricade. Pulling up to the wooden barriers, he lowered his window as an officer approached. "We're Internal Affairs," Speedy said as he flashed his badge.

"Do you need to drive in there? It's still chaotic," replied the officer.

Tory interjected, "We need to drive in!"

He didn't mean to speak so forcefully, it just came out that way. The officer nodded and backed up as he and another officer made way for the patrol car to drive through.

As Speedy pulled onto Spencer Avenue, they saw two fire trucks in the middle of the street. Hoses were deployed, now laying across the asphalt and concrete. Firefighters moved about the extinguished fires that partially consumed the vacant shop and the fried chicken restaurant. The liquor store didn't appear to have been touched by flames. But what it had in common with the neighboring structures was the complete destruction of the front windows. The proof of it being looted was evident in the assortment of broken liquor bottles littering the sidewalk and street. As Tory turned away from that part of the destruction, he saw that the store of the gas station had also been left desecrated with broken windows.

A throng of police vehicles filled the street along with three ambulances. The city darkness illuminated by an array of flashing lights. Paramedics and fire fighters tended to wounded civilians. A few police officers were also being treated. From a distance, it didn't seem that any of the injuries were life threatening. Those providing medical care didn't move with the intensity that often accompanied more serious conditions. The worst appeared to be a woman being treated with an oxygen mask.

In the near distance, beyond the injured, were the remnants of Martin's memorial. Now a disarray of broken and trampled upon items scattered about by the chaos of people fleeing the scene.

Speedy parked the car at the gas station. Tory exited with his helmet in hand. He surveyed the street, stupefied. Speedy stood beside him, lowering the visor of his helmet to cover his face. As they walked toward the street, a familiar voice called to them from the side.

"Givens, Dillenger... Over here." Tory and Speedy turned to see Gulley approaching. He wore a riot helmet and a bulletproof vest over his shirt. As he stood by Tory, he nudged him, warning, "Put your helmet on. We still got random rocks flying from all directions."

As Tory put on the helmet, Speedy asked, "What happened?"

"Madness. Complete madness." Gulley shook his head to emphasize his words. "We still got cops chasing down looters in the area. It might be a long night into dawn."

◆ ◆ ◆

Within an hour things had calmed down. An eery absence replaced the usual activity and sounds that filled the streets. The people weren't there but the tension remained. A lingering tension.

It wasn't long before most of the responding units were allowed to go, including Speedy and Tory. But they were told to keep their riot gear with them, just in case they were summoned overnight to respond to another uprising.

He sought to make the drive home intentionally uneventful. He didn't turn on the radio. Kept his eyes only on the road before him. His mind wanted to wander but he was too tired to engage the thoughts. So he let the moving collage of mental entities pass by randomly like the passing scenery, giving no attention to anything in particular. He pulled into the driveway, knowing it would be a while before his mind would let him sleep. That's if he would sleep at all. Perhaps he could find something mindless on the television to dull it into slumber.

As he entered the back door, she was in the kitchen with a cup of tea. Dressed for bed but restless. And she wasn't really drinking the tea. The agitation she hoped it would calm was impervious to the soothing liquid. So instead she held it as a prop, subconsciously hoping the appearance of its pacifying might alleviate the disturbance still running rampant through her mind.

But that disturbance was immediately re-energized upon seeing the riot helmet in his hand. His fatigue made him oblivious to the rising tension behind her trying-to-be calm facade. And, in his unawareness, he only increased her anxiety by holding the helmet in clear view.

He looked at her and could see the repressed alarm in her eye. "Are you okay?"

She too felt ashamed to admit she was disturbed by the sight of the helmet. A shame she tried to hide by her reply. "Can't sleep."

But the night had been too much for her. Too much acting calm and collected. Too much suppressing emotions bulging for expression. The apex reached as the rush of descending emotions bent her frame and frowned her face. Tears, uncontrollable sobs joined the avalanche. Somehow she placed the cup of tea on the counter as her body hovered in a state of standing collapse.

He put the helmet down and rushed to embrace her. Holding her in an attempt to comfort her within his own comfort-yearning fatigue. "It's okay. Everything is fine now." Not even he believed the words as he uttered them. Nor did they become more believable in the moment of silence that followed. She refused to believe them. Nor would she allow them to go unaddressed.

"No, it's terrible! We were just trying to do right by Martin and these people came. They weren't protesting. They just came and mixed in with the crowd. Then all the sudden they started breaking windows with rocks and everything became crazy. The crowd was peaceful until then. Upset but peaceful."

The weight of the night's events could be held back no longer. And she felt personally responsible for it all in some convoluted way. Yet in his fatigue, the detective within him responded to her words. Not the husband.

"Do you think you could identify any of them?"

"No, but it was our people. Young people. They've been so upset by this. But it's just..." She couldn't continue, hiding her own feelings behind youthful discontent. A lingering struggle she had been trying to avoid for too long was now unveiling itself. And it needed her words in her own voice.

"This one has been weighing on me so deeply." She stepped away from her husband's embrace. She needed the space to finally say it. "It's not the first Black guy killed by a cop in our community. And it won't be the last. But it's just like... what am I doing in this whole situation? Educating our youth isn't changing anything. Neither is the organizing..."

He saw where she was going. And intuitively, he didn't want to go there. At least not now within his numbed fatigue. "You're being too critical right now."

But she wouldn't relent. No. "If Martin was an A-student in one of my classes, would that have stopped that cop from shooting him? What, if anything, could've been done on Martin's part or our community's part to stop that cop from shooting him?"

Silence. These were exactly the types of questions he was trying to avoid on the ride home. Yeah, his mind was clever enough to dress such inquiries as random thoughts that danced in and out of the case and other ideas related to the shooting in some way. But he didn't have the honesty to admit that he saw nothing in all the things being done to address such issues that was working: that was actually pre-venting unarmed Blacks from being killed by cops for reasons that didn't make sense. Or maybe it wasn't a lack of honesty as much as a lack of courage. A courage that would demand he take a real stand to confront and finally resolve these long-standing issues.

He didn't have a hopeful answer to her question. And he was too tired now to face something he didn't have the willingness to examine on his own. So he offered a way out, a route by which to escape. "That's part of what your orga-nizing work is for."

No. Something in her wouldn't let this conversation be evaded. "But it's not working: Martin is dead! And there's nothing in place to stop the same thing from happening again tomorrow. Like it's happened last week. Last month. The months before that for years. If cops want to kill us, they just kill us! And usually with no consequences!"

The words struck like a dagger in Tory's heart. Although he wanted to refute it, he knew it was true. Beneath the surface of it all, this was one of the things deeply nagging him about this investigation.

"You know," she continued, "when they started rioting there was something deep within that just wanted to burn shit down! Just destroy everything!"

Tory was startled because Loretta rarely cursed or spoke in an angry tone. She then looked up with eyes that were more lost than filled with rage.

"But I ran," she confessed in defeat. "And truth be told, that's what's keeping me up more than anything else. Yeah, I know it's wrong to riot. Something I could never justify. But I ran. I wasn't even willing to stand my ground for a peaceful protest. So what am I really doing?"

She looked at him as if hoping he might provide an answer. Or a semblance of one. But she also knew that wasn't a question for him or anyone else to answer. The question was really for her. And he knew he couldn't answer it. He wouldn't even dare. So he gave no response beyond his empty stare.

Somehow in the silence that haunted the kitchen, they each found ways to exit within the lingering awkwardness. She made her way to the bed before he did. And again, she was sleeping with her back to him. Or at least she appeared to be asleep even with the constant tossing and turning.

It was deep into the middle of the night when he climbed into the bed. He lay motionless with his back upon the mattress. But his mind was an unyielding deluge of passing thoughts. And worries. And frustrations. And grasps at a hope he seemed unable to hold. Nothing clear. Nothing conclusive. Until he fell into an unconscious numbness of the body as the mind continued to recoil upon itself in a state some would call a night of not really sleeping.

❖ ❖ ❖

"Baby, get up... Tory, get up! You need to see this..."

In his grogginess, his first thought was the house must be on fire. Why? He didn't know. The couple hours of disgruntled sleep gave his waking moments no logic. But instead of fleeing, she was turning on the bedroom television with a remote.

As the screen flashed on, he was able to formulate words. "What's going on?"

"The news is showing cell phone footage of the shooting."

"What shooting?"

"Martin Little."

His semi-sleepiness was instantly shed. He sat up, alert, as the black screen flashed to show three reporters sitting at a news desk. The "Breaking News" text was prominent on the screen beside the logo designed for coverage of the Martin Little shooting.

"It all happened overnight. And rather quickly," said the Black woman reporter. Her words were directed to the White man and White woman news anchors at the desk. It seemed to be an impromptu moment, lacking the usual scripted feel news segments have. "And, as she said in the interview, the reason she contacted us is that she trusts us more than she does the police." The reporter then addressed someone off-screen, "Do we have that clip ready...? Okay, let's play it."

The broadcast cut to a recorded interview of the reporter and another Black woman. The reporter sat in a chair within a different television studio. Her guest sat nervously on the adjacent sofa.

"I felt guilty," the guest confessed. "I called 9-1-1 because he was acting weird. Like he needed help."

"Would you say he was dangerous?"

"More to himself than anyone else. Like maybe he needed psychiatric help." As she continued, the following text appeared on the screen: LaVonne Watkins, witness to the Martin Little shooting. "But back to your question. I called 9-1-1 to get him help and they killed him. I felt a little responsible because maybe if I didn't call the cops, maybe he'd still be alive."

She paused. The sadness in her eyes seemed more profound in the silence.

"So after he shot him I just ran home and didn't tell anybody. I wouldn't even answer my phone. But then the media..."

Her voice wavered off in hesitation. But the reporter encouraged her to go on. "You can say it."

"The media started making it seem like he was a criminal. Digging up all this stuff that wasn't relevant to what happened in that moment. And then even after the riots, it just made me feel like I had to let people see what really happened in that alley."

The broadcast cut back to the live shot in the studio.

"So again, that's LaVonne Watkins who, overnight, gave us cell phone footage of the Martin Little shooting. Let's show it again. And just a warning, the footage is graphic and may not be appropriate for children."

Tory's cell phone rang from the night table. He answered it as his eyes remained on the screen. "Detective Givens... I'm watching it now... I'm on my way, Chief Smitts."

◆ ◆ ◆

The mood in Chief Smitts' office was tense. The chief, Tory, Speedy, and Gulley were watching the cell phone footage of the shooting on a large television. It was shot across the street from the alley, opposite from the office building. Handheld and chest high, her wide-angled view was partially blocked by the parked patrol cars.

As the footage began, Martin could be seen in the alley, standing near and facing the office building's wall. Although the cell phone was too far to give a clear shot of his face, one could sense that he was upset. Officer Easthill also stood in the alley, a short distance from Martin. There was nothing but open space between them, Easthill's fear covered by a veneer of toughness. His gun was already drawn and aimed at Martin, who had his back to Easthill. Officer Peters stood between the two police cars, his hand on his holstered gun. Officer Stevenson stood by the back of the second police car. He had a taser in hand, ready to use but presently pointed to the ground.

Easthill is seen saying something, but the camera was too far to clearly capture his words. There was a moment of silence as Martin didn't respond. Easthill then spoke again, a brief forceful statement. Martin suddenly turned around yelling at Easthill. In a volume muted by the distance, Martin's voice could be heard.

"Leave me...!"

The sentence was brutally interrupted by the sound of two gunshots immediately fired by Easthill. Officer Stevenson simultaneously raised and shot the taser but quickly ducked in response to the gunshots. As Martin's body dropped to the ground and out of view, Officer Peters ducked between the police cars and pulled out his gun.

It all happened so fast. In an unexpected instant. "Oh my god, oh my god!" LaVonne's reactionary commentary could be heard clearly. The cell phone camera jolting with her shock.

Moments later, Officer McDonald cautiously approached the alley from the bus stop. Her eyes peeled and gun drawn. Her body camera was small yet noticeable on her chest to those who knew to look for it. Peters approached Easthill who remained frozen in the alley with his gun extended. Peters lowered Easthill's gun to the ground. Stevenson moved to the fallen body and spoke into his radio. He then pointed for McDonald to return to where she was by the office building, probably to keep people away from what was now a crime scene. As Peters walked in the opposite direction, toward the liquor store, the cell phone was stuffed into the darkness of a purse. LaVonne's shoes could be heard hitting the sidewalk as she ran away. The footage is paused on the black screen.

Tory watched the clip twice before rushing to police headquarters. Watching it again only increased his concerns about what he saw. Yet he felt he shouldn't be the one to break the silence permeating the office. What occurred was obvious in his eyes, undeniable in plain sight for anyone willing to acknowledge it. But would the culture of "blue" view this through a different, more doubting lense? A doubt more partial to siding with Easthill.

Tory was also very cognizant of the fact that he was a Black man in an office with three White men who just watched a White man kill an unarmed Black man in cold blood.

"Well, it clearly shows something was going on with Martin Little," Gulley suggested. "That Easthill clearly gave a series of commands that Martin didn't follow."

"Or was unable to follow. He may not have been mentally coherent enough to obey the commands."

"True," Gulley conceded to Tory's point.

He would not allow them to simply spin this as an *objectively reasonable* course of actions. But he would have to be reserved and measured, he was treading two worlds.

"It also shows they had him contained," Tory volunteered. This should have been enough to manage the situation in a way that didn't require the use of deadly force. Especially with Officer Stevenson having a taser in hand.

"Yeah," added Speedy, "but without the audio and it being shot from a distance, he's going to argue there was some threat the video doesn't show."

The point was valid. But beyond the words, Tory was trying to determine where Speedy stood on the spectrum of defending or denouncing the shooting. For some officers, any threat justifies any response an officer engages. Even if that response is unnecessary and excessive.

"If Martin was a threat," reasoned Tory, "why was Easthill standing directly in front him and not using his car or something else as a protecting barrier?" Officers are trained to employ such means for their safety, although it is not always applied in the field.

"That's what I would have done if I felt the need to pull out my gun." Speedy's remark, although somewhat encouraging, didn't reveal any certainty of his position in Tory's eyes. But the chief had a different agenda and didn't waste any more time shifting the discussion there.

"Let's just concede Easthill's judgment can be questioned. What I need to know now is if there's anything in the footage that makes this undoubtedly a crime." The query was addressed to all and Tory already knew his response. But he also knew the unwritten rule which dictated he should hold his opinion until Gulley, his superior, spoke.

"It's questionable but I wouldn't say it's outright murder or manslaughter."

Speedy quickly chimed in, "I agree."

Tory felt abandoned. That the others were diminishing the clarity of what was clearly an unnecessary shooting and, thus, at minimum manslaughter. Words uttered by Alton Lewis, the Little's family lawyer, at yesterday's press conference echoed in his mind: "If a regular citizen did what Officer Easthill did, he would already be arrested and charged with murder." But being a cop, Tory couldn't say that. Not even within the confines of what was supposed to be a confidential investigative meeting. It would somehow get out that he was violating the code of the blue fraternity. And surely his superiors wouldn't look at him with the same trust if he betrayed this code. So he took a moment to cautiously parse his thoughts before speaking.

"How about you, Givens?" Chief Smitts asked, interrupting Tory's calculation.

"Watching the whole thing, I don't know why he shot him. It seems like unnecessary force. But is it unquestionably a crime? The footage doesn't show that."

He couldn't call it an outright crime. He just couldn't, although that is what he felt. And the technicality of the footage not providing indisputable evidence gave him a way out. A way to not have to be honest and courageous. The absence of footage prior to Easthill pulling out his gun and the indecipherable sound compromised the ability of the video to implicate him. Points his lawyer would absolutely play on, as had been done by lawyers in previous cases similar to this. With things leaning considerably in Easthill's favor, why should Tory take on an unnecessary risk? One he would surely suffer consequences for. He said enough to hint what he really felt without actually saying it, he thought to himself.

But he felt alone. Isolated. Ashamed. Although he was being asked for his honest opinion, in reality it was only welcomed if it fit within an acceptable range. Cops don't convict cops unless there's indisputable evidence. This creed is only broken in the most extreme cases. Cops are expected to give other cops the benefit of a doubt. Even if that means looking the other way. Or through a lens that diffuses clarity from what is otherwise obvious to frame things in questionable terms. This is what is expected to secure the unquestioning back-up and support of other officers in the array of dangerous situations one may face. Yet in this instance, it felt defeating to uphold this creed while merely implying his disapproval of Easthill's actions.

"Then let's see what comes out of the interrogations this afternoon." Chief Smitts was ready to bring this meeting to an end. "And I'll need all of you on Spencer Avenue tonight.

Although there's a curfew, there will definitely be protests now that this video has gone public."

◆ ◆ ◆

Tory was the first to exit Chief Smitts' office. He headed to his office without looking back. Moving through the corridors in a rapid pace, his cell phone rang. The display showed it was Devin Scott.

"Hello, this is Detective Givens."

"Good morning, this is Devin Scott."

"Thanks for returning my call."

Devin beat him to the punch. "If you want to talk, I'll give you a few minutes. But I only want to talk to you alone."

The request seemed a little odd. But Tory was willing to accommodate it. "Okay. When can we meet?"

"This morning if you have the time."

"That would be fine. Where?"

"If you're in the Water Hole area you can come to my apartment."

"How about at ten?"

"Let me give you my address."

◆ ◆ ◆

A sign by the elevator door in the lobby stated, "Out of Order." To which someone added in bold handwriting: "Again??" So he had to walk up the four stories of stairs, which left him slightly winded.

He headed down the hallway and turned the corner, arriving at his destination. He rung the door bell. Moments later, the bearded elder opened the door. The look on his face was pleasant but not smiling.

"I'm assuming you're Detective Givens."

"Yes, sir. I can show you my badge."

"That's not necessary. Come in."

There was a quick left turn and then a right into what was intended to be the apartment's living room. But it had been converted into a wood sculpture studio featuring flawless pieces of West African art. There were carvings of people and animals. Sacred masks. Short stools with engravings. Wood panels of various portrayals. In a corner, an assortment of tools lay upon a thick cloth. Against one of the walls there was a love seat covered with an African print.

Devin motioned his arm for Tory to sit on the love seat. "Can I offer you a cup of tea?"

"No, thank you."

"Well, I'm making a cup for myself. I'll be right back." Devin exited.

Tory settled upon his seat. He scanned various works throughout the room. Some completed. Others in various stages toward completion. He didn't know much about African art but the quality of the craftsmanship was exquisite. He wondered if Devin's work was showcased elsewhere, in art studios or museums across the country. Or even around the world. He had no idea Martin's uncle possessed such a talent. And for it to be hidden in an aged apartment building in the ghetto of Water Hole was mind-boggling to Tory.

Eventually his attention settled upon a piece that looked like a cross with a large disc upon it. On the bottom of the disc was a simple face, with patterned etchings extending above it to cover the rest of the disc. The horizontal crossings were short, taking on conical shapes that narrowed toward the ends. The length of the vertical round base was such that it could be handheld, as if in a ceremony of some type. Like a blessing ritual.

Devin returned with a steaming cup, noticing Tory's gaze. "You see something you like?"

"Just looking."

"It's not done yet," he said stirring his cup with a spoon. "It's a gift for Martin's girlfriend. *Asase Yaa*, the Ashanti goddess of fertility. Although she's already pregnant, it can keep her and the baby protected." He paused. "But it also takes on a different connotation in light of what happened. *Asase Yaa* is also the goddess who gathers our souls when we die. So they say."

The silence seemed as intentional as it was poignant.

"But you didn't come here for a mini-lesson on Ashanti deities. You came to discuss the murder of my nephew."

Tory felt slightly uneasy as Devin pulled up a hand carved stool and sat across from him. Devin made it no secret that he intended to dictate the tone of this meeting. And if Tory was lucky, he might get some of what he came in quest of.

"First, let me say, I wasn't planning on talking to the police about this. With all due respect, you're part of the gang that killed my nephew. So why would I discuss it with you? Especially since it's highly unlikely anybody will do any time for this. But you're married to Loretta, right?" Tory nodded affirmatively. "That's the only reason I returned your call. She's a remarkable sister and I trust she wouldn't marry someone completely oblivious to *our* plight." Tory knew what the emphasis on "our" meant.

"As you can see, my life is immersed in African culture. Literally reconnecting with the ways of our ancestors through the work of my hands. So I know the death of the body isn't final. That Martin's soul lives on. And we pray he is guided to reach the ancestral realm.

"But this doesn't negate the brutal injustice of how he was killed. From a place of dignity, I can't participate in a police investigation in any way. Especially with the video now going public, only confirming what we said all along. That Martin was doing nothing wrong when he was killed. That it was an unnecessary use of force. A viscous murder."

"What was his mental state in the days leading up to the shooting?"

Devin paused before replying. He was willing to answer the question but also wanted to maintain control of the conversation.

"Did you grow up in the 'hood, Detective Givens?"

"Yeah."

"So you may understand what I'm about to say. Martin was a sensitive soul in an environment that discourages sensitivity. Especially among men. We're supposed to be hard and tough. Able to bear whatever. But he wasn't built that way. This is at the root of all his struggles, from his prior drug abuse to his recent problems trying to find a job.

"He never felt it was okay to show his pain except to a few people. He either tried to cover it up or repress it, which only works for awhile before it starts to break a person. I told him constantly that it's okay to show your weakness, your vulnerability to others. Granted, in certain situations you have to be tough, but that wasn't his natural demeanor. I used to tease him, when things were good, that if he ever learned to cry in public his whole life would change drastically for the better. There was a kernel of truth in that which he heard but never really embraced.

"So when I see him standing in the video, close to the wall with his back to the cops, I see a sensitive soul on the verge of breaking. And trying to hide it from the world. I knew he was stressing out over not being able to find a job. Over becoming a father. Over knowing things had to change in his life but not seeing how that was going to happen. And I see a scared cop yelling at him. And so not understanding where my nephew is that he points a gun at him. As if he's a danger. You don't push a person on the verge of breaking to the edge of a cliff. But that's what that cop did. My nephew got killed for reacting to being pushed to the edge by a cop.

"If someone would have just taken a moment to talk *with* him, not *at* him, Martin would still be here. But that's not the job of the police. Their job is to enforce order. Not to care in any way about the people they patrol. Especially in the 'hood. It's an old paradigm. One whose origin lays in the days of the old South where slave patrols roamed the roads and backways for runaway and "disorderly" slaves. Or in the North where police departments were organized to oversee the poor workers, especially if they were engaged in labor strikes against the ruling class.

"A more friendly face may be put on it now, but police are not here to serve and protect our community. They never have. They're here to oversee it. And in their oversight, a sensitive person teetering on the edge of his own breaking point is an expendable threat that can be killed for not acting right."

It became clear to Tory that Devin would only use any questions asked to speak to his desired points. Yet Tory felt a certain sympathy for him. Who else in the police department would give him audience to vent his views? If history was an indicator, the department would never admit any wrong or apologize for the shooting. Even as evidence clearly showed an unarmed Martin being contained by three officers. Even if the city paid a legal settlement for Martin's wrongful death. At most, the department might publicly express regret the shooting occurred, say it was unfortunate, but without taking any responsibility for it. Maybe.

And was this not part of the problem? The refusal to admit wrong only exacerbated the decayed relations among Blacks and police. And fueled the frustrations Devin now wished to vent. Clearly, mistakes will be made in policing. Danger exists everywhere in this country, in the 'hood and elsewhere. At times, police and civilians will make bad, sometimes deadly, decisions regarding actual or perceived dangers.

Such is a collateral consequence of a society immersed in high rates of violence. Yet the fallout of bad decisions is only amplified when parties refuse to admit wrong. Often, in part, trying to protect themselves from unwanted consequences and liabilities.

But a lecture from Devin to Tory would go nowhere. He had no influence to affect changes in the police department or offer any amends to Martin's family. His role was limited to investigating the shooting and offering recommendations based on his findings. Recommendations that could easily be ignored. Besides, the past day's fatigue and forthcoming chaos of the present day left Tory in no mood to bear a lecture that would amount to nothing substantial.

"Well, Mr. Scott, what you shared with me has been helpful."

Devin gave a scowl that Tory was ending the conversation. But he wouldn't resist its conclusion. He had gotten some of what he wanted off his chest. It also became clear to him that Tory wouldn't become an ally of his position.

Devin stood to escort Tory to the door. Tory stood to follow. The measured steps of departure felt awkward and heavy. But there was probably no way to have a pleasant exit within the circumstances.

"Thank you for your time," Tory said, extending his hand.

"Be well, Mr. Givens," Devin replied keeping his hands withheld.

It quickly became clear that Devin would not shake Tory's hand. So he retracted his hand and exited into the hallway.

❖ ❖ ❖

CHAPTER SEVEN:
Questions

H e went home to take a much needed nap. The fatigue had reached the point where not even coffee was helping to sustain his mental functioning. It didn't take long after laying his head upon his pillow before he was unconscious. Dead asleep. When his alarm awoke him hours later he felt physically refreshed but still mentally burdened.

He put on one of his "court" suits: slightly more formal than the casual suits he wore on normal days. He sat in silence as he ate a full meal, knowing the coming hours might be extremely stressful as well as unpredictable. He maintained silence as he drove through the city streets. Taking solace in having a temporary escape from the constant pulls of this case which had become his past two days. Just two days. It felt like so much more time had expired since being summoned to that alley on Spencer Avenue.

It was not lost on him that he was driving to the Prosecutor's Office to sit in on the interrogations of the four officers involved. The prosecutors moved with an accelerated speed in this case, organizing the interrogations only a day after taking over the investigation. In past cases, it was not uncommon for the prosecutor's interrogations to come a few days later, sometimes weeks later. But the pressure of a controversial national case seemed to be increasing the pace of the city's legal machinations.

Just outside the building was a life-sized sculpture of Lady Justice. The grey stone molded as an European woman wearing a long dress with the classic symbols. In her left hand was a set of scales, suggesting the law would fairly measure the strengths of all sides in each case. Her eyes were covered by a blindfold, implying the law would not view persons through the usual partialities which color how favorably or unfavorably we perceive others. Thus, the poor or wealthy, the strong or weak, famous or unknown would be afforded the same impartiality equality demands. And in her right hand she grasped the handle of a long sword, its broad blade extending to the ground. A reminder of the law's pledge to be swift and decisive in power, as well as to enforce its promise of justice.

The placement of the old statue on the walkway leading to the main entrance of the building was intentional. A reminder of key virtues the legal system vowed to uphold. A reminder placed by someone in the past to speak to present and future passers-by. Yet how often did people walk by it without offering a glance? Pass by it without giving mind to the explicit symbolism it proclaimed? Tory was guilty of this. He had probably walked by this sculpture at least a hundred times in his years as a cop. Yet this was the first time he really paid heed to its unspoken message.

After going through security, he was directed to an office where his picture was taken to place on a temporary photo identification. He wore the guest badge on his suit jacket as he moved through the halls. The building seemed filled with an unstated excitement and anticipation. A security checkpoint was set up at the entrance of the hallway leading to the interrogation room. Two additional officers stood guard outside the room itself. He showed his badge to the attending officers, his name checked against a list on a clipboard. He was then allowed into the guarded room.

A large table was the centerpiece of the room, surrounded by chairs and room for people to gather privately away from the table. Upon the table were two recording microphones, one for each of the adversarial sides of the table. The prosecutors were already set up on their side. Upon entering, Tory saw an older man berating two younger assistants. A woman, sitting beside the man, noticed Tory's entrance.

"Is this what I asked for!" The man wouldn't relent to the look of shame upon the younger faces. "I want the full report, not the summary. And I need it like ten minutes ago!"

One of the assistants immediately rushed out of the room. The woman nudged the man to alert him to their awaiting guest. He first glanced at, then turned to address the newcomer. "Are you Detective Givens?"

"Yes."

"Have a seat over here." He then directed the other assistant, "Go get a coffee or tea for the detective."

The assistant looked at Tory as if asking what he preferred. "A coffee with milk will be fine." The assistant quickly exited.

"Make yourself comfortable. I just want to finish arranging this."

As the man resumed organizing papers in a folder, the woman extended her hand to greet Tory. "I'm Doris White." Her pleasant smile and frizzy hair offered a sense of life to the otherwise sterile room.

Tory responded, "Detective Tory Givens."

"Yeah, she's my assisting counsel," the man said perusing the papers. Having completed his task, he turned to Tory and extended his hand. "I'm Lucas Garfield, lead prosecutor on this case." He leaned back and then smirked to say, "You boys down at the precinct sure handed us a doozy with this one."

There was an invitation to relax within his cynical sarcasm. The chubby, balding man had no qualms about this space being his terrain. His demeanor flaunted it. But don't let the thick glasses and puffy mustache fool you. He was a calculated legal assassin behind the flash of sneering arrogance.

"But let's be blunt, off the record," Lucas continued, "cause I'm not one to play around with shenanigans. Is this involuntary manslaughter or not?"

Tory was slightly taken aback by the question. "That's not for me to say but I question if the shooting is justifiable."

Lucas wasn't interested in playing politics. He wanted a definitive answer to his inquiry. "If it's not justifiable, is it a crime?"

Tory paused. He was open to giving an honest answer yet hesitated since nothing is truly "off the record." Within these circles, words stated in private had ways of reaching the ears of those not present. He decided to give a hint of his opinion within guarded remarks.

"The officers had Martin Little contained. I question if deadly force was necessary."

Having given Tory two chances to state his opinion, Lucas decided to move on. "He's going to come in, coached by his lawyer, saying it was," he said referring to Easthill. "That despite what the video and other evidence may show in retrospect, in the moment the incident occurred he had reason to believe Martin was a threat. Without concrete evidence to argue otherwise, unless he incriminates himself we don't have much of a case. Especially since, with that wonderful blue wall of silence, all the other officers are going to be mums.

"Now I can build a strong enough case to get him indicted. But I wouldn't want to waste my time trying it in court cause he's going to get off. And I'm a straight shooter. I'm going to tell it to you plain without all the sticky and smelly political vaseline."

"I appreciate that," Tory chimed in.

"With that said, I'm gonna grill him hard. You kill an unarmed civilian I get the right to try to make you shit your pants. Especially since he just cost the city millions of dollars with the forthcoming wrongful death civil suit. But I'm also realistic. Right now I don't have a solid case in criminal court. So if there's something you need from me for the Internal Affairs aspect of it, let me know and I'll try to get it for you."

"I just want to know why he thought deadly force was necessary when none of the other officers had their guns drawn and one officer had a taser in hand?"

Lucas looked at Doris and said, "Write that down for me." He then addressed Tory again. "Anything else?"

"That's the main thing."

"Well, if anything else comes to mind during the interrogation, slip a note to Doris and she'll feed it to me. But once we start, I'll be the only one to address them."

◆ ◆ ◆

When it was announced that Officer Easthill and his lawyer had arrived, the tension in the room immediately spiked. Lucas went off to use the bathroom before the questioning began. Doris checked messages on her cell phone. The two assistants talked quietly to each other as they sat ready to serve any request. But Tory didn't want any distractions. He wanted to eye Easthill as he entered the room, to see what his body language might convey.

Lucas was back in his seat by the time Easthill made his way down the hallway. He talked to himself under his breath, as he examined the stapled pages that contained his long list of questions. A deep silence seemed to permeate the entire building as an officer opened the door of the interrogation room. Easthill entered following his lawyer. His gaze was stern, his body reserved and slightly stiff.

Lucas motioned for them to sit on their side of the table. The lawyer, Adam Dunlop, took a moment to retrieve some documents and a pad from his briefcase. He then whispered some words in Easthill's ear before signaling that his client was ready to begin.

The interrogation began with an introduction explaining how the questioning would proceed. Lucas then set to gathering preliminary information, having Easthill state his name, rank, how long he had been on the force, etc. The tone of interrogation questioning is not as dramatic as often portrayed in films and television. It composes of simple and direct questions that seek to tediously reconstruct the concerned event piece by piece.

The mood was cold and formal. There wasn't even an attempt to present a pleasant facade upon the hostile atmosphere. The intensity quickly began to rise as the questions moved through Easthill receiving the initial radio call and proceeding to Spencer Avenue.

"So after arriving on the scene, what did you see?"

"I saw Mr. Little pacing back and forth by the entrance of the alley."

"Was he carrying anything?"

"A manila envelope," responded Easthill.

As Lucas continued, Tory made a note on his phone to check if such an envelope was collected as part of the crime scene evidence.

"Did you exit the car?"

"Yes."

"Were you on the passenger side?"

"Yes."

"Was that the side closest to the sidewalk?"

"Yes."

The coaching Easthill received from his lawyer was evident in the series of calm, unemotional, brief responses that only addressed what was queried.

"Was there anything between you and Mr. Little?"

"No."

"Did you consider him a threat at that moment?"

Easthill, unsure about answering the question, looked at his lawyer. Adam nodded that he should respond. "No, I did not."

"How did Mr. Little appear to you?"

"Something didn't seem quite right with him."

"In what way?"

"His mental disposition."

"And so then what happened?"

"I attempted to talk to Mr. Little. But he ignored me. He just walked back and forth by the alley."

"When you say "ignored," can you be more specific?"

"He did not respond to any of my words."

"Then what happened?"

"He took a few steps into the alley and started screaming. He also crumpled up the manila envelope and threw it on the floor."

"What was he screaming?"

"Just sounds. Like sounds of rage."

"Then what happened?"

"That's when I started to fear for my safety."

Lucas rolled his eyes and asked, "Why?" His body language shifted as if he knew a scripted reply was coming.

"It's a high-crime neighborhood. And by him not responding to me in any way I was concerned we might need to detain him."

"Him being Martin Little?"

"Yes."

"Then what happened?"

"My partner, Officer Peters, called for back-up."

"What did you do while Officer Peters did that?"

"I kept my eyes on Mr. Little."

"So after Officer Peters called for back-up, what happened?"

"We contained the area."

"Can you be more specific?"

"What do you mean?"

"Who was standing where?"

Easthill looked at his lawyer again, who nodded that he should answer the question. "I was standing on the sidewalk by the alley, close to the liquor store side. Officer Peters was standing on the other side of the parked police car, closer to the bus stop. He had to tell some people to cross the street..." Easthill stopped, realizing he was offering additional, unnecessary information.

"What did Officer Peters say to the people?"

Another glance to his lawyer, who nodded that the question was safe. "He had to tell people, civilians seeking to walk by the alley, to cross the street to get to the other side of the alley."

"At that time, did you withdraw a weapon of any kind?"

"I had my hand on my gun."

"And where was the gun?"

"Still in my holster."

"How about Officer Peters, did he withdraw a weapon of any kind?"

"I, I don't recall."

"Did you say anything to Mr. Little at that time?"

"I told him if he didn't calm down and talk to me, I would have to arrest him."

"Did you state any charges?"

"No."

"Then what were you going to arrest him for?"

Easthill gave a quick, deep exhalation. The tension in the room was very, very high. "Disorderly conduct and public intoxication," he stated.

"Why?" Lucas' follow-up question was quick, as if pouncing on the last of Easthill's words. Lucas felt Easthill was becoming uncomfortable and didn't want to cede the momentum.

"The loud outbursts were disorderly and his non-responsive, erratic behavior gave me reason to suspect he was high on some drug."

"Do you have training in recognizing the signs of intoxication of various drugs?"

Easthill seemed flustered. "I don't understand the question."

Lucas was in full bulldog mode now and would not relent. "You said you suspected Mr. Little was high. I'm trying to understand what informed that. If you've been trained to make such determinations or if you're just making decisions off the cuff?"

"Objection!" retorted Adam.

"Question withdrawn. I'll just check his personnel file."

Tory nodded to himself. He sensed the intent of this series of questions was to unnerve Easthill, to nudge his discomfort a little more to see if it led to a slip-up. After pausing for a moment, Lucas returned to his list.

"So how long was it before the responding unit arrived?"

"About two minutes."

"Do you remember who the responding officers were?"

"Officers Joe Stevenson and Silvia McDonald."

"How long have you know them?"

"I've only had passing interactions with them while on duty."

"So they arrive. What happened next?"

"They parked behind our car."

"And then what happened?"

"I don't remember all the details because I was keeping my eye on Mr. Little. Officer Peters is the one who interacted with them. But I remember that eventually Officer Stevenson was by his car, by the bus stop side, with a taser in hand. And Officer McDonald went to back up, I mean move back the crowd of people who were forming by the bus stop."

"And where did Officer Peters end up?"

"He was standing between the two police cars to help contain the area."

"So Officer McDonald was not by the alley. Is that correct?"

"She was by the bus stop."

"And she's the only officer who was wearing a body camera?"

"I believe so."

"Do you recall if there was a reason why she was the one sent away from the alley?"

Easthill looked at his lawyer again, who nodded for him to answer the question. "I don't know why she was sent away."

"Was it because she was wearing a body camera?"

"My client already answered the question," Adam interceded.

"He did. I just wanted to make sure he didn't want to add anything more. Question withdrawn." Lucas took a moment to stare at Easthill before continuing. "So yourself, Officer Peters, and Officer Stevenson have Mr. Little contained in the alley. Is that correct?"

Easthill nodded.

"You have to give a vocal response for the record."

"I'm sorry. Yes."

"And Officer McDonald is over by the bus stop?"

"Yes."

"What happened next?"

"Seeing the other officers in place, I ordered Mr. Little to stop pacing and put his hands up or we were going to arrest him."

"Where were you when you said this?"

"Just inside the alley, about ten feet away."

"Ten feet away from Mr. Little?"

"Yes."

"What happened next?"

"He stopped by the corner of the office building, facing the wall."

"Where were his hands?"

"Down around his waist."

"So what happened next?"

"Since he was not responding to my police commands, I became concerned and pulled out my gun."

"What did you do with your gun?"

"I aimed it at Mr. Little."

"Did he still have his back to you?"

"Yes."

"Did anyone else pull out any weapons at that moment?"

"I believe Officer Stevenson may have had his taser out, but I can't say for sure."

"How about Officer Peters? Did he have any weapons out at that moment?"

"I don't know. Honestly."

"What happened next?"

"I ordered again more forcefully for Mr. Little to raise his hands and turn around slowly."

"When you say "forcefully," what do you mean?"

"I used a louder and more stronger tone of voice."

"Then what happened?"

"For a moment there was no response. Then all of the sudden, he lunged forward, yelling. I couldn't tell if he had a weapon or something, so I immediately fired two shots. I have to say I was never so scared in my life. The look on his face was pure evil."

Tory cringed hearing the words. The seemingly intentional portrayal of Martin as "pure evil" was utterly disturbing to him. And so fabricated, in Tory's eyes.

"Did any of the other officers use any weapons at that time?"

"I don't recall."

Lucas paused to see if Easthill would offer more. But no, he remained firmly within the guidance of his lawyer's coaching.

"Why did you think a gun was necessary while another officer thought a non-lethal taser was sufficient?"

Adam intervened, "My client is not here to speculate about the decisions of other officers."

"I'll rephrase the question." Lucas then looked Easthill squarely in the eye and asked, "Why did you think deadly force was necessary to arrest someone for disorderly conduct and public intoxication?"

Tory appreciated the question. But he also sensed Easthill had a coached reply for it. And then it came.

"Water Hole is a high crime neighborhood with a lot of gun violence and other types of violence. He was verbally non-responsive and did not obey my reasonable police commands. So when he suddenly turned and lunged at me, I had no choice but to protect my life and the lives of my fellow officers."

◆ ◆ ◆

The questioning continued, reconstructing what followed after the shooting. Easthill basically sat in his patrol car as the other officers called an ambulance and transitioned the alley into a crime scene. His supervisor arrived, he gave a brief oral report. He was then ordered to return to the precinct and write up the police report he submitted. After that, he was released for the day.

When Lucas was done, Easthill and his lawyer quickly exited the room. They didn't even say goodbye. Lucas, Doris, and Tory debriefed for a couple of minutes. The prosecutors agreed that, as expected, Easthill didn't offer anything that would incriminate himself. That the prospects for a criminal conviction remained weak.

Then it was on to the other officers with their accompanying lawyers. Officer Peters was already waiting in another room to be questioned. The interrogations of Officer Stevenson and then Officer McDonald followed.

None of the officers provided anything that would strengthen a potential criminal case. Which wasn't surprising. Although they didn't pull the trigger, pursuit of criminal charges might expose them to unwanted scrutiny. Probably not criminal sanctions but perhaps internal department discipline or a diminished reputation. Or perhaps a mark on their records that might hinder future promotion and other career moves by being associated with a negative controversy. It was in all their best interests for this investigation to quickly pass without a finding of any wrong; for its clouds to blow away like a storm of days past forgotten in light of the present weather.

When asked, Officer Peters stated that he thought Martin might be intoxicated. The responding officers declined to answer any questions regarding that matter. They asserted they were there to back up the primary unit in whatever determinations and course of actions were already decided.

Officer Stevenson admitted that he ordered Officer McDonald to tend to the small but growing crowd by the bus stop. Since he was trained in using the taser, and she wasn't, it made sense for her to handle the crowd as the other officers dealt with Martin.

Lucas asked Officer McDonald if the reason she was sent to the crowd was because she was wearing a body camera. Her lawyer objected, refusing to have her answer the question: declaring he wouldn't allow his client to be put in the situation of speculating about others' motivations. Yet it wasn't lost on Tory that she, the Black female officer wearing the body camera, was sent away as three White male officers surrounded the distraught Black male in the alley.

The officers' descriptions of the moment of the shooting also stayed safely away from any criminal incrimination. Officer Peters said he saw Martin lunge at Easthill, immediately followed by gunshots. He said he ducked when he heard the shots, claiming that the "pop-pop" sound echoing through the alley made him unsure at first where the bullets were coming from. This inferred the "danger" of the situation. That they were working in an environment where gunshots could be fired without warning or cause, indiscriminately, from unseen perpetrators. He only realized after ducking for safety that the source of the shots lay with his fellow officer who stood holding the extended gun toward the fallen body.

Officer Stevenson said he shot his taser when Martin lunged toward Easthill. He then reactively ducked to the ground upon hearing the gunshots. He wasn't sure if Martin was hit by the taser and didn't become aware Martin had been shot until he stood. Tory noted in his mind that all the officers in the alley used the same *lunge* word to describe Martin's action as he turned from the wall.

Officer McDonald said she didn't see the shooting or what immediately precipitated it since she was dealing with the civilians gathered by the bus stop. By the time she turned after hearing the gunshots, Martin was already on the ground, unconscious.

After Officer McDonald departed with her lawyer, there was an emptiness in the room. Everyone present was fatigued. The weight of probing four accounts of the shooting was exhaustive. And the officers' collective guardedness was obvious. Lucas and Doris agreed to meet in the morning to discuss next steps. They promised to give Tory a call to update him of their decision. They then invited him to join them for dinner but he had to decline. Gulley ordered him to report to Spencer Avenue as soon as the interrogations were done. A major protest was planned despite the imposed curfew.

◆ ◆ ◆

Driving back to police headquarters, certain racial dynamics of the afternoon ran through his mind. Aside from the last session, when Officer McDonald was being questioned, Tory was the only Black person involved in proceedings inquiring why a White officer killed an unarmed Black man. And even his presence was only as a courtesy to the White police chief. He was there to observe, not participate. But the questioning prosecutors were White working for a White District Attorney. Even their two assistants were White. The officer who shot Martin was White. The two assisting officers were White. The police chief who assigned him to the case was White, working for a White mayor. Even his boss and his partnering detective on this case were White. White. White. White.

All the major players in this case aside from the dead, unarmed Black man were White. And his corpse couldn't speak for himself. In theory, the District Attorney's Office was there to represent his interests within its larger mission of representing the people of the city. But in practice, the prosecutors had their own agendas and perspectives which differed from his. Even the admission that there weren't strong grounds for a conviction, and that this was informing their approach, showed they weren't truly representing Martin's wishes. If he could speak from the grave, would he say it's okay to dismiss the plausibility of seriously pursuing criminal charges because the odds were unfavorable? Would his ghost proclaim contentment with Lucas trying to get Easthill to "shit his pants" instead of seeking a conviction? Would Martin deem a likely monetary settlement to his family from the city as sufficient justice? Would all this be acceptable in Martin's eyes?

Even the non-response of the prosecutors when Easthill described Martin as having a look of "pure evil" was telling. Would anyone representing Martin allow such a depiction to go unchallenged? Especially with what it inferred about him as a person and the larger social group he was part of. Yet

Lucas simply went on to the next question, allowing the statement to stand unchallenged.

The more these thoughts reverberated through Tory's mind, the more upset he became with the resignation to cede criminal charges. There seemed to be an ease of dismissing or minimizing the value of Black life among all the Whites involved, even if such devaluing wasn't maliciously intended. Tory felt that if most of the Blacks in the city were asked their opinion, they would overwhelmingly support pursuit of criminal charges even if the chances for success were limited. Were they not part of "the people" the District Attorney had the duty of representing? Especially since there seemed to be a vigor to prosecute Blacks for lesser crimes. In the 'hood, you could get indicted and convicted on *suspicion* of stealing a ham sandwich. But there seemed to be a different standard for pursuing charges with a White cop who unquestionably killed an unarmed Black man.

Even the fact that Officer McDonald was directed away from what was unfolding in the alley troubled Tory. Not to belittle the importance of crowd control in an escalating situation, but was it just coincidence that she, the only Black officer at the scene, was sent to deal with the less important factor while three White men tended to the more pressing situation? One so dire they were prepared to use a gun and a taser. Again, matters of life and death were being decided by Whites with the exclusion of Blacks. Even if such exclusion wasn't deliberately motivated.

And what was the point of the investigation, and the accompanying flurry of activity, if it was pretty much decided by the prosecutors that pursuit of criminal charges was not a worthwhile cause? Why even have interrogations when it was already known that the cops would be coached and not yield anything that might remotely incriminate any of them? And if the officers started to stumble amidst questioning, the lawyers sitting beside them would intervene to protect not only their client, but all the cops involved. What was really going on?

Was the chosen "blindness" to these factors the modern reason imposed on the blindfold covering Lady Justice's eyes? Were the scales fixed to appear equal although more favorable weight was placed on the side of the White officers? More weight given within a system of law enforcement and prosecution content to limit how it challenged them. And if this was the case, then surely the long sword would remain in a position of show, not unleashed in force against the officers.

Yet this same sword was not withheld from cutting fury when it came to investigating and prosecuting Blacks and other disadvantaged groups. Even with lesser crimes that didn't result in someone's death. Did not Martin feel the might of this sword when he was convicted on drug charges for essentially being an addict? And was this same sword present in the alley when the bullets pierced Martin's chest, rendering a guilty verdict upon the unproven suspicion of wrong-doing and danger? At most, he would have been arrested for "disorderly conduct" and "public intoxication" if he wasn't shot. And maybe "resisting arrest" if a struggle ensued. But instead the sword of justice delivered a more severe verdict through Easthill's hand. A life sentence of two shots fired commuted to death.

But time was short. And to keep pondering such questions would only make him angry. And he didn't want to be angry, not when he had to go police a protest that would likely possess enough anger. And justifiably so.

As he changed from his "court" suit into the riot gear uniform he was ordered to wear, he turned on the small television in his office. The local news cable station was in the midst of a report on the Martin Little shooting. The news reporter was also White.

"... sources state that all the officers involved were questioned by prosecutors today. While neither the District

Attorney's Office nor the officers' lawyers would comment on what transpired in the interrogations, Adam Dunlop, the lawyer for Officer Oliver Easthill, did take questions from the media. Here are excerpts from his comments."

The impromptu news conference happened a short distance from the main entrance to the Prosecutor's Office Building. Adam stood in the foreground. Easthill stood behind him holding hands with a White woman, perhaps his wife. Behind them a number of uniformed police officers stood in line. Attentive and in solidarity. All White. And all men except for two women officers. Tory had seen this media tactic before. The police union made it a priority to have other officers be visible in support of fellow officers immersed in public controversy, especially when media cameras were present.

Also in the background, the statue of Lady Justice stood. Quite noticeable to Tory's eyes within the residue of his preceding thoughts.

"My client has unwaveringly maintained his innocence from the beginning," Adam declared with a calm boldness. "We should not forget he was responding to a 9-1-1 call about a man acting weirdly in an alley. His behavior was so erratic it prompted a Black resident who lives in Water Hole to call the police to deal with this dangerous situation."

The news segment cut to another clip of Adam speaking.

"The video doesn't capture the entire encounter, particularly the numerous attempts by Officer Easthill to peacefully resolve the situation. And it borders on being extremely irresponsible for the media to continue showing the video without emphasizing this point every time. It gives the impression the incident began with Officer Easthill aiming his gun at Martin Little when clearly that was not the case."

The news segment cut to another clip of Adam speaking.

"He ignored clear, repeated reasonable police commands. He lunged at Officer Easthill forcing him to defend himself.

In retrospect, we now know he did not have a gun. But in the heat of the moment, within a dangerous situation, my client had to defend himself. I don't think any reasonable person would deem it wrong for an officer to protect himself in a life-threatening situation."

The news segment cut to yet another clip of Adam speaking. "There is no basis for any charges to be brought against Officer Easthill or any of the officers. In fact, and this is my personal opinion, we should be applauding their service, especially since they risk their lives everyday in a dangerous, high-crime neighborhood..."

The reporter reappeared on the screen to say, "That was Adam Dunlop, the lawyer representing Officer Oliver Easthill. Officer Easthill declined to give any...

Tory turned off the television, certain that the reporter would say Easthill gave no comment. He was already running late. So he grabbed his helmet from the desk, the completing piece to the combat gear he now wore. He was covered head to toe: from the steel-toed boots, to the protective armor covering his torso and limbs, to the leather black gloves upon his hands, and the riot helmet on his head. He felt more like a storm trooper than a cop. Like a soldier going to join a military operation rather than a member of a civilian police department entrusted to serve and protect the community.

CHAPTER EIGHT:
But on the third day he did not rise

The movement of the night quickly took on a pace of its own as Tory sped his way to Water Hole. The calm of little traffic precipitated the storm converging on Spencer Avenue. He was directed to a side street nearby that the police were using to park cars. A police captain then told him to hurry up and get on the "frontline." That was literally the word used. *Frontline.* As if he was being sent onto a battlefield. A theater of war.

Jogging toward Spencer Avenue, he could feel the weight of his riot gear. The feel of the padding and hard shell paneling taking on an additional heaviness that was more mental than physical. His anxiety increased. Something was brewing in the air. Or maybe it was already there and just now being realized. Exposed in a way that could not be ignored.

As he approached the corner that turned onto Spencer Avenue, he stopped at an equipment checkpoint. "You got a gas mask?"

"No."

The officer grabbed one from the back of the utility truck. "Here. Take it. Everyone has to have one." Holding up a transparent fiberglass shield, he offered "These are optional."

Tory shook his head to decline.

"Are you authorized to use a riot shotgun? It shoots non-lethal rubber bullets." Tory, puzzled, didn't reply. "Just take it if you want it. It's about to be get real crazy."

Tory declined again and put the gas mask around his neck. He then continued toward the corner.

The idea of non-lethal bullets seemed bizarre to him. Anything fired can kill. He even remembered responding to a police call once where a man was killed by a punch to the head. And he was apparently healthy, fit enough to give his killer a bulging bloody eye and busted jaw before receiving his death blow.

The thoughts were quickly diluted in the frenzy of noise that was becoming louder. "No justice, no peace! No justice, no peace!" A distinct refrain being intensely repeated over a din of vocalized discontent mixed into the rumble of idling vehicles and human activity.

He turned the corner to see a sight of bedlam barely being contained. He walked past the riot tank, its angled metal vibrating to the engine's idle roaring. The torso of a man wearing night vision goggles protruded through the turret's hatch. The word "POLICE" was boldly painted on the sides of the military-styled vehicle ready for action on civilian streets.

Other police vehicles formed a line with the tank. Ready for combat, only a few feet from the alley where Martin's body fell a couple of days ago. Passing the tank, Tory bumped into another captain. "Where you been?" barked the older man. "Get back in line! There in the middle!"

Tory was confused because this was his first time seeing the man tonight. But to avoid adding to the suffocating chaos, he joined the line of officers standing a few feet from the metal barricades. This was the point of demarcation between the opposing sides. The hard steel extending across the sidewalks and street, from the fenced off lot to the closed shop. Or perhaps one should say what remained of the looted shop behind the large sheets of wood covering the large windows destroyed last night.

Tory stood in the middle of the line, shoulder to shoulder with other officers dressed in full riot gear. They seemed cold and fierce behind the helmet visors that muted their distinct facial features to a veneer of a faceless armed force. Yet Tory was very cognizant of the fact that most of these faceless faces were White men ready to confront a throng of mostly Black faces unveiled.

Some officers stood with their arms folded across their chests. Some had their gloved hands on their batons. Others had their hands on their guns. Some held large shields donned across their forearms, a transparent protection against the opposing side. The local residents and citizens they were charged to "serve and protect" were now the enemy.

The protesters had their own frontline, their anger surging beyond the bodies packed behind the barricades. The refrain they chanted was accompanied by other words. Most unpleasant. Some cruel and insulting.

Tory glanced to the side to see a few news cameras and other spectators standing by the gas station. Although they were there to witness what was happening, everyone present was somehow active in this bizarre, volatile unfolding. No one could be mere observers in the midst of this delirious hysteria.

The outpouring intensity moved a man to boldly reach across the barricades. Two officers quickly stepped forward with billy clubs raised, commanding him to back up. Really threatening him. Other protesters pulled the man back as a bottle, hurled from a distance and unseen in the night air, crashed upon an officer's helmet. He fell with the descending shattered pieces of glass. Other officers ducked. He hurriedly returned to his feet with the assistance of other officers. Some protesters pointed and laughed at him as the majority continued to chant the fury of their discontent.

Moments later, the second captain emerged from behind the officers. He was emphatic as he walked before the line of cops, yelling his instructions. "We're clearing the street! Prepare to clear the street...!"

His voice was drowned out by the loudspeaker that blared loudly from behind in an ominous tone. "Attention citizens, a curfew has been imposed in this neighborhood. This is your last warning to clear the area or risk being arrested."

The response from the protesters was instantaneous and more unified. They all chanted louder and more defiantly. Another bottle descended from the night sky, this time landing before the line of police. Parts of the broken glass shattered upon the legs of the cops and the frontline protesters.

The captain rushed back across the line of officers, his face flushed red with anger as he yelled. "Put on your gas masks! Everyone, gas masks! Now!" He then yelled into his radio, "Get the gas ready! They're throwing bottles at my guys!"

As the captain continued on, more officers emerged from behind the line. They carried large bags of plastic handcuffs, handing bunches to the lined officers. As soon as Tory finished placing the gas mask over his mouth and nose, a handful of the plastic strip handcuffs was forced into his hand. He stuffed them into one of the pouch pockets of his pants.

He then looked up at the protesters. They were fully aware of the escalating preparations. Yet no one ran or turned to depart. None wavered in hesitation or fear. Instead their increased fervor seemed to welcome a clash with the well armed and armored paramilitary force on the verge of attack. A bravery in face of the fact that most of the protesters were unarmed, Tory assumed. Their only weapons being their voices, their bodies, and a willingness to stand strong together.

"If you do not leave now," the voice blared again from the loudspeaker, "you will be arrested. And we will use tear gas to clear the area."

Still, none of the frontline protesters flinched for fled. Another bottle descended from the night air, trailed by a few rocks which landed near or hit the police. The captain's voice barked with a clarity that seemed to penetrate all the other surrounding noise. "That's enough! Let's get 'em!"

The people's resistance had been tolerated long enough. They would now be met with the might of an army unleashed.

The police erupted upon the unmoving protesters. Literally charging over the metal barricades, some of them crashing to the ground where the protesters could get out of the way. And where they couldn't, the surge of the police pushed the hard metal frames upon the bodies that could not evade them.

Most of the chants and calls of courage instantly became reactionary screams mixed with anxiety and fear. The potentiality of attack doesn't resonate with the same ferocity as that attack coming upon you. And the initial rush of officers was viscous: with clutching hands, swinging batons, and pepper spray flying through the air. Most of the protesters backed up into the crowd that staggered into a slow, crushing retreat. But some refused to run. Some even fought back, to be bombarded by an indiscriminate wave of coercive violence. Having declined the opportunity to avoid the coming fight, they would be beaten into submission as determined by whatever means the officers they encountered chose to use.

Tory wasn't among the first who charged. But when he felt the push from behind, he had to go forward. He decided in his own mind that he would not use force preemptively. If the point was to clear the area, he would let the protesters run if they fled. And if they chose to stand their ground and be arrested, he would use the minimum amount of force needed to handcuff them and lead them to the holding area. But if they resisted with force, he would not hesitate to use all his power to yield them into submission.

Yet he couldn't help but notice that most of the officers blitzed ahead with a callous, adrenaline-filled zeal. They were intent to run down and capture the enemy. And make them pay. In the officers' eyes, the protesters' defiance of the warnings to leave and their willingness to stand among those who were attacking the police -- throwing bottles and rocks -- warranted them being exposed to the full range of force reserved for threatening criminals.

It was intoxicating and terrifying in the same breath. And the breaths kept coming in relentless rapid succession. Steps forward as gas-emitting grenades skipped forward along the pavement. Cries, coughs, and more screams filled the pandemonium as the growing fog spread.

The rule of brutal authority was choking the life out of the mounting crisis. Despair and agony became the unseen flags waved in defeat as the protesters quickly realized this battle was lost. As a mass, they had not the weapons to sustain a defense. And the individual shows of courage would not change the overall outcome to secure a victory tonight. But now even escape proved to be a challenge as those fleeing had to struggle through the confusion of a scene congested with no clear sense of direction. And the cops kept coming. Unrelenting without mercy. Intent on capture and inflicting suffering. Maybe even brutality. The descent into chaos eradicated all rules. Only willing martyrs welcomed the sacrifice of the coming pain.

The police reclaimed most of the occupied territory in a matter of protracted seconds that took on the feel of lingering minutes. The battle was being won through an imposing assault playing out through a series of simultaneous encounters. Two cops tackling a man. Another cop knocking a middle aged woman to the ground, unconscious, with a baton. Four cops shooting pepper spray indiscriminately at three youth who were yelling and swinging their arms wildly as an officer behind them pulled out his gun, ready to shoot. Another cop kicking a fleeing man to the ground from behind, his palms and forearms scarred bloody upon the coarse asphalt to protect his falling face from impact.

Although unwilling, Tory had to participate in this ruthless conquest. His return without a capture would have surely been noticed. By grace, he noticed a man standing in a gap within the fog. He was already holding his hands in the air as his voice bellowed, "I ain't running from you fucken cops! I ain't running from shit!"

Tory approached the middle-aged man who did not resist. He almost seemed out of place with his colorful cowboy hat and sunglasses. He complied as Tory grabbed one of his arms to cuff it. The point of his refusal to flee was to maintain his courage, not to fight the police.

As Tory grabbed the man's other arm, he heard a loud yet familiar scream nearby. He turned to see Loretta backing up and yelling at an officer, pushing his hands away as she continued to scream non-verbal sounds. She appeared more panicked than threatening, but that didn't stop the officer from pulling out his pepper spray. She retreated to the ground in complete fright, terrified of the coming spray that would steal what was left of the breath being yelled from her body.

"Put your hands up now! Or you're getting sprayed!"

Her screams evolved into uncontrollable cries as he grabbed her shaking, raised arms. As the officer cuffed her, Tory rushed to intercede. The middle-aged man was no longer important. The duty of his badge superseded by the sight of his wife in need.

"I know her, I got her," Tory said to the officer who had his wife bound.

A look of confusion. It was taboo for an officer to interfere with another officer's arrest. Especially on the battlefield of an uprising being quelled. But why be bothered, there were other loose enemies to fight and capture.

The faceless officer left the crying woman to the stranger officer and then disappeared into the fog that was now upon them. As Tory bent to comfort her, the gas took hold. "Loretta, Loretta..."

She wanted to reply but couldn't, the gas now enveloping her face. Her ability to communicate was reduced to uncontrollable coughs and gasps and cries. So he picked her up to carry her to safety, her body starting to go limp within his arms. Along the way, he passed the middle-aged man with the colorful cowboy hat and sunglasses. Still free with the plastic handcuff upon one of his wrists, the fog descending upon the space where he stood. His nonviolent resistance continuing between the coughs that now started to steal his words.

"I ain't..." A cough. "...fucken running..." More coughs. More gasping breaths which melted into the frenzy of a surrounding cacophony as Tory carried his crying wife away.

◆ ◆ ◆

The street now echoed silence. Its emptiness marred by marks of the battle expired. The mental aftershocks left him in a state beyond words. An indescribable yearning of mixed emotions seeking answers beyond the obvious yet ignored solutions within reach.

The night replayed through his mind as he approached a shiny object on the ground. Taking the gas mask but refusing the riot shotgun. Non-lethal bullets in a situation turned deadly. "POLICE" painted boldly on a tank built for military combat. Glass bottles descending from above to break. Stormtroopers surging forth. Metal barricades crashing to the ground. Screams, cries, bodies moving in a convoluted mass. A cowboy hat and sunglasses. A cop attacking my wife. My wife...

He couldn't even speak to her as he carried her from Spencer Avenue. Her body wringing in his arms from uncontrollable and violent coughs. A bottle of water handed to him, he poured little sips into her mouth and on her eyes. Irritated eyes that would not cease emitting streams of tears with the descending trails of water.

He felt odd tending to one of the "enemies" in the midst of other officers. He could feel the questioning looks, the doubts of his loyalty. She was extremely uncomfortable too, being surrounded by cops in riot gear. So he led her to his car to be away from the whole scene. And to remove the plastic handcuffs. It would have been too awkward to remove them around the other officers. But that meant he had to walk her through the streets still handcuffed, like a prisoner.

After cutting the plastic strips, he mumbled words barely decipherable, "Where did you park?"

She didn't even reply with words, just started to lead the way. He walked beside her until they reached her car. She looked at him, the awkwardness obvious. She wasn't going to embrace him in his riot gear. He resembled too much the faceless officer who ran her down to the ground and cuffed her.

Besides, what could he say to alleviate the lingering discomfort? Especially since he felt partly responsible: he was part of the officers who charged the protesters. So he just reached to open the car door. It was locked. She unlocked it by pressing the button on her keys. He opened the door. She sat inside. He closed the door and walked away. Wiping away a tear underneath the helmet's visor as he heard her drive away.

He was then ordered to question a few arrestees. Including a man who had a large bandage taped on his forearm. He was among the dozens of civilians injured. Fortunately none were life-threatening. Earlier, word had spread among the cops that one woman had a heart attack. It actually turned out to only be an anxiety attack. Only. And she was still arrested. Taken away in an ambulance in handcuffs.

Although no one was saying it, Tory noted that no injuries were reported until after the police charged the protesters. Was there another way to deal with the unruly few, those transgressing the bounds of legal protest, without attacking the others? Who knows. And who among the police would ask that question since order was now restored without any causalities, major injuries, or significant property damage.

But he had to follow orders, so he questioned nine of the people arrested. All had been charged with "disorderly conduct" or "refusal to obey police commands." Those charged with more serious offenses like "resisting arrest" or "assaulting an officer" were immediately shipped off to jail in metal handcuffs.

The topics Tory was told to inquire about seemed pointless. And it didn't help that the people were still bound by the white plastic cuffs. No one could or was willing to identify who threw the bottles at the cops. Neither did anyone admit or know of a deliberate plan to attack police or property. Then after asking questions Tory already knew would yield no useful information, he led them to a nearby paddy wagon to be transported to jail. Likely to spend the night there being processed into the system before being given a citation to pay a fine or appear in court at a later date.

After completing that pointless task, he walked back to the former frontline. He needed to regain a sense of something. What? He didn't know. But he knew something was lacking and felt the need to search for it somehow on that now desolate asphalt.

He caught whiffs of how the media was reporting what transpired: "More Riots in Water Hole." "Protests Erupt into Violence." "Protesters Attack the Police." These headlines seemed absurd to him. Yes, the people were protesting vigorously. And were perhaps intimidating in the eyes of some. But aside from the unidentified persons throwing bottles and rocks from the distance, the majority of people were within reasonable bounds. Upset but restrained. What turned an intense situation into a "riot" was the police rushing the people with indiscriminate force. Even arresting people who clearly weren't throwing things. Who decided to stand defiantly in disapproval of something they considered a grievous injustice. Yes, one can say they disobeyed the police order to disperse; but if they weren't given an outlet to express their dismay, what other options were the people supposed to take?

A quote from John F. Kennedy came to mind, one Martin Luther King, Jr. quoted in one of his speeches: "Those who make peaceful revolution impossible will make violent revolution inevitable." Perhaps "revolution" was too strong a word for what was unfolding in Water Hole, but the sentiment of the assassinated president's words registered deeply with Tory in that moment.

A sudden gasp bowed his head to the ground. His knee bent to the asphalt toward what caught his eye. He took hold of the shiny object. A slim silver chain with a silver cross, the left side of the horizontal bar bent. The connecting clasp was broken. He imagined the cross hanging around the neck of a protester and somehow being torn away within the throng of those fleeing danger. Or perhaps it was forcefully ripped from the owner's body in the midst of struggling with a cop. Or maybe dislodged in the passion of chanting dissent over Martin's death.

He put the damaged cross back on the ground to rejoin the protest's refuse. Damaged signs, scattered leaflets, and other trash. An empty tear gas grenade nearby. A few loose papers blowing in the night wind.

He stood again and looked around. The street felt haunted, but not by human spirits. Some imperceptible energy mass was weighing upon the air and only made him feel more confused. More unsettled. He almost hoped a ghost would come instead. Even if it couldn't speak. Maybe its presence could grant his mind a focus. Or strike a fear within to penetrate the vague web of eeriness.

But instead he stirred, realizing his eyes staring at the dark alley. In the dimness, he could see the memorial that was set up for Martin had been trampled and scattered about. Then the lines spoke forth:

But on the third day he did not rise.
Maybe because his name wasn't Jesus,
Or because he had not yet reached
The mystical age of 33.

Words from a poem Jelani once wrote about police brutality. I need to write to Jelani.

Jelani's words had a way of resurrecting their remembrance spontaneously. Another late night conversation on a street much like the one Tory was standing on. All the other guys had already peeled off into the night. Only he and Jelani remained. Each drinking from bottles to take in the moment of silence they found themselves within. But Jelani had that piercing look. The one he would get when he really wanted to get to the heart of a matter.

"So you're serious about doing this cop thing?"

"I passed the test."

"That's not what I asked."

Tory shrugged his shoulders to say, "Yeah, I want to be a cop."

"So how about this as a hypothetical? Rodney King, 1991. You're called to a scene where a bunch of White cops got a Black man on the ground. And they're just beating the shit out of him with billy clubs. What do you do?"

The question was daunting. The naivete of Tory's ambitions never pondered him being face to face with police brutality as a cop. It seriously wasn't something he had considered. And not something he really wanted to although he couldn't deny the possibility of such occurring. So he tried to sidestep the question.

"That's like a historical... I mean, an event. That type of thing that doesn't happen regularly. Like an extreme case."

"How do you know? How do you know that wasn't just one of the rare ones that got videotaped." These were in the days before the prevalence of cell phone cameras. "But fuck it, even if it is a rare occurrence," Jelani conceded, "you're there. What do you do?"

A moment to reflect with a mind slightly impaired by beer. "I tell them to stop."

"I say you don't even do that, although that's weak. I mean, someone's on the ground, getting hammered by billy clubs, his face literally exploding onto the asphalt. And you, as an officer of the law, with a badge and a gun, respond by saying," his voice taking on a characterized inflection, ""Please guys, don't beat that Negro on the ground." That's upholding the law?"

Although the question was serious, the unexpected change in voice made Tory smirk. "But why you gotta make my voice like that?"

They both laughed. A moment of true joy shared. But the one friend wouldn't let the other friend off the hook so easily.

"But all jokes aside, I say you don't even do that. I say you end up doing what the other cops did: being a spectator to police brutality."

"Why?" asked Tory with a touch of sarcasm. "Cause I'm just one of those "types" of cops?"

"No. Because of the reality of mental conditioning. And your need to survive on the streets. You don't have a martyr spirit, someone who's willing to die for what is right."

The words hurt but Tory knew they were right. He was looking at being a cop as a profession -- a job. Not something to die or endure great suffering for in quest of upholding justice.

"The cops are a gang," continued Jelani. "And if you want your fellow members to have your back on the streets -- no questions asked -- when they do dirt, you turn the other way. And you'll turn."

The silence gave Tory more time to reflect. He wanted to mount some type of defense but in his heart of hearts he knew Jelani's assessment was correct. Even on the streets, he kind of just went along with the flow. Preferring to not make waves even when the fellas did things he didn't agree with. If his disagreement was strong enough, he would just depart instead of engage a conflict. But never take a stand unless it was absolutely necessary and unavoidable. Fortunately, he was never really placed in such a situation. And when he was, usually Jelani or someone else spoke up on his behalf.

Even the older Tory, remembering this conversation, had to acknowledge that Jelani's words had proven true. As an officer and detective, he looked "the other way" from numerous improper acts committed by fellow cops. These occurred regularly enough that he conceded tolerating them was just part of the job. It wasn't necessarily because cops were nefarious, although some were. And most improprieties weren't as big as an unarmed person getting shot. Yet in the midst of surviving on the streets or wishing to get things done, officers sometimes chose to cross "that line." A line sometimes vaguely defined or inconsistently enforced.

He took solace in the fact that he very rarely crossed "that line." And sometimes the other party deserved it, got what was coming to them, if you understood how "justice" played out on the streets. But such acts were part of the everyday terrain of policing. Choices made by grown men and women, often by their own initiative, to abuse or over-exert the police powers entrusted to them. And if circumstances played out certain ways, they would have to pay the consequences for their actions. Besides, Tory reasoned then, he was just an officer and then a regular detective. He wasn't a supervisor charged with oversight of other officers. Neither was it his job to investigate other cops: that's what Internal Affairs was for.

Yet this attitude continued even when he joined Internal Affairs. He usually leaned toward giving officers the benefit of the doubt. As long as they didn't cross certain blatant lines, he could frame evidence and situations in ways inclined toward innocence or inconclusive findings, avoiding a determination of guilt. There was an unspoken understanding within the ranks that certain things if done and caught would not escape penalty. But other things could find their way under the rug as long as you didn't get caught too often, establishing a pattern that couldn't be reasonably ignored. And, of course, it didn't hurt if you avoided burning certain bridges, especially with high ranking officers in the department.

"I don't know if you heard," Jelani said, breaking the silence of the memory, "last week this kid my cousin knew got smoked down by a cop. Just cold blooded murder. The kid was selling rocks and had a gun on him but he didn't make a move for it when the DTs rolled up." Tory knew DTs meant detectives. "In fact," Jelani continued, "my cousin said he had his hands up and told the DTs he had a piece. Then they just shot him.

"So they go to arrest him, presumably for selling drugs. He doesn't resist and becomes the victim of a "justified homicide." And it won't get any media attention as a police brutality case because he had drugs and a gun on him. That always makes whatever the cops do justified.

"I don't know his government name but on the streets they called him Jelly Bean." Jelani paused to take a drink. Despite no specifics being given, certain characteristics were obvious although not stated. That he was Black and from the neighborhood. And maybe he was skinny with a nickname like Jelly Bean. Or maybe he really liked to eat them.

"I know people say, going in, they would never do something like that. Or be part of something like that. No cop would get hired if he said, "Hey, I'm just gonna shoot any ol' Black guy whenever I feel like it for whatever reason I deem worthy." But that cop mentality eventually kicks in. Especially with the stress of the job. I mean, let's be real: it's hectic out here on these streets. Even when you're careful, death could sneak up on you and snatch you up. So sudden and unexpected.

"Everyone who puts in work out here got dirt out here." Jelani smiled to appreciate the spontaneous gem that spoke itself out of his mouth. "That's kinda smooth. I should use that in a poem.

"But back to what I was saying. There's no way you could be a cop, a gangsta, a regular on the street, and not eventually end up in some dirt. These streets are grimy. Even if as just a person witnessing a situation in which everyone knows something foul is going down but acts like they don't know nothing. You feel me?"

"I'm listening."

"But this is where it gets more tricky for those with a persuasion of darker melanin. That despite how things play out through all the individual motives, agendas, and particulars of a specific situation; in the grand scheme of things, the pattern remains the same: more often than not Blacks are getting the worst of it. We end up being the overwhelming majority of victims of police brutality, street violence, drug selling and addiction -- whatever. And as much as you may try to dodge it, as a cop, situations like that are going to find their way to you.

"So for the sake of survival -- life and death survival, keep-your-job survival, day-to-day I need to get along with these other cops survival; for the sake of all that, you'll go along when the dirt's on a cop's hand. Maybe not participate but look the other way. Not intercede when morally you know you should. Not make a stink of what smells blatantly putrid. And then try to find a way to still live with yourself."

It was tough medicine to take. Tory couldn't even speak, even if just to interrupt the flow of this potent dose.

"Cause when I look back at the Rodney King video, the cops who were beating him, we know they're sick. That's indisputable. And maybe they're so sick they're oblivious to how their soul is eating itself inside. But I look at the cops who stood on the side and watched. They're just as sick but in a more slick way. They're just as morally depraved and inhumane. Cause as a cop, if it's your job to uphold the law and protect society, how can you be a tacit witness to such an obvious and brutal injustice? They may not admit it but they can't deny the hypocrisy of that. And that's what deteriorates them from within.

"They may try to spin it by saying, "Well, I wasn't the one swinging the club." But how could you let someone do that when you have the power and responsibility to stop them? To not do so, to be so cold or unconcerned, is to stop being human. And for a human to not be human, that's worse than being an animal.""

The words couldn't read truer to the moment. And he smiled in appreciation. That even now, years into the separation prison imposed on them, Jelani was still being his friend. His best friend. That truest friend who has the courage to tell you what you refuse to hear but can't ignore. And does so because he or she sees what's better for you better than you can see for yourself in the moment. The wonder of Jelani's friendship somehow intuitively placed these words in Tory's life years ago, only to re-emerge of their own spontaneity now. And so appropriately. In the midst of an odd feeling experienced in the middle of the night, only a few feet away from the alley that forever changed his life.

Tory nodded to the friend who was no longer present, knowing what he should do. What he had to do despite how difficult or uncomfortable it may be. So he walked away from the disfigured cross laying by his feet. Walked by the alley where what was left of the memorial lay as scattered shambles upon the dark concrete and asphalt. Walked by the now motionless tank that remained in the middle of the street. Walked by the equipment truck where he declined the riot shotgun offered to him. He walked to his car and sat in the driver's seat. He exhaled deeply as he put his head upon his arms resting on the steering wheel. And in the shadows of the idle vehicle, he just let go: releasing the heaving cries that were weighing on his eyes and in his chest for too long.

CHAPTER NINE:
Martin - Martin - Martin

He had been forewarned that certain cases would steal his night's sleep. And on those nights, to let the case be his mistress. The drive back to police headquarters afforded him a time to decompress. To allow the rawness of suppressed emotions released to seep away.

With his mind reinvigorated and returning to a sense of clarity, he was too awake to go back to sleep. He sent a text to Loretta to inform her that he would be at his office working on the case. The empty halls of the headquarters felt like a mausoleum, as if there were dead and decaying things behind the closed doors. Things better left undisturbed and unexamined lest they become something more than death. Things that could not be ignored once revealed.

Sitting at his desk, he checked his cell phone. He saw the note he wrote to himself about Martin's manila envelope. He called down to the evidence room. Although it was outside the normal hours of operation, sometimes the clerks on night duty would allow him to check some things. Sometimes.

Fred answered with his usual cheery voice. He was usually accommodating. Besides, he said he was bored and would help if Tory brought him a glazed honey bun from the vending machine. The stipulation was half joking, half serious.

Fred was all smiles as Tory entered the evidence room. "If it ain't my man, Detective Givens." His smile became even bigger as his greeting was returned by Tory holding out the honey bun. "My man," he said accepting the treat. "Now you know I was only joking?"

"I know."

"But that won't stop me from eating this." Fred raised his eyebrows to accentuate his humor. "I'll put this to the side so as not to make you jealous. Cause with these things here, I never share." He roared with a laughter that ebulliently echoed throughout the room. Giving a sense of life to the dead of night.

Tory genuinely found pleasure in seeing Fred. Unashamed of his southern swagger, he was gracing his senior years still dressing in the latest youthful fashion. He once said, "I believe in having the finer things of life, but I'm not materialistic" -- the sarcasm of his joke evident in the bellowing laughter that followed. He was a visual display of his statement. Adorned with the "movie star eye frames" (fancy glasses), "flashy neck pieces" (necklaces) and "glimmering finger toys" (rings). He even had on his signature gold watch with matching cufflinks, which he named "Lord Have Mercy" and "Hot Damn One" and "Hot Damn Two." But his smile was the pinnacle of his wardrobe, a voracious bundle of joy. He was one of those people who smiled and laughed the wrinkles onto his face. And was not afraid to further deepen them with his constant displays of delight.

"So what you looking for?"

"I want to see if a manila envelope was brought in with the Martin Little crime scene evidence."

His look shifted from its jovial residue to a more serious countenance. He looked to make sure the door to the hallway had completely shut before speaking lowly.

"You know, I... I usually avoid making comments on police matters. Having an opinion on things can become an occupational hazard in some settings, if you know what I mean."

"I do."

"But that there case," he said, pointing to his heart, "really hit me here. Especially after I saw the video."

The admission alone was significant. Except for a few janitors, Fred was one of the few Black faces Tory encountered as regular staff at the headquarters. And aside from a few passing jokes when no one was around, the prevailing norm at the headquarters was to mute any sense of expression that might be construed as Black. Even Fred's attire, with touches of urban flashiness, was probably tolerated only because it was limited to the corner of the basement where the evidence room sat. So to offer commentary on a controversial case involving the killing of an unarmed Black man: this was noteworthy. And Tory welcomed it, understanding it was to be kept private.

"I have some concerns too," Tory acknowledged, "which you know I can't speak on."

"I heard you were investigating it." Tory was somewhat surprised Fred knew this. "I hope they actually let you do your job on this one. You seem like a stand-up guy, someone who'll tell it like it is."

"That's what I always try to do."

"Yeah, but sometimes they put a Black face up front in situations like this and censor what that man can say. But just between me and you, we really need the truth with this one. Like things are at a breaking point that will only get worse if things are covered up. I mean, I got family from across the country texting me about this one. So that shows you how big it is."

Fred paused before asking, "You got a minute?"

"Sure."

"You see, I got a great nephew named Martin. A teenager. Fairly good kid, but he got some knucklehead tendencies. And he got his hair in them dread things, something I'll never understand.

"But anyway, watching the news, seeing the pictures of Martin Little with the same hairstyle, hearing "Martin - Martin - Martin" over and over again..." His voice stopped, his eyes stained with a tinge of gloom. "What if that was my little Martin who was there and got shot? I know it sometimes seems cliche to say something like that, but the name and hairstyle were too similar. Made it so real to me. Personal. "I love that kid. He's like my grandson." His lips quivered slightly as he said, "It would break my heart if they killed my nephew like that."

There was a silence. Fred needed the moment to let his emotions settle. And Tory would not intrude upon the moment.

"You know what's one of the weird ironic things about it for me?"

"What?"

"My grandnephew was named after Dr. Martin Luther King, Jr. Martin Luther-Scott Jacobs. I felt so proud when my niece named him that cause Dr. King is one of my heros. But could you imagine a young man named after that man -- a hero who lived and died for peace; someone one named after him being killed so cold-blooded in the street by a cop. And so unjustly. Or at least it seems that way to me.

"But just to name a kid after a person who lived such an extraordinary life, who died so young men coming after him wouldn't have to get killed the same way. And still it happens. And like," he snapped his fingers for emphasis, "that! In an instant! I could receive a call right now, at any moment, saying little Martin Luther-Scott got killed by a cop for doing nothing. That someone *took* his life."

The look of sober resignation was a powerful summation. Reflecting an unsaid yet understood reality weighing on both men in that room. That despite their individual triumphs and successes in life. Despite the changes and limited progress transforming the landscape of how Blacks are treated in America. Despite the glimpses of hope for better days still on the way, there was nothing neither of them -- two adult Black men -- could do to prevent the younger generations from suffering the same tragedies that afflicted their people for centuries.

In fact, if they were honest and looked beyond their individual circumstances, which could belyingly suggest otherwise, neither of these "accomplished" men could save themselves from these same tragedies. In an unexpected instant, they could be seized. Killed in cold blood by a cop. Including Tory with his badge and gun. The continuing reality of police brutality remained a strong current among the wide river of tribulations afflicting Blacks in America and around the world.

"I was ten years old when my father -- a great man. He never made a lot of money or did anything that gets written in the history books, but he took care of his family. And he taught me what it means to be a man. More so through deeds than words.

"But I was ten and it was a hot September day out in the boondocks, out in that ol' shack that was called a school. We're in there sweating with that noisy fan blowing hot air all over the place. And our teacher, Mrs. Watson -- still remember her name. She pulled out a cassette player and said she had a special presentation for us.

"She started talking about how some of us may have heard about that big March on Washington that happened last month. I heard a little bit about it, mostly the church ladies gossiping about it. But she said she was able to get a tape recording of a news program that played some of the speeches.

"That's when it happened. That voice. Even on that crackling tape with all the static. That voice was a thunder resounding through the heavens. Majestic. It was more like he sung when he spoke. And so much power. Not just the force of his voice but also the power of what he was saying. Simple but powerful.

"I didn't remember the specifics of what he said, but I knew I was moved. That he was saying something to make things better for all Black people. Years later, when I had a little bit more sense about me, I found out that was the "I Have a Dream" speech. One of the greatest speeches ever given in the history of America.

"But, and I know I'm going off on a few different tangents. But it all connects. You still got time?"

"Absolutely," replied Tory.

"I went home that night and all I could talk about was Martin-Luther-King-this, Martin-Luther-King-that. I even asked my daddy to officially change my middle name to Martin. Never happened, but it shows how much of an impact he made on me. Maybe you can see why that name is still special to me. If I had a son I would have named him Martin. I petitioned my daughters to give one of their sons that name, but they ignored me. But my niece fulfilled that wish for me..." Fred's voice faded to a sweet smile of appreciation.

"But I'm taking too many scenic routes to where I'm trying to get. Back to where I started, the following May. I'm still ten years old cause my birthday's in August. My father wakes me up at four in the morning and makes me put on my church clothes. He puts me in the back seat of the car, pretty much asleep, but when I wake up he tells me we're on our way to Ebenezer Baptist Church. That's in Atlanta. We find some parking and walk over to the church. And there's like an excitement in the air, all the Black folks there are beaming and smiling. My daddy still ain't tell me why we drove all them hours to Ebenezer for.

"But we're moving through all the people, dressed up to the tee and glowing with pride. Squeeze into the back where we're crushed in there with other folks, all hot and sweaty. My dad's trying to keep me cool with one of them church fans, the piece of cardboard on a stick. And the choir was singing, but I'm hot and bothered. I figured if we drove all this way to be uncomfortable for some choir singing, we could have gone to one of the churches in town and be more relaxed. But then this big man, I'm assuming a reverend or something like that, comes out to introduce Dr. Martin Luther King, Jr."

Fred smiled, shaking his head, unable to contain the childhood exuberance of the memory.

"When he said that name, I started shaking -- speechless, I became so excited. And I looked at my daddy like: "You got me, Daddy. You got me good this time." Then he comes out, and everything is cheering and applause. I literally lose my mind. To see him there in the flesh, just like shining. Like an angel, man. Then everything got quiet and... that voice! I didn't even hear what he said, just mesmerized by his power. Words can't even describe what it was like."

Another silence. A glimmer of hope within struggles wading within past and present waves.

"So Dr. King has a place in some of the happiest moments of my life. But also one of the saddest. The moment I heard he was assassinated, I broke. I was at home and just went out to the back porch to cry in the dark of night. Even now, I don't know if you've seen one of the photos of the motel balcony. The one where his aides are all pointing in the same direction toward a nearby building, right after he was shot. And Martin's body is there on the landing, his knee bent up in the air while the rest of his body is laid out flat. Dead. I can see it now. And an hour later, they pronounced him dead at the hospital. Just gone.

"I was so sad and so angry. Didn't even sleep that night. I always said God be thanked I wasn't living in one of the cities where they rioted. Cause I probably would have died that night. The only way they would have gotten me off the streets was in a body bag, that's how mad and distraught I was."

The similarities were stirring through Tory's mind. Two unarmed Black men named Martin. Both not doing anything that warranted being shot. Their bodies dropped to the ground by the force of unexpected bullets. Both not living more than an hour after being shot. And did not the first Martin struggle in his life, in part, so the second Martin wouldn't die in an eerily similar manner? The first death sparked anger and discontent that ravaged city streets with riots. A pattern repeated on a smaller scale with the killing of the second Martin.

One could look to the life of the first Martin for teachings and guidance. A living example of working toward healing and solutions to address social ills still afflicting the everyday lives of Blacks. Were there similar lessons to be found in the life of the second Martin? Although not adorned with fame, prestige, and worldly recognition, were there still lessons in the fold of his life that could address the continuing injustices?

"Thanks for letting me get that off my chest. And I'm sorry if I'm holding up your work."

"No, I... I needed to hear that. Really."

"Well, I know you didn't come down here to get a lecture from an old man. What did you want?" Then he remembered before Tory could speak. "Right, a manila envelope in the crime scene evidence. Let me go check the inventory before I have you fill out any paperwork."

Tory stood in quiet reflection as Fred disappeared into the back. Thoughts of Martin, Martin, and Martin roamed through his mind. Although he never met any of them, and two of them he would now never meet in this life, he felt in a personally impersonal way that he somehow knew them. Not intimately, but just like having shared an experience with them. Even if brief and passing, it was significant enough that they were no longer strangers.

A few minutes later, Fred returned holding up a manila envelope within a transparent plastic evidence bag. "Is this what you're looking for?"

"I have no idea. Is it sealed?"

"I don't think so," Fred said as he handed it to Tory.

He carefully removed it from the plastic bag. The creases and dirt stains on the envelope revealed it had been crumpled and thrown on the ground. One of the metal fasteners were also broken off. Tory carefully lifted the other one to open the envelope's flap. Inside there were a few copies of Martin's resume and a looseleaf paper with handwriting on it, also bearing creases.

Tory examined the resume first. The top stated his objective: "I am seeking employment with a company where I can use my talents and skills to grow and expand the company and become a better person." Three things were listed under the Experience section. From June 2014 to December 2015 he volunteered as a part-time assistant cook and food server at a church soup kitchen. The next item noted his time as a stock clerk at one of the local supermarket chains from November 2007 to February 2010. The gap in activity from February 2010 to June 2014 stood out. Tory remembered Martin was arrested on February 10, 2010. Thereafter, he pled guilty to cocaine possession, serving about three years in jail. He was then released to a halfway house before entering a long-term drug rehab program. But these were not details one would put on a resume and still expect to be called for an interview. And from April 2007 to September 2007, he worked as a part-time newspaper delivery person. The sole item under the Education section was that he graduated from Lincoln High School in June 2004.

It wasn't what many would consider a strong resume. But it was probably honest, cause if he was going to fabricate anything why not make the resume more impressive.

But the weight of the obvious unspoken was something Tory knew Martin would struggle to overcome. Unless he had the favor of personal connections, many employers would deem him undesirable once he admitted his drug conviction. And it was very unlikely an employer would not ask about his criminal history, since such had become a standard employment question. Once asked, if he didn't mention his conviction, he would be fired or no longer considered for employment when a criminal background check revealed his criminal past. And most employers who asked would conduct the background check.

How many people would look upon felony cocaine possession with a tone of compassion for his struggles with drug addiction? How many people would hire him, trusting he wouldn't commit a criminal act against their business? Or assume the other often unstated suspicions of recovering addicts? Like that he might slip back into using and become a burden to manage. Or do something that might prove to be a liability for their business. Or that his addiction was a sign he was morally untrustworthy and likely to commit other crimes or vices.

The sparsely filled page was a loud pronouncement of his struggle to find employment. A struggle that probably would have continued if he wasn't killed. One that was not promised an easy resolution, if it was ever to be resolved. Tory had seen in Jelani's case how such could drive a strong and conscious person to resort to crime as a desperate means to address unending employment rejection.

And yet, that envelope contained proof of Martin's hopeful resilience scribbled in curvy penmanship upon the looseleaf paper. "Remember to smile. Talk slowly and clearly. Don't slouch. Don't chew gum. Be polite and patient. Stay calm. Stay positive. Trust in God."

Although Tory wasn't sure, he imagined it was likely Martin's handwriting. A reminder to himself of things to help him navigate this struggle stacked with immense odds against him. Something to read before going into situations where he was more likely to meet rejection instead of fair consideration. He made mistakes and took actions to pay for and correct them. Yet still he would more likely be viewed through the lens of his former faults instead of what he did to address them. And who he had become as a result of overcoming them.

"Can you make a copy of this paper and one of the resumes for me? Then I won't have to sign them out?"

"I got you," said Fred. He took the papers to the nearby copy machine. "Just black and white?"

"Yeah."

The machine hummed as Fred copied the resume. While copying the looseleaf paper, he looked at the resume. He then returned to Tory with the copies. "I can see why he was having a hard time getting a job."

"And you know he had a drug conviction?"

"I know. We don't give people a second chance like we used to do. Or maybe I should say: we don't give it to some people."

Tory was thinking the same thing but wouldn't vocalize it.

"Anything else I can get for you?"

"No, this is all I needed. I'll leave you in privacy to enjoy your honey bun."

They both smiled. A warranted pleasant ending to their emotional confessional. And bonding. Fred then extended his hand. A firm handshake of love.

"I'll see you around, detective."

"For sure."

◆ ◆ ◆

Tory sat at his desk inspired and determined. The last watch of night was upon him. His mind and body were immersed in fatigue, yet there was a clarity in his thoughts and a precision in his movements. He navigated the various pieces of evidence constructing a synopsis of the incident. He then listed all the persons he interviewed, with summaries of what relevant information was gathered. He cited points of the department's standards of policing and relevant policy, noting where he felt these were upheld and violated. But he paused as he reached the section for "Findings and Recommendations." It was clear in his mind what these should be yet still there was a hesitation.

In the midst of the vacillation, he peered to the side. The breaking light seeping through the partially shut blinds. He stepped away from his desk and raised the blinds all the way up. Although he knew the window of his office faced east, it took on a greater relevance in this moment.

The sun was rising, its light expanding beyond the silhouette of buildings blocking view of the distant horizon. Yet there was an invitation to witness the sun's continuing ascent, to catch a glimpse of its unveiled sphere as it slowly soared above the city roofs.

Introspection. In the midst of this investigation which was dragging him back and forth between life and death, hardship and hope, tragedy and injustice; in the midst of these, the weight of his age fell upon him. Forty-three years had passed since he emerged from his mother's womb. The days of his infancy and youth spent within urban enclaves, where concrete and asphalt were more common than green grass and leaves. Where strife and tribulation were constant intruders upon their pursuit of happiness and peace. A mother always there. A father sometimes, an intermittent presence between the weeks and months away as a railroad man. Until one day he was just gone. The sum of days absent amounting to him never coming back. It didn't seem like a big deal at the time since Uncle James was often there, a reliable source of male guidance and support whenever Tory needed it.

Yet this divergence from the perceived norm of fatherhood could not be discounted. The vague presence of a father in his life undoubtedly had some effect on Tory. Even if he couldn't state how in specific terms. Martin was a father following the footsteps of his father, footsteps left for his future generations to follow. Martin was looking forward to being a father, an aspiration that would now not be fully realized. His child left to continue its journey into this world despite his sudden removal from it. And another Martin was still meandering the paths of footsteps left for him, perhaps with a father. But surely he had the love of his uncle to help him navigate his own path in a world imbrued with uncertainties.

The questions became increasing urgent in Tory's mind, reflecting on these three Martins and fatherhood. Who am I following? To whom am I leaving a legacy to be followed? Have I become my father's son? Or a man capable of being a good father? Will I even have children of my own so late in life?

Watching the glowing light rise beyond the shadowed buildings, it settled upon Tory that he would probably never have a child of his own. At least not biologically. That, as things stood, he had become the final point of a branch in his family tree. A dead end in his family's lineage.

Forty-three years. He had most likely lived at least half of his life already. The end was probably closer than the beginning while still being unknown. Martin was dead at thirty-two. Martin lived till thirty-nine. And another Martin was on his way to an eventual end that might be less than or surpass the former two.

He remembered how The Professor said that when the autopsy was done, the thirty-nine year old Martin had the heart of a sixty year old. And yet, the bullet that dropped him on that balcony wasn't his first brush with his own death.

How years earlier, at a book signing in New York, a woman stabbed him in the chest with a letter opener. A Black woman. Mentally ill. Tory could see The Professor's face as he described how the blade of the opener laid upon Martin's aorta. If he would have sneezed that major artery would have been punctured, leaving Martin to drown in his own blood. There he was, bleeding with the letter opener protruding from his chest, only a sneeze away from death.

He needed surgery to have the letter opener removed, which left a cross-shaped scar upon his chest. Something Martin noticed often. Its sight was obvious upon his naked chest, in clear view of any bathroom mirror while brushing his teeth or washing his face. A constant reminder that any day could be his last. That death's seizure could be swift and unanticipated. Forging his conviction that if you don't have something you're willing to die for, you're not fulfilling the duty of life. An evoking, living call to make sure that whatever you're doing with your life is something worth dying for.

And even Martin and his struggles with drug addiction. Tory had seen enough through his time on the streets to know that urban addiction was never far from death. There was death in selling drugs. Death in using. Death in overdoses or the slower decay of health that eventually brings many to the grave. Death in doing what many users do to get drugs, especially in the desperation that can overtake those who no longer have the resources to support their habits. Death in the relationships lost because of addiction. Death in people being forever changed from who they once were, with recovery sometimes offering a chance to partially reclaim their former selves. And even for those who survive and overcome the bondage of drugs, there's the mental scars that linger with the imprint of death. Life within such proximity to death doesn't leave anyone unscathed.

What am I living for? Am I willing to die for it? Or even suffer something significant for it? These weren't new questions for Tory, given his few brushes with death. A few bullets dodged or errantly off-target in the line of duty. A police chase crash that totaled his police cruiser, yet he was fortunate to walk away from it. The dozens of bodies he had to tend to as an officer, cooling to become stiffening corpses. Most from natural causes but some due to human affliction. These questions weren't strangers to him, but in the past he could ignore their haunting. Or find distractions. Yet as the sun's sphere began to peek above the skyline of edifices, he could no longer avoid or escape the questions.

He took his badge in hand, the gold shield with the engraved star. The drilling of his academy instructor still embossed in his mind. Each point of the star represented a cardinal virtue of being a police officer. *Honor*, the privilege and duty of upholding and enforcing the law. *Integrity*, to live with an unwavering moral character that is worthy of and will never betray the public trust. *Chivalry*, to serve and protect the people with respect and justice, especially the weak, oppressed, and innocent. *Courage*, the willingness to lay one's life on the line as a public servant. *Excellence*, the uncompromising standard all officers must strive to maintain, free from corruption, bribery, and undue influence.

He wore the symbol of these values upon his chest for nearly half his life. As a patrol man, he donned it proudly upon his left shirt pocket. As a detective, the inner left pocket of his suit jacket became its common abode. He never left home without it. He polished it every two months, maintaining the habit he began as a rookie. The badge, and all it represented, became a pillar of his life. Not far behind his marriage, his family, and his friendship with Jelani. But was he truly living its values? Willing to die for them? Suffer for them?

The inclination to quickly say "yes" became a pause that had to confess a reluctant "no." And he could offer no comfortable justification for this. His compromising, his obscuring hypocrisy was undeniably exposed as the sun beamed its light upon his sullen body. Like the sphere of blinding light visually cut in half by a distant rooftop, he felt himself being severed between the facade he tried to uphold and the failings he was too ashamed to admit.

Yet nothing was fixed as the sun continued its rise. Within his internal shifting, he still had a chance to change. His breath of life still breathing. His heart still beating. His body still able with potential acts at hand. Martin died living for what he was willing to die for. And Martin was in the midst of a change, striving to find a way to live for a child who now will not see his living face. The other Martin will eventually be presented with a similar dilemma of what to live, and perhaps be willing to die, for. And then the lines spoke themselves again:

> *But on the third day he did not rise.*
> *Maybe because his name wasn't Jesus,*
> *Or because he had not yet reached*
> *The mystical age of 33.*

It was the third day since his death and Martin would not rise. Neither did Martin rise on the third day after his assassination. Will the other Martin rise when the moment of death comes? Probably not. And Tory had to confess that he also probably wouldn't either on the third day after his last breath. That if he was going to live for something that was worth dying for he had better do it now. Before death, which is often sudden and unexpected, comes and denies him the chance he now has. A denial that may bury him with regrets in the grave and whatever there is beyond this earthly life.

◆ ◆ ◆

When the sun completely rose above the buildings, he lowered the blinds and made his way to his car. The halls were still empty as he carried a different manila envelope in his hand. Large and stuffed with various papers. Navigating the pre-rush hour traffic, he drove to a part of the city he rarely entered. The "old neighborhood" where Dusty lived remained segregated: it was virtually all White.

The house was just another house along the row of houses. The paint faded, the porch cluttered with a hodgepodge of items. He stepped over the rubber-banded newspaper that had been thrown before the front door. He knocked loudly and waited, expecting no response. Dusty rarely answered the front door. But Tory had to follow the established protocol. After about thirty seconds, he approached the side gate. As usual, it was locked. So he hopped over the fence, being careful to not catch his pants on the top of the wired mesh. He moved through the pathway between the side fence and the house. He then turned sharply as he reached the backyard, keeping his gaze low. Dusty could be rather weird at times, his backyard becoming the canvas for bizarre experiments. Like one time, there was a naked scarecrow with an erect member extending to the sky. And a pitiful looking scarecrow at that. An image forever impressed into Tory's mind, one he could never suppress when passing by the backyard. He didn't want to add another such sight to his mind's inventory.

The back door was slightly ajar. This meant Dusty was home and welcoming select guests. Although not required, Tory knocked on the door as a courtesy before entering. As he started to enter, he heard a voice from behind.

"I figured you'd be here sooner or later." Tory didn't want to turn around but knew that he should. "Aww, you can look. There's no scarecrow sculptures right now."

Dusty laughed. Tory turned to see him poking his head out of a tent set up in the backyard. The blue fabric had streaks of black paint upon it. Clothes, food wrappers and containers, newspapers, and an assortment of batteries were scattered by the tent. Dusty noticed Tory's puzzled look and smiled. "Don't ask. Just go ahead in. I'll be in in a minute."

He didn't ask. He knew, since retiring, that Dusty was constantly engaging in various "experiments" to find and reconnect with parts of his "lost" self. An attempt at "self-recovery," as he called it, after spending so many years as a tough guy detective.

The next step in the protocol involved patience. Tory walked through the cluttered kitchen into the cluttered dining room. The theme of Dusty's house, and perhaps his life, was unending clutter. The eccentric mix of items seemed to have no connecting logic. But there was always a method to his madness. And often it was better to let the madness remain unexplained.

There was a cleared spot at one end of the table, perhaps from the previous visitor. In general, Dusty didn't have guests. But his wealth of policing knowledge made him a sought-after source of guidance to certain leaders, veterans in the department, and those fortunate to hear about his wellspring of wisdom. He was not only an expert of the practical science of police work but also a superb advisor for dealing with the politics surrounding it. Especially with controversies. He would often joke, "Although I retired from the force, the force didn't retire from me." And with his reputation of being an insomniac, people would come without calling at all hours of the day and night. That's why Tory didn't hesitate to go even at the crack of dawn.

Dusty wouldn't accept money, yet still a price was to be paid for his time. It would vary from person to person. Since Tory was his last detective partner and he really liked Tory, his price involved eating, without questions, whatever Dusty decided to make. And the rules of Dusty's grandmother applied: the plate had to be bread-wiped clean. She had a thing of being extremely annoyed by anyone who would waste food in a world where people are starving to death. Yet one difference between Dusty and his grandmother was extremely significant. His grandmother was an exceptional cook, from what he proclaimed, whereas he was a "horrible food burner." Those were the very words he used to describe his lack of cooking prowess.

In a matter of minutes, Tory heard Dusty enter the kitchen and slam the back door shut. The shut door was an indication that he was unavailable if other select visitors came seeking advice. Tory was already in the midst of checking messages on his phone as an array of loud bangs emitted from the kitchen. First what sounded like something being beat -- literally, beat -- in a metal bowl. Then pots being heavy-handedly removed from cabinets, rinsed in a sink, and then clanged on a stove. The sound of frying was quickly accompanied by the scent of eggs, then the smell of burning as smoke rolled along the heights into the dining room. Dark smoke. The hacking sound of a spatula soon followed, with some expletives mixed in. The rattling of the silverware drawer being pulled all the way open and then slammed shut. Then heavy footsteps approaching as Tory put his phone away.

Dusty entered placing a plate and silverware before Tory. He had an apron on, which Tory always found amusing. The contrast of this old tough detective wearing a frilly apron would have made a good picture. No words were exchanged but the looks in both of their eyes indicated another food failure was forthcoming.

Dusty exited to return carrying a hot frying pan with a hot mitt. With a spatula in the other hand, he practically tossed the burnt omelette upon Tory's plate. The crashing sound upon the porcelain didn't increase its appeal.

"As you can see, I'm still perfecting the art of the perfectly burnt cheese omelette. There's salt and pepper there, though you probably won't need much pepper with the char. I'll be right back."

Dusty exited again. Tory looked at the pitiful and very burnt attempt at a meal. He only stared at it. There was absolutely nothing appealing about it. His gaze was momentarily broken by another loud bang from the kitchen: the frying pan being dropped into the sink. Then his stare returned to the plate with dread. He didn't have the courage to place that "thing" in his mouth. But he knew he would soon have to.

Dusty returned without the frilly apron. He was peeling a grapefruit as he plopped himself in a chair nearby. He took a moment to smirk at Tory. The glow of his eyes shined within the framing of his salt and pepper hair and beard. He allowed it to grow out after decades of daily shaving the leathered skin that was now tanned. It brought him joy to see Tory stare at the unsavory omelette. It wasn't his original intention to torture Tory but he would enjoy it nonetheless.

"No charred cuisine for you?" asked Tory.

"I'm on a diet. Too much char is making me fat." Dusty laughed loudly. He then grabbed a model ship from the middle of the table. It was still in the process of being assembled. "Look. It's supposed to be a historical replica of the Piñata."

"The what?"

"One of the ships Columbus sailed on."

"A piñata is like a stuffed animal or something filled with candy. They blindfold you and you try to break it with a stick."

"Why would he name his ship that?"

"I don't think that was the name of the ship."

"Oh."

They would both look it up on the internet later to see the name was "Pinta."

"Well, eat up. Since you didn't come over for a history lesson, you have to at least make me feel like I'm a good cook. Otherwise, I won't let you pick my brain."

The inevitable could no longer be avoided. Tory grabbed the fork and knife. The crunching sound was loud as he cut into the thick burnt bottom of the eggs. The initial bite confirmed what he already suspected: the omelette was burnt through and through. The charred bottom caught on his teeth as he chewed delicately. He added salt but there was no way to masquerade the nasty taste of burnt. It just became salty burnt.

Chew, chew, swallow. Past experience taught him this was the only way to minimize the burnt taste. Break the former food into pieces small enough to go down the throat. To be followed later by an antacid.

And maintain a poker face. To display displeasure would only invite Dusty's cruel ridicule. The mentor smiled, enjoying every moment of Tory's suppressed disgust.

"Martin Little, right?"

"Yeah," Tory said in between chews.

"The chief was here yesterday. His manila envelope is over there on the chair, so you can keep yours. But what are your questions? Concerns?"

"I'm planning on submitting my Internal Affairs report and..."

"Whoa, what's the rush? Did the D.A. already decide on charges?"

"No, but I want to make my recommendations before they do."

Dusty took a moment. This was different than normal. But instead of asking about it directly, he would give Tory the chance to say why in the natural flow of conversation.

"So this report, what kind is it? One that tells what really happened or one that suffices to check off the necessary boxes? Cause, as I always say, the two don't always coincide..."

"The two don't always coincide," overlapped Tory. "Especially in this case where so much politics are involved."

"You're preaching to the choir."

"What's your take on it?"

"On what happened? He was stressed out, got scared, and shot. Probably didn't intend to kill the guy but shit happens when guns are involved. And he was going to make sure he got home to see his family that night. Remember, it's not like he really wanted to work in the Hole anyway. That's what my gut tells me."

That was one of the things Tory always appreciated about Dusty: he always told it how he saw it. Unapologetically. And he was rarely wrong when it came to police matters.

"So what's the right thing to do?"

Dusty almost chuckled at the question. "This whole thing has moved beyond right and wrong. It's all about people protecting their interests now. And that includes people not at the scene of the shooting." He raised his eyebrows before saying, "It might even need to include you."

Dusty's look conveyed he understood that "stuff" was afloat within the undercurrents of the activities of the players involved. He had been through enough political struggles at the department in which people used cases as fodder for personal ambitions and collective agendas. For years, he would fight for some sense of decency and justice within the sausage making of such politics. That is until he burnt out. Reached the point where he no longer cared. From there on, he just put his head in the sand to get things done, stomaching what could not be avoided until he reached the grade of pension he wanted. Then he abruptly quit, not even showing up at the retirement party he told them not to plan for him but held anyway.

Tory hadn't reached that point. At least not yet. There were still aspects of the job he cared about. Still had faith in. He still sought to view things through the prism of what was right. What was moral. What was just. And this perspective still informed his work.

Despite his skeptical view of the department, and all the politics surrounding it, Dusty chose to speak to the searching hope within his mentee. He put the grapefruit to the side and leaned forward to be more tactful, looking Tory squarely in the eye to proceed with a surgeon's compassion. There would be some pain in cutting straight to the heart of the matter.

But when there's a serious illness, rarely can a treatment occur without some pain. A pain that offers the opportunity of healing instead of continuing an ongoing deterioration progressing toward demise. He would ensure Tory wasn't blindly succumbing to an ideal that would only break his heart while the machine uncaringly rolled on.

"Look, it's obvious what happened. Obvious. An unarmed and probably innocent Black guy got killed by a White cop for reasons that go beyond what happened in that alley. And there isn't a cop or prosecutor with any sense in his head that can deny that. The racial dynamics cannot be ignored even if people downplay and spin them in a thousand different ways. But the brutal truth is these types of incidents are part of how the system works. And most people in the system would rather not rock the boat. Even if they're bothered by what happened.

"So it'll be a controversy that gets attention now and will fade into the background soon enough. And the factors that caused it to happen will go unaddressed. So it'll happen again. Eventually. That's how things go. "

"But can't they be changed?"

"Who wants things to change? Who's willing to endure the burdens and repercussions that will surely come? And the loneliness? To be among those rare few who end up putting everything on the line to only suffer and maybe be appreciated some time in the future? Maybe.

"But isn't that the real issue at hand for you, Tory? It's obvious things need to change but everyone else just wants to go along with how things are. Figure that out and all the detective issues will be resolved according. Cause like I said, it's obvious what happened."

"I agree."

"Do you want to be the hero on this one? Is that it? Catch the bad guy and put him behind bars for a crime he'll otherwise get away with? Although that's not your job."

"It's not that. Honestly."

"Then what are you eating that nasty-ass omelette for?"

Tory smirked before returning to the serious issue at hand. "I just can't go along with this one. It's too..." Tory paused, searching for the words.

"Fucked up?"

"Yeah."

"But you've gone along with fucked up cases before. Racial ones too. Cases where everyone knows it was wrong but no one pressed it. You wouldn't have ended up in Internal Affairs if you didn't."

Dusty paused to allow Tory to realize the truth of these words himself.

"This, whatever you want to call it, it's not about the case. It's about you. This isn't the first time a Black guy got killed by a cop and didn't deserve it. Whatever's bothering you now, don't put it on the case. It's you."

"So you're saying I'm personalizing it."

"You may be doing that too. But that's not what I'm talking about. It's more that something in this case tugs at the core of who you are. Exposing you."

Dusty's gaze became even more intense, as if seeking to convey with his face what his words could only scratch the surface of. And Tory got even quieter, hoping his mentor would say something to resolve this inner turmoil Dusty knew he was struggling with.

"That's not something I can help you with. I offer work advice, not psychological counseling. Or self-discovery. Shit, I'm still trying to figure out who the hell I am. And I'm an old fart. But at some point, we all encounter a case like this. Actually a few cases over the course of our careers. But I can't tell you what to do. I refuse. Cause whatever you choose, you're going to have to live with it for a long time. Maybe the rest of your life. And I want no part in that."

There was a silence. As much as Tory hoped for more explicit direction, he couldn't disagree with Dusty's stance. Within he knew he had to choose how to proceed. He alone. He knew this walking in the door. And it was fitting that Dusty wouldn't give him a way out by telling him what to do. Or even suggesting something.

"Either choice comes with consequences," Dusty stated. "I chose to go along with the flow, thinking I might be able to escape them. The consequences. And I always justified it. Change in the department is supposed to come from the top. So as long as the chief and top brass continue to tolerate it, it's not my job to address it. Or I didn't want to mess up a possible promotion. Or my pension. Or I needed to work on my second, third, fourth marriage. Relationships flawed from the beginning, bound to end in divorce.

"They were all just excuses cause it was easier to keep my mouth shut and just do my job. And I was honest with myself: I didn't want the hard shit that comes with trying to change things nobody else wants to change. But you know it needs to be changed. So you suppress a sense of yourself to get by, go along even when you feel like you shouldn't. Yeah, I avoided some really hard blowback but found out later that's the path of delayed suffering and retirement regrets. Stuff I'm still working through. Had me so mixed up inside I ended up making naked scarecrows with exaggerated hard-ons."

They both chuckled. Tory knew, from the established pattern of their talks, the joke was Dusty's way of saying he was done. Yet there was still half of the burnt omelette on the plate. It had to be devoured before Tory left. So the discussion turned to the latest struggles of the various sports teams Dusty followed. They all seemed to be having hard times. And how he was trying to recapture parts of his fragmented childhood by sleeping in the tent in his backyard. It was something he always wanted to do but his parents never let him. But the tent's blue fabric didn't replicate the pitch black darkness he became accustomed to in his curtain-draped bedroom. So he tried painting it black, but immediately realized it wasn't going to work. It just ruined the appearance of the tent.

When the last bit of char was swallowed, Dusty said he had to kick Tory out. That he needed the clear end of the table to continue working on the Piñata. More laughs. Tory thanked Dusty who ceremonially rejected all words of gratitude. Besides, this time he didn't really offer any advice.

A firm handshake, a wink of the eye, and Tory made his way out the back door. He always thought Dusty was being such a jerk by making him have to climb the side gate again instead of allowing him to exit through the front door. But great mentors are allowed to have their peculiarities and their ways of irking their students. And in the long run, climbing a fence, bearing the taste of burnt unsavory food, and tolerating mild indigestion was a small price to pay for priceless wisdom.

◆ ◆ ◆

He drove home thinking he might catch Loretta before she left. But she had already departed by the time he arrived. He took a shower, more for the comfort of the warm water than anything else. Then he laid down to take a short power nap. What was supposed to be a half hour rest became about an hour after repeated presses of the snooze button. Slightly refreshed, he put on one of his regular suits. He then started to the car but turned back at the door. He forgot to feed the fish.

Standing over the tank his gaze wandered to the portrait of Uncle James. At moments like this, he wished his uncle was still around. Not that he would offer any direct advice, but just his presence might help Tory settle into an answer within. An answer he already knew. Again, it was obvious to him what he needed to do. But still the hesitation.

He drove through the city streets to arrive at police head-quarters. He didn't stop to check in with anyone, walked straight to his office. He refused to check the awaiting phone messages and emails. Instead he opened up the investigation report for the Martin Little shooting on his computer.

He moved to the end of the document, the cursor flashing beneath the title for "Findings and Recommendations." A moment of stillness. The chatter of thoughts revolved around a single point. Just do it. You already know what you should do. What you need to do. Why am I hesitating? Why am I... The thought dispersed behind the physical tension of his fingers frozen motionless upon the keyboard. He was shocked at how stiff they became.

Then he just did it. The first keystroke followed by suc-ceeding finger movements comprising words, sentences, and paragraphs. The flow of activity was easier than the preceding inertia, as the conclusion pretty much completed itself. The section, once typed, was reread and a few minor revisions were made. Touches of clarity expounding upon what was already obvious.

The anxiety arose again when it came time to print. The hesitation to send it to the printer which was shared by others in the Internal Affairs Division. Just print it. He did. And then rushed to the printer to grab the pages as they emerged.

He was relieved to find no one was by the printer. He col-lected the document and returned to his office, again shutting the door. He browsed the document again, not so much for typographical errors rather in hope of finding some sense of reassurance from the pages. From what he was doing. But nothing more came. He was still torn about seeing the task to completion.

He grabbed a report cover and inserted the pages. Now he just wanted to get it done. He didn't think to call the chief's office, he just walked over there. But the chief was in a meeting. And he didn't want to leave the report with the secretary. So he said he would just come back later, that it wasn't a big deal.

He walked back to his office and placed the report on his desk. He just sat there staring at it, the white pages laying flat under the thin flimsy plastic cover. Time passed. Then there was a knock on the door, followed by Speedy's usual walking entry. Tory picked up the report with a sense of alarm in his eyes. He wanted to put it in a drawer, but didn't. That would have only brought more unwanted attention to the document he wished to hide.

"Is everything okay?"

"Come on in, Speedy."

Speedy entered and shut the door. "I left you a message but I guess you've been busy."

"I haven't checked anything yet," Tory said, placing the report to the side, faced down. "What's up?"

"I just wanted to see if you had anything planned on the Little case today. Cause Gulley gave me a new case. Nothing major. One of those inappropriate behavior complaints. I'm available if you need me, but if you had nothing planned I might as well get started on this."

"No, I don't have anything planned."

"Okay. Well, if anything pops up give me a call. And get some rest, you look beat."

As Speedy started to exit, Tory called out to him. "Well, actually Speedy, there is something I wanted to mention."

Speedy turned around, asking, "What's up?"

"I wanted to tell you that I'm... I'm submitting a preliminary report on the Martin Little case."

Speedy's eyes widened with a questioning look. This was totally unexpected. "Did Gulley or the chief ask for it?"

"No. I'm doing this on my own."

An awkward silence. Tory's decision was not only out of character but totally contrary to how things usually proceeded with cases like this. No action was necessary until after the District Attorney declined to press charges. Or, if charges were pursued, until either a verdict was rendered, a plea deal reached, or the case was dismissed by a judge. Then Internal Affairs would resume their investigation. It would usually be months, if not over a year, before a report was submitted to the chief, citing findings and recommendations. To act quicker than that would send shockwaves through the department as well as incite others to suspect that a personal agenda was in play. Or politics. Such action would also exile Tory from any good standing in the force. And there was nothing pleasant about being a pariah in the department.

"Should I ask what your findings are?"

"I already stated I have concerns about the shooting."

"Concerns that require you submitting a report prior to the D.A.'s decision? To move so quickly would mean potential career suicide."

Tory sat stoic-faced. Speedy tried to read beneath the expression but couldn't. So he grabbed a chair and sat across from Tory.

"What's this really about?"

"The facts of the case and his poor judgment."

"If you're trying to get this guy, I'm not against it. But why not be patient? You can reach the same point without ruining yourself."

Again, Tory was expressionless.

"Look," Speedy conceded, "I know this one has..." His voice drifted off in search of the right words. "The racial stuff in this one is... it's there. Can't be denied."

Tory chuckled.

"What?"

"It's funny -- no, ironic that you bring that up after first assuming I have some personal agenda."

"I don't get what you're saying."

"We're partners, right? So we can be honest?"

"Of course."

"When have we ever had a real discussion about race?"

Speedy searched for an answer. Eventually he had to admit, "Rarely, if ever."

"Yet do you think what I deal with on a daily basis in this department "rarely" involves race?"

Speedy leaned back. He felt somewhat uncomfortable about where this might be going.

"I'm not going to spill my heart out to you now when I've never done so before. And we've been partners and associates for many years. But every day being Black in a predominantly White police force brings up racial things most Whites are oblivious to. Including you, with all due respect."

"So what does this have to do with this case?" Speedy was then quick to add, "And in all honesty, I'm saying this more as a friend than a partner. Someone who genuinely cares about you."

"I don't doubt that. But why do we, as a force, constantly look to excuse things that are obviously wrong? Including the obvious racial factors in this case?"

"I'm not looking to excuse anything. I'm just saying there's a way to do things without going nuclear."

"It's going nuclear to say that Easthill shouldn't have killed Martin Little? What did he do to warrant being shot?"

"I can see your side and I can see Easthill's side."

"Really?"

"If Martin obeys Easthill's commands, he doesn't get shot."

"So it's proper procedure to shoot someone for not obeying orders?"

"Procedures are one thing, survival on the streets is another."

"And even that statement, you think that has nothing to do with race?"

"I don't get it."

Tory was done dancing around the issue and just said it directly. "Do you think Easthill would have shot Martin if he was White?"

"Maybe."

"Then where are the comparable number of cases of unarmed Whites getting killed compared to Blacks?"

"It happens."

"Far less frequently. Far less."

It became evident that neither side was going to be moved to the other's position. That the roots of their disagreement went deeper than what the present conversation could mediate. That perhaps it was better to leave things as they were, since any further division might do irreparable damage to their relationship. A relationship that would most likely be less personal going forward. Certainly more distant. And probably forever changed.

Yet there was something Tory had to get off his chest, that had to be said to some aspect of the White force he was working within.

"You know, it amazes me, Speedy, how when you're Black, working in a situation like this, there's an expectation that you're supposed to tolerate White racism. To just live with it as long as it's not too extreme. And I guess a White cop killing an unarmed Black man is not considered too extreme. It rarely gets punished. Continues to happen over and over again. And nothing substantial is ever done to address it."

"So that's what this is about?"

"It's about me being able to live with myself by telling it like it is!"

"Again, I get it. Or to a certain extent, as I guess you would say. I would just not rush it. And I say that out of a genuine concern for you as a friend and fellow detective."

Another silence. They both realized any further words would be pointless.

Eventually, Speedy stood up. He gave a look warning that Tory may regret what he was about to do. "It's your case, your call. I was only assigned to assist you."

With that, Speedy turned and left. And Tory felt even more alone in an isolation he was coming to realize was always present. The diminished rapport with Speedy was one less veil concealing it.

CHAPTER TEN:
Memorials for lost uncles

Tory sat in the dim of his office. The stress was mounting, the intensity of the isolation increasing. The report was still laying faced down on the side of his desk when his phone rang. The chief's secretary called to say his meeting had ended and he had a few minutes free before he would be off to meetings that would last into the afternoon. She didn't have to call, but she was being considerate. Tory thanked her for her thoughtfulness and said he was on his way.

Moving through the halls he kept his gaze low. His replies to others' greetings were very reserved. He felt they might soon diminish significantly, if not completely disappear. Although no one would say it, such courtesies were conditional upon towing the unofficial officers' code.

Upon reaching Chief Smitts' office, he was allowed to go right in. Tory knocked on the door to the private office before entering.

"Come in, Givens." Tory entered carrying the report. Chief Smitts sat behind his desk reviewing paperwork. "Have a seat." As Tory sat, "What do you have for me?"

Tory leaned forward to place the report on the chief's desk. "A preliminary report on the Martin Little shooting."

An awkward silence. Chief Smitts made no movement toward the report. After quickly eyeing the cover, he returned to looking at the paperwork before him. He didn't even give a moment's glance to Tory. The message was clear.

"What are your findings?"

Tory straightened up in his chair to speak with a calm conviction. Yet his anxiety remained a strong undercurrent. "I find the shooting to be unjustified. I suggest the department recommend Officer Easthill be charged with involuntary manslaughter. Also, in the event that the District Attorney doesn't press charges, I'm recommending Officer Easthill be ordered to go before a department disciplinary trial for charges of "unnecessary use of deadly force" and "poor judgment.""

"But the D.A.'s Office isn't done with their criminal investigation." This echoed Speedy's words supporting the status quo of the current police culture. It wasn't surprising but still upsetting.

"That doesn't prevent us from offering a recommendation," countered Tory, "and being prepared for whatever choice they make."

Chief Smitts paused, his eyes shifting from the paperwork to Tory. His glare was another warning. A warning then communicated through the veils of coded words.

"You don't want to wait until after conducting your own questioning of the officers before submitting your report?" In other words, I'm giving you one more chance, perhaps your last, to back away from this edge, officer. You're moving too quickly. Stop.

But the lower ranked officer reluctantly stood his ground. "I doubt additional questioning will reveal anything significant that hasn't already been revealed. I also wanted to submit this report prior to the District Attorney making a decision, which she promised would be soon."

In Tory's mind, his words sounded more confident than he felt. Especially since he sensed what was coming.

"Okay."

In a single word, all was conveyed. Tory's quest for what was right, his pursuit of justice, would go no further. The work of his investigation, and the accompanying personal struggles, would only amount to delivering recommendations to the chief. Recommendations which, although fair and justified, would only come to fruition if Chief Smitts chose to act upon them. Yet his intentions, although unspoken, were clear: he had absolutely no interest in acting upon Tory's suggestions. In his eyes, they were unnecessary and premature. And dangerous within police circles.

There was an established course for how these things should progress, with a slowness and procrastination that weighed in favor of inflicting no penalties upon Easthill. Or any officer whose infractions weren't considered too extreme.

But more, Tory's suggestions reflected a conscious and deliberate break from conforming to the current police culture. A volatile violation of the code. This code facilitated a strong bonding within the police fraternity. A fraternity that sought to vehemently protect its own and exorcize even potential traitors and betrayers. Upholding these values was, in practical terms, deemed essential to serving as a viable police chief. One who not only occupied the position of commander, but one the rank and file would respectfully follow. And if the chief upheld these values, the overwhelming majority of officers would embrace them too. Components of a cycle reinforcing itself. And within this self-sustaining cycle, those who abided by this culture would be granted significant leniency to display their displeasure to the betraying Tory once the word got out.

"In the meantime," continued Chief Smitts, "you can start on a new case I gave Gulley this morning: a captain accepting questionable gifts in the Fifth Precinct. Any further work on the Little case can be put on hold until after the D.A. makes her decision."

Only a few seconds had passed after that ominous "okay," but it felt as if the tides of all time had been shifted within that quick expanse before directing Tory to another assignment. And despite what the chief said, Tory doubted he would do any more work on the Martin Little case going forward.

Some reason would be found to place the investigation in the hands of another detective. One trusted to conform.

Tory knew his course of action was soundly based in points of department policy. Points honoring the spirit of the policy and the department's purpose. But his course was eviscerated in an instant to the reigning culture of the department. At the foot of the chief's desk.

He also knew in that moment any efforts to push the matter further would amount to nothing more than more hardship being inflicted upon himself. The parties responsible for deciding any pursuit of justice and punishment were set in their ways. Ways inclined toward accommodating the existing norms. Ways that would likely spare an overreaching cop from the sword of justice or any official accountability. The District Attorney and Chief Smitts had little to gain, but possibly much to lose, if they sought to punish Easthill. Yet they would suffer no significant losses by not pursuing his punishment.

The exclamation point to this realization was Tory watching Chief Smitts place the report on the side of his desk. He had strong reason to doubt the chief would even skim through its contents, let alone give it a serious read. Sentiments of rejection and repudiation were boiling within Tory. And regret. Didn't the chief say he wanted the facts of what happened irrespective of all the other stuff surrounding them? Yet here they were, hand delivered to his desk, and they were being dismissed without any consideration. Probably to never be read.

Maybe he was just being used as a Black face to address a simmering Black controversy.

The chief returned to perusing the paperwork before him. A clear sign he was done with the matter and that Tory could leave. Yet Tory refused to stand. He wouldn't walk away from this indignity. He wanted his displeasure to be looked in the eye. To be granted at least that much acknowledgment, since he knew most of the forthcoming reprisal would be done beyond his eye's purview.

Eventually, Chief Smitts looked up and asked, "Is there anything else?"

"No, sir."

As their eyes met, Tory knew their relationship would never be the same. That any favored trust he enjoyed from the chief, or possibility of such, was gone. That he was nothing more than just another officer under a line of command. One that would be regulated to the normal functions of his role, not given any special or significant tasks. And certainly not given any meaningful power.

And to Tory, Chief Smitts became just another politically appointed man with a decorated badge. A man with a powerful job in a flawed department of government. Not a leader. Not someone serious about justice.

Tory stood and exited the office. Although he didn't see what happened next, it would not have surprised him. After Tory left, Chief Smitts grabbed the report and tossed it in a red plastic bin behind his desk. Falling upon a stack of other papers and documents that would be shredded by the end of the day.

◆ ◆ ◆

He didn't even go back to his office. He went straight to his car. He called Anne to inform her that he would be out of the office for the rest of the day finishing up loose ends on cases other than the Martin Little investigation. He emphasized this as he sensed Gulley would be informed of the transpired events and would check to see that he was no longer doing anything in relation to the case he was now essentially removed from.

But he needed some closure, even if it was something symbolic. He wanted to apologize to Martin. Why? He wasn't sure. But it felt like the thing to do. Something he had to do.

He thought about going to the morgue to apologize to the corpse. But his presence there would surely reach the ears of his superiors. Then he remembered the alley last night in the aftermath of what was labeled a riot. The scattered mess of Martin's memorial. Maybe placing flowers at that tragic spot would suffice.

He grabbed a bouquet from a nearby shop and started toward Spencer Avenue. Along the way, he pondered why he felt like he owed Martin an apology. Although he immersed himself into the integrity of conducting a fair and thorough investigation, he never had any great expectations that Easthill would be charged. It was a possibility, but certainly nothing guaranteed. In fact, from the beginning things leaned toward nothing being done. Just as nothing had been done in past similar incidents.

Yet he remained meticulous, maintaining a standard of excellence in his investigating. He stood up for things others wouldn't have, asked questions others would have omitted. And did so with an unwavering conviction. He was careful to keep in mind that Martin wasn't just a corpse or a sensational news story garnering a lot of attention. Martin was a person worthy of dignity and respect. And justice. Tory's intention remained the pursuit of actual justice, not motions performed in its name that wouldn't actualize it. He wouldn't reduce the investigation to an item to be checked off the list of things routinely performed in these types of recurring tragedies. Tragedies that often resulted in officers not being held accountable.

But why apologize when he had given his best, sincere efforts? Perhaps the apology was due for what he felt were the failings of others. Was it his place to apologize for a police department and legal system that would not respect and honor the loss of Martin's life? Or perhaps an apology was due on behalf of his generation. An older generation which had not made the necessary changes in society to prevent Martin's death. That they had failed or not resisted enough to end or transform the societal forces that still prey upon, belittle, and destroy so many Black lives. Why was it still normal for men like Martin to be killed? And boys too? Killed by the very same government endowed with the responsibility to serve them as citizens. As human beings.

Isn't the government supposed to be a creation of the people, with the duty to serve and protect them? If so, why are people allowing the government to inflict and be unresponsive to the continuing destruction of the people? Why are people being complicit with and supporting such a government? Are not Blacks part of the people who create and are due to be served and protected by the government? A part that has died for, endured great suffering, and continues to dedicate their lives to the sustenance and continuing evolution of this country?

The scope of such an apology felt too large for his shoulders. He was but a small cog in the moving machinery of society. One so tiny he couldn't even get his report read in the police department he worked within. It dawned on Tory how little influence he had within the overall scope of things. Yet Martin had even less and still sought a place within this society. He had less power. Less means to survive. And still he strove to build a life within such conditions.

Was that what an apology was due for? That Martin would no longer have the chance to continue to struggle in the midst of this society's rejection of him. That he wouldn't live to be a grey-haired old man in a nation that, at best, might grant him a limited acceptance. Maybe. That he would never get to hold his child in his arms in the midst of a life filled with hardships. Never melt at the sight of his baby's first smile. First laugh. First step. Never get to kiss his baby and tell him or her how much he loves his child in a world that was so lacking in love for him. Was an apology due for the fact that he would never be with his family again? I mean, maybe spiritually there might be a togetherness, but that living physical presence we become so accustomed to was now banished by a cop's bullets. Should someone apologize for denying him the likelihood of continuing to struggle to find a job? And if one was found, it probably would have been something that would only perpetrate the adversity of living in this society as a poor Black man. Not a job that would deliver him from such. That's if he was able to get a job.

Uncle James. The sight of him laying broken-bodied upon that hospital bed remembered. Exhausted from the unending crying, the fear of not wanting to die. The inevitable was inescapable. A pause as his tear ducts had run dry and his chest needed a temporary reprieve from the constant heaving. Terrified, he turned to the side to look at his nephew who didn't know what to say or do to offer comfort. He pointed to a drawer beside the hospital bed, his finger extremely leaned by his near approach to his final breath. Then a voice rasped out to a loud whisper.

"The Ten Commandments. I want you to read," a breath, "the Ten Commandments."

Tory was puzzled but opened the drawer to find a Bible inside. The King James version. He then read aloud the words God spoke to Moses. Ten commands the Lord gave to those brought out of bondage. They were familiar to Tory through his many years of attending church as a youth. By the time the nephew read the last command, the tears had resumed flowing from his uncle's eyes. But they weren't part of the previous cries of desperation and terror. Instead a calm regret being accepted in the dwindling of his body's life force.

"Tory..." He reached out to his nephew but had not the strength to raise his hand far enough to touch him. So the nephew stepped to the edge of the hospital bed, offering his hand. "Tory," a swallow as he gripped the younger hand tightly, "I tell you, live everything through those words. Everything!" His body seemed to jolt with emphasis upon that last word, fainting to an even more drained defeat. The grip of the hand loosening. "Whatever life may come, live through those words. I didn't and that's why I can't..."

His voice faded but the meaning was clear. The regrets haunting his last hours were a result of abandoning the guidance of these holy words.

"There's so much more I could have done but..."

Again, vocalizing the completion of the sentence would have been too much to bear. And he was suffering enough. But the warning was clearly conveyed. Do more when you have the chance, cause if you don't there will come a time when it's too late. Too late to do the more you could have done. Too late to escape the consequences for not having done so.

As he maneuvered his car through the streets of Water Hole, Tory ran them through his mind. *To have no gods before Me.* He remembered how one preacher explained that this was not just worshiping idols, but applied to anything that might deter us from doing what God says to do. Material things, ambitions, desires, fears: anything we allow to have more influence than the All-Mighty, that moves us to act in ways contrary to what God deems we should do.

Did he do this with this case? He would say for the most part he did, but there may have been some things where he deviated.

To not make a graven image to be worshiped. Doing so will bring punishments that will afflict the present and future generations. But honoring God will bring mercy upon even more future generations. Thousands. Although this didn't seem to have a direct connection to the case, the principle of what we do now affecting those who follow after us was relevant. So relevant. Tory wondered if his diminished religious living played a part in a punishment that was resulting in killings like Martin's? Not to excuse Easthill's acts, but maybe a more committed religious life could somehow serve as protection from these kinds of incidents.

To not take the Lord's name in vain. He may not have used the Lord's name in vain, but was he fully honoring it? He felt he needed to get back to going to church, being more religious in his overall life.

To keep the Sabbath holy. He knew he didn't do that. Again, the need to get back to going to church and living righteously.

To honor your parents. He promised to call his mother later, to just make sure she didn't need anything. It dawned on him how her determination that he go to church every Sunday imprinted a lasting memory of these commandments. One that survived his long absence from the pews.

Then came the core of the commandments, in his eyes. *To not kill, steal, commit adultery, lie, or covet your neighbor's possessions.* He felt he upheld these but reflecting on these moral abstentions spurned the affirmative sentiment that he could do more to honor Loretta as his wife. And that he could be more appreciative of all they were fortunate to have in their lives.

But did he uphold these abstentions in the Martin Little case? He felt a sense of relief in being able to say "yes" without delay. Yet he wished Easthill had applied these in the incident. To have not killed and stolen Martin's life. And then to not lie, even via the omission of truth, in the aftermath. It could have brought a sense of healing to what remained an open-wounded tragedy.

As he rested in the residue of these thoughts, he realized he was already parked at the gas station. He grabbed the flowers on the passenger seat and exited the car to see Mandy standing by the barricades that closed off the street. Argumentatively animated, she spoke loudly at an officer who was denying her entry past the boarded up shop. A Black officer. Chunky stood behind her holding a bunch of flowers, a glass candle, and a large photo of Martin.

"But I'm his sister!" she said, holding her driver's license in her hand. Tory was already on his way as she continued in vexation. "And look how messed up it is. I just want to fix his memorial."

"I have my orders," replied the officer. "No one is allowed beyond this point."

Tory quickly interceded with a greeting. "Hello, Ms. Little."

"You're Detective..." She paused. She had forgotten his name.

"Detective Givens," Tory completed her sentence without any offense. "What's the matter?"

"They won't let me fix my brother's memorial. He said I have to set it up here," she said, pointing at the officer.

Tory was disturbed by the insensitivity of the officer, especially a Black one. He couldn't help but wonder if she would have been allowed to tend to the memorial if she and Martin were White. Allowing a loved one to honor a recently deceased relative. Allowing humanity and due consideration to trump blindly following a given order.

Tory's agitation was evident. He displayed his badge to the officer and pronounced, "I'm with Internal Affairs. I'll walk her in."

The demeanor of the officer immediately cowered. "Yes sir, detective," he muttered as he moved the barricade to allow entry.

Mandy walked by him, still with an attitude. Chunky and Tory followed. Tory made a point to look the officer squarely in the eye as he walked by. The officer lowered his head to avoid the chastising gaze of a superior. As if something in him knew better, that he could have found a way to accommodate Mandy without Tory having to impose his rank and will. But, Tory thought to himself, this is part of the dynamics that play out when a Black face is put forth to uphold blue values. An officer can suppress one's own sensibilities to be a cop first and foremost. Something Tory had been guilty of many times over the years, so there was a touch of compassion behind his external displeasure.

Daylight gave full view to how wrecked the memorial was. Very little of the growing collection of assembled items remained as placed. If one didn't know what had transpired in the past few days, the sight would have looked like just another dirty alley with trash that needed to be swept up. It became too much for Mandy. Her eyes welled with emotion as Chunky, also affected, leaned against her. She wanted better for the spot where her brother was fatally shot. Only three days ago. Martin deserved better.

Tory stepped forward and bent to the ground. He put his flowers to the side and began to gather the ravaged items. He didn't care that he was touching unclean and sullied garbage with his bare hands. Or even broken glass and sharp objects with his exposed flesh. Martin did deserve better.

Mandy stepped forward to join in clearing the area but he stopped her. As a family member of the deceased, this was something that should be done for her, not by her. To be served and protected. "I got this. Give me a minute to clean it up."

Anything that wasn't damaged too badly he put to the side. He collected the rest of the ruined stuff into a pile of trash. And then dusted the asphalt with his hands, mildly scratching and scraping some of his skin. He then picked up the trash and approached the nearby dumpster. The echo of his footsteps in the alley took on a solemn meaning. Respect was due to honor Martin. And it needed to be genuine, with true reverence.

He placed the trash in the dumpster with care, making sure to not let the cover slam after he was done. He then walked back to the spot now cleared for the memorial. Wiping his dirty hands on the inside of his suit jacket, he stood beside Mandy and Chunky. "Now you can set up the memorial."

He watched as Mandy bent down to help Chunky reconstruct the memorial. The photo of Martin placed in the center. The glass candle set before it. The flowers Chunky brought were laid at base of the candle. Tory told Chunky to use the ones he brought too. So flowers were laid on both sides of the candle. Then the salvaged items situated around the perimeter of the flowers. To convey a sense that others were also mourning this tragedy and wanted to show their concern and hurt.

The new memorial was smaller than what was previously there. But it was a memorial nonetheless. With it being complete, Mandy stood as Chunky pulled a book of matches from his pocket. He looked up at his mother, his face distraught by sadness. He bit his lip and struck the match across the dark bar on the book's back. The first strike merely scarred the match head. The second strike produced a flame. With that flame, he lit the candle. The candlelight was invisible within the sun's rays. Yet the inconspicious symbol was no less sacred. No less sincere.

Chunky looked up at Mandy again, a tear pouring from his eye. Her eyes swelled with tears as she nodded to her son. He hugged her leg. And Tory quietly took a step back. He felt it was the right thing to do. His heart pouring out sympathy to the bereaved family. Especially to young Chunky. Because he knew too well what it was like to lose an uncle. To mourn unendingly for a beloved uncle no longer here...

EPILOGUE:
A poem from Jelani

There was a greater crime that preceded
The committed crime,
    Or supposed crime.
There was a greater alarm before
The flashing lights danced with the sirens' song.
There was an overseer with an agenda
That set the paradigm for officers with badges.
There was a legacy of oppression and horror
That continues to live through today's injustice.

The justifications are often similar:
He was resisting.
Non-compliant.
Acting suspicious.
Threatening or violent.
Threatening and violent.
He had something in his hands.
He didn't show me his hands.
I thought he had a weapon.
He made a sudden move.
He attacked me and I had to defend myself.
I feared for my life.

Justifications given
For some cop with a gun
Who became so afraid
That he or she shot a Black man.

Or sometimes a woman.
Or sometimes a child.
Sometimes in the chest,
Sometimes in the back.
Sometimes in the head.
Sometimes surviving.
Sometimes dead.

And life for us is never the same again,
As those sworn to serve and protect
Remain an ongoing source of brutality
Upon the innocent and guilty.
Our is trust murdered again with each recurring incident
As more Black corpses decay into familiar tragedies
That decompose to become more of America's soiled soil,
From blood spilled upon the surface to bones buried deep.
And headlines come and go:
The same film remade with a different cast.
Prequels and sequels of police brutality surround my life.
Flicks I'm tired of watching with stale buttered popcorn,
But the producers and filmmakers are too invested in their storylines
To come up with a different type of script.
Especially since these old formulas
Continue to be big box office hits.

So when my man died in police custody,
After the funeral,
        I went to the corner where we used to drink.
I stood there and poured out my soul with words
Instead of a little liquor.
I went to give him his due honor.
I tried to tell the world
How another whole life got shortchanged.
That even if we try to do right with the cops

They can kill us in the wrong.
And blame us for doing something
That justified their use of force.
And walk away unpunished,
Pretty much every time.
Situations that sometimes draw protests,
And sometimes don't catch a glimpse of the public's eye.
Then it falls on us to bury the corpses.
Falls on us to try to heal the wounds of sudden losses.
Falls on us to try to render complete
Families now made permanently broken.
Friendships severed.
Communities fractured,
And we are rightfully afraid for our lives.
As our collective fate drowns more
Into unending, inescapable tragedy.

And on and on went my testimony for almost fifteen minutes.
But the passers-by looked at me like I was crazy.
And the traffic roared on disrespectfully,
Not giving ear to the words commemorating my dead friend.
Even a patrol car passed by rudely,
The cops grilling me with saucy looks.
So I sought refuge in the pews of the nearby church
That was now empty after the funeral service for my homie.
I went to pray to God in silence.
Staring at that cross with a White Jesus
hanging above the place where my man's coffin just laid.
And a verse rang through my ears:
    "Those who would seek to save their lives
      Will lose their lives
      But those who lose their lives for my sake
      Will live forever."
It goes something like that.

So I said to myself,
That maybe in the midst of whatever funky deal went down,
Maybe my man took that cop's bullet for the Lord.
And maybe if I just wait
Some angels will come to take him from the grave.
Or maybe Jesus will come himself
To open his casket like he did for Lazarus in his tomb.
But on the third day he did not rise.
Maybe because his name wasn't Jesus,
Or because he had not yet reached
The mystical age of 33.
His coffin remained cold and covered
While the cop who shot him went on living.
And I went on crying
Over the flowers at his grave that were withering to rot.
Because the solution lays in something
This country is awful at:
    Building true community.
Because the solution lays in something
This country is awful at:
    Love, respect, and justice truly for all.
So I swore from that point forward
To take a moment every morning
To say aloud how my friend was killed:
By a cop,
For reasons that shouldn't warrant death.
Murdered by a cop,
when he should still be alive...